Storm in a Teacup

BOOKS BY KAT PAIGE

Love In Edinburgh
Bumps in the Road
Down to a Science
Storm in a Teacup

STORM IN A TEACUP

A NOVEL

KAT PAIGE

AUTHOR'S NOTE

Hi readers, thank you for picking up this book! In lieu of my standard content warnings page, I am writing a whole author's note for *Storm in a Teacup*. If you do not believe you need the content warnings and/or do not want any potential spoilers, please feel free to flip ahead.

In this story, one of our main characters, Linny Jenkins, has a neurodegenerative eye disease called Retinitis Pigmentosa. This is an eye disease that she and I share. While I did further research into RP, most of Linny's experiences are pulled from my own life (namely her minor injuries, frustrations with dark spaces, and color troubles) and how I personally interpreted them.

Symptoms of RP include night blindness, loss of peripheral vision, and eventual complete loss of vision. Linny is at the same stage of degeneration that I am while writing this, so she is experiencing night blindness and declining peripheral vision.

On a separate note, I would like to mention that Linny has a cat named Oscar Wilde who has three legs. Oscar is based on my real cat nephew, Dorian, as is his story of how he lost his leg. I promise he is not injured on page, as the accident happened years prior to the events of the book. And yes, he *is* confused as to why other cats need four legs because he is excelling with three.

Full list of content warnings:

- Explicit sexual content
- Mention of a miscarriage (happens before the events of the book)
- Mild medical descriptions
- Mention of severe leg injury and leg amputation of a cat, non-graphic (happens before events of the book)
- Mention of past emotional/verbal abuse by a romantic partner and displays of emotional/verbal abuse by an ex
- Mild ableism relating to a visual impairment
- Legal drinking and a character intoxicated on page

To my mother,
who showed me shit eyesight
is only a deterrent if you let it be

Storm in a Teacup

CHAPTER ONE
Ben

Whoever spread the egregious lie that *bravery* is a good thing deserves a proper kick in the nuts.

I shove my hands in my jacket pockets as I walk briskly down the dark streets of Edinburgh. Today, I moved here from Newtonmore, my hometown in the Highlands. This was a brave endeavor.

However, too much bravery in such a short stint has thrown my karmic scale off balance. The nerve of me, honestly. Everyone knows you can't move to a new city *and* confess romantic feelings for your best friend on the same day.

Especially when you are well aware that he does not feel the same.

But I did that. Me. Brave boy. After months of pining, a bat of courage bashed me over the head.

We were leaving the pub after I had spent all goddamn day staring at his perfect face, listening to his perfect laugh, and wanting to kiss him on his illegally perfect mouth.

As we stood on a street lit only by dim lanterns hung on either side of the pub door, I grabbed him by his broad fucking shoulders and said, aloud, "David, I'm in love with you. In a romantic way. In an I-want-to-kiss-you-on-the-mouth sort of way."

Oh? How did that go?

Well, with hesitancy in his voice, he said to me, "Ben…you know I love you. You're my best friend, but I-I don't…love you in that way. I…I'm with Callum." He sighed before he added, "Even if I wasn't…"

He didn't need to finish that sentence, as I knew what he meant to say. He would still never love me even if he did not have someone else. Ridiculously, his words did not come as a shock. Not at all, despite every fantasy I've ever had about this moment going in a very different direction.

Even so, I didn't know being this utterly broken was possible.

I shattered into granules when he asked me, "Are you sure, Ben? I mean, I'm so happy you figured out you're attracted to men—congratulations, really—but are you sure you're not directing this toward me because it's easier?"

Because he's my best mate, and he's gay, is what he meant by that. But his assumption was wrong.

I shook my head slowly. "Falling in love with you is the hardest thing I've ever done. Of course I'm sure."

That's when I walked away.

I don't even know where I'm walking. I needed to get away after that. Positively mortifying, right? Confess love, get rejected, run away.

Welcome to the world of bisexuality, Bennett Pyeon.

I spot an empty bench along the street and sit heavily on it, head in my hands. Stupid. *Stupid, stupid, stupid.* Why did I do that? Especially now. Especially when I just moved to this city to be closer to him. Well, him and my sister. I moved here for a business venture—Isla and I are opening a café. It wasn't *just*

David. But it's only him I can focus on.

It was David who held me back from moving here for so long, but it was also David who convinced me to make the jump. David and the damn café. I let myself get too excited about the café—figured if that was going to work out, *everything* might work out.

At least opening preparations will keep me busy. So busy that maybe I can dig myself out of this abyss of embarrassment. It'll be fine. I'll go no-contact for a week, and then I can face him again. I'm being overdramatic, surely. It's what I do. Make a big deal out of nothing. Everyone says so. This is another nothing.

My eyes squeeze shut. It doesn't feel like nothing. It feels like my insides have been pulverized, yet I'm being forced to strut around as though I'm whole.

I've felt like this for months—since I realized my feelings. I've spent time hinting at them around David, trying to get an inkling of whether or not there was a chance. Every time I *knew* there wasn't, but I held on to hope that maybe if he *really* knew how I felt, it would be different. I mean, up until thirty minutes ago, he was under the impression I was straight. Up until four months ago, as was I.

But then I realized how I look at him. How I feel about him. How I've looked at other men. How I'd ignored these feelings for so many years because I'm also attracted to women.

I remove my head from my hands. It doesn't matter. I've worked through this, sexuality and all. Now, I just need to get over my feelings. I did the thing. It didn't work out. Time to move forward.

Easier said than done.

I'm not sure how long I sit on the bench staring at a mixture of nothing and the tree planted fifteen meters away, but it feels like it's been a while when a ginger-haired lass plops down next to me with an audible exhale. A quick survey of Grassmarket proves that there were plenty of unoccupied benches to choose from, but I'm of no mind to judge. When she lets out another sigh, I figure she needs to be alone without actually being alone, thus choosing to share my bench.

Then she lets out a third sigh, and I start to wonder if she's waiting for me to ask her what's amiss. I'm craving a distraction, so I bite.

"You alright?" I ask, tapping away at the silence the night has created around us and her plentiful sighs.

She peers at me out of the corner of her eye. "Oh, sure," an American accent answers me. "Just saw someone I was not expecting to see, so now I'm sitting on a bench staring at him like a stalker."

My eyes follow the direction of hers, landing on a group of blokes having a laugh in front of the pub cattycorner to our bench. There are pints in each of their hands with the light overhead shining down like a spotlight.

That explains the choice of bench.

"An ex?" I guess.

"Ex-fiancé," she confirms with a click of her tongue. "Ex-fiancé who lives in London with his new fancy finance job. New fancy finance job that was supposed to *keep him* in London." She crosses her arms and mutters, "Edinburgh is mine."

If I were an arsehole, I'd point out that one cannot claim ownership over a city, but I don't say that. She's an upset woman sat on a bench on a dark street in Edinburgh watching her ex-fiancé without his knowledge. She can claim whatever she wants, in my opinion.

Instead, I choose to ask, "Why are we watching him, then?"

Another sharp exhale. "Great question."

"You could walk away," I offer.

"I could, but I don't know how to walk away while he's there having a grand old time when I'm still—" She cuts herself off.

I consider her. "You want him back?"

"Absolutely not."

"Are you planning to speak to him?"

"Absolutely not," she repeats. Her eyes don't leave the pub.

"Suit yourself." I mimic her crossed arms and watch the group of men as well. I've no idea which of the five is the object of observation, so I give them all a general glare. Probably all wankers, anyhow.

A chorus of laughter erupts from them, causing the woman to swear and duck toward me. With the breeze, I catch a whiff of citrus I assume is her. It's nice.

"Is he looking over here?" she whispers.

I assess the group of men. One does seem to glance our way, but not for long enough to assume he's taken any notice of us. "Which one is he?"

"Brown hair, beard…baby-blue eyes."

I snort. "Can't see those orbs from here, love."

She glares. "Don't call them 'orbs.'" With a cautious turn back to the lads, she notes that none are looking at us, so she leans back into the bench with a grumble of, "Red shirt."

Ah. The tall one. He stands about five inches taller than the other men with him.

We continue to watch him in silence. I'd say I feel like a creep, but I am so grateful for the distraction that the option to feel weird about surveilling this man doesn't even occur to me.

Then, his head snaps toward us.

"*Shit,*" the woman hisses, ducking into me again.

This time, he does spot her. His eyes linger as he fixes on her in the dark, trying to determine if she is who he thinks she is. He seems to decide the affirmative as his mouth presses into a line.

"We've been compromised," I comment.

She sucks her teeth. "Would you mind compromising me again, then?"

"Pardon?"

"Kiss me." Then, she adds as an afterthought, "Please?"

My mouth drops open. This has taken an unexpected turn. "I don't even know your name."

"Not sure that matters. It's Linny. Kiss me."

I chuckle. She cannot be serious. I glance at her ex to find him still watching us, then look back at her, her deep blue eyes pleading. Well, kissing a beautiful woman would turn this night around, even if it is just at the expense of her ex-fiancé. Kissing a beautiful woman is a fantastic way to forget about what a complete and utter arse I made of myself earlier.

"Alright."

That's the only word she needs. She leans forward, pressing her mouth to mine. Her lips are soft and tentative upon introduction, but as we become acquainted, she urges more firmly into me. My hand finds her hip, clutching it over the gauzy fabric of her black, floral dress.

Abruptly, she pulls away to whisper, "Is he still watching?"

I check. He is—staring, in fact—his face aghast by what he's witnessing. Shocking this man fills me with a guilty, horny kind of joy. "Aye."

Her lips find mine again as she shifts to perch across my lap. The weight of her body on mine sends an ease through my chest. *Goddamn*, I needed this. My hand glides up to lace in her silky hair, grasping tightly, tugging a little. A small moan signals her approval, even if only for the aspect of the show we're putting on, as her mouth moves more fervently on mine.

At what I find to be a terrible moment, she draws away and directs, "Kiss my neck."

I do as I'm told. My mouth travels down her throat before I improvise, pushing her thick jumper off her shoulder to place my attention there. Her soft and positively delectable flesh tempts me to sink my teeth in.

Breath labored, she asks, "Still watching?"

I scrape my fingers across her neck to draw her hair away and clear my vision. He's gone back to talking with his mates, but his body is angled in our direction as he steals frequent peeks. No one else in the group seems to have taken notice, which means he has chosen not to share that he can see his ex-fiancée aggressively snogging a random bloke on a bench across the square.

"Yeah," I whisper into her throat.

"Then grab my boob."

I tow myself away to gaze at her full-on, eyebrows raised.

"Grab my boob, *please*," she amends, eyes cast bashfully downward.

My mouth is drawn in by the heat of her skin, trailing along her jaw before I locate her lips.

"Only because you said 'please.'"

Her palm rests on my cheek as we reconnect. I graze a hand up her side before finding the small, firm breast, encompassing it in my grasp.

A true whimper escapes her mouth and—*bloody hell*—that sound alone gets me instantly hard. She pulls at the tie on her dress, a bow atop a keyhole resting in the center of her chest, then guides my hand under the fabric so my palm is skimming her taut nipple. I adjust my touch so my fingers can find focus on the pebbled bud, rolling it gently between my fingers.

"*Fuck*," she breathes into my mouth.

I shift us slightly to ensure she is completely covered from everyone besides myself as my mouth moves to her neck again.

"Still watching?"

It takes great effort to drag my attention away from her, but I manage only to discover he's gone. The group must have left.

Desperately, I do something I'm ashamed of: I lie. "He is."

She pulls my mouth back up to hers, body grinding into me, drawing a thick groan from the base of my throat. Just a bit longer, then I'll tell her he's gone. Her tongue traces the inside of my mouth, and I can't remember a time when her tongue wasn't in my mouth, because what is the point of remembering anything beyond this moment?

Fuck.

My conscience gets the better of me. I draw away, internally kicking and screaming, to whisper, "He left."

Staying on my lap, and pressing into a very sensitive appendage of mine, she directs her attention toward the pub. "He did. Cool." Linny climbs off me, standing as she re-ties the top of her dress in a tight bow and smooths down the skirt. "Well, thanks."

"Yeah," I manage to get out, head clouded by the shock of her absence from my lap.

"What was your name?"

"My name?" I ask like a numpty, concentrating too much on her long hair mussed by my hand.

Her mouth quirks. "Yeah, I'm assuming you have one of those?"

"Ben?" I say as though I'm not sure.

"Ben," she repeats, running quick fingers through those fiery strands to fix them. "Well, thanks again, Ben."

Linny goes to stroll away, but I call, "Wait!"

She turns back, head cocked.

"Let me walk you home. Or to a bus. Or your car. It's late. And dark."

Amusement crosses her face. "I'm not scared of the dark." Her eyes pointedly go toward my crotch. "It's probably best if you stay here and cool off."

Well, she has me there. I shift uncomfortably, really wishing I were not on a public bench at the moment.

Turning around again, she says, "Goodnight, Ben."

I ground out, "Goodnight, Linny," as I watch her walk away, wondering if I'll ever see her again.

Wondering if what could be our only meeting was exactly what both of us needed.

CHAPTER TWO
Six Months Later
Linny

My fingers delicately trace over the silky white fabric of the dress hanging before me. The bodice is fitted with buttons going up the back and paired with a light, flowing skirt lined in flower-stitched tulle. It's the most gorgeous wedding dress I have ever seen. Far prettier than the one I picked out.

The one the shop allowed me to return because no alterations had yet been done.

Melanie, my cousin, slips back into the dressing room, a pair of white, satin heels in her hands. "These should do," she says, handing the shoes to me. "Not an exact match, but the same heel height. I cannot *believe* I left the shoes back at the flat."

"Exactly the same height?" I ask jokingly. "Because a single half a millimeter could—"

She cuts me off with, "Oh, quiet, you. You know I measured the damn heel. Now put those down and help me into my dress."

I set the heels on a small stool in the corner of this compact dressing room. We're in a bridal shop in London picking up Mel's wedding dress after its second round of alterations. The dress ended up too big in the bust after the first round, so we're back again, hoping to get it right this time since her wedding is in less than two months.

"You know they have shop assistants who are meant to help you into the dress," I remark.

"I don't need a random shop assistant commenting on my knickers. You'll be helping me into the dress on the day, so you may as well have a practice."

"And Julien will be helping you out of it," I tease with a wiggle of my eyebrows, referring to her fiancé. I remove the dress from the plush hanger.

She snickers as she undoes her trousers, dropping them to the ground, followed shortly by her shirt. I hold the dress open for her to step into, and together we guide it up her body.

"I can understand why you didn't want anyone else to see your neon pink thong," I say as I start to button the microscopic back buttons of the dress.

Mel reaches into the bodice to pull her boobs into a more desirable position. "It's the same style as the pair I bought to wear on the day, but I'm saving those." She starts to fuss with her blonde hair, shuffling her bangs over her forehead, then pushing them back again.

"The fringe was a mistake," she whines.

"The fringe looks great," I argue, still buttoning. "But if you keep touching your hair, it'll get greasy and it won't look great."

She exhales a groan, reluctantly dropping her hand while I finish the buttons and then step back. As I do, I yank open the curtain of the dressing room right as Kensie, Mel's closest friend and maid of honor, enters the shop, clackity heels echoing on the tile floor.

"Sorry I'm late!" she shouts, long, dark ponytail swinging

aggressively behind her. "I took a bus because it was more direct than the tube, but the traffic today is horrendous." She drops her leather bag in a chair, then looks up, slapping her hands over her heart. "Oh! Mel, you're gorgeous!"

She approaches as Mel steps fully out of the dressing room and onto the little raised platform in front of a three-way mirror.

I say lightly, "It looks like it fits. Does it feel like it fits?"

Mel stares at herself in the mirror, eyes watering.

"Shit," Kensie and I say together. We step onto the platform, taking our places at Mel's side.

"You're beautiful, Melly," I say, squeezing her arm.

Kensie hums in agreement, hand finding its place on Mel's shoulder. "This is the perfect dress. Are you happy?"

Mel nods, a tear slipping down her cheek. "It's perfect," she whispers.

Kensie thinks quickly, hopping back down from the platform to fetch tissues from her bag. Stepping back up, she offers the pack to Mel.

Mel takes one and dabs at her tears. "Sorry," she says. "I don't know why I'm getting so emotional."

Kensie nudges her. "Because you're excited."

"And hot," I add.

"I do look hot, don't I?" She's practically glowing, so elated. So in love.

When I was engaged, I was never at the level of excitement Mel is. Don't get me wrong, I loved Atticus at the time, but marrying him would have been a mistake. I was happy, sure. There were a lot of things to be happy about during my engagement, and I embraced them all, but I wasn't *this* level of happy about marrying the man himself. So, I'm very glad I didn't.

Marriage isn't really for me, anyway. I'm not anti-marriage, I'm just anti me being in any sort of romantic relationship. They never work out, and that's okay.

The tailor comes out and claps her hands together. "Oh, gorgeous, darling. It's perfect. How does it feel?"

Kensie and I step aside so the tailor can fuss over Mel.

I ask Kensie, "Anything you need me to do for tomorrow?"

Mel's bridal shower is the following day, which is the main reason I'm in London for the weekend.

She shakes her head. "I think it's all sorted. I have all the party favors packed into my girlfriend's car and have printed out all the games and such. You and Mel just need to show up." She squeezes me on the arm. "She is so happy you were able to come for this."

"Yeah," I say. "Me too. It's not that far of a trek, though."

"For an American, I suppose. You lot act like it's perfectly normal to drive three hours one way for a concert."

I laugh because she's right.

Kensie continues, "Anyway, she knows it can be hard to step away from the shop."

I manage an antique shop up in Edinburgh. My Auntie Carolyn owns it, but as she is aging, I have taken more and more control of everything. "Carolyn gives me grief about *not* stepping away from the shop more than I do."

Mel finishes up with the tailor as they decide the dress does indeed fit perfectly. Kensie helps her take the dress off, then we pack it into a garment bag and are on our way.

The sky is dark by the time we leave, so Mel hands the garment bag to Kensie to carry and loops her arm through mine. "Steps," she says as we exit the bridal shop, down two concrete stairs.

I squeeze her on the arm and mutter a thanks. I saw the steps, but she'll warn me about them in broad daylight as well. I took one little tumble down a step exiting a shop once, and now she expects me to take that exact tumble every time we come across any variety of stairs.

Mel says, "Do we want to head back to mine? Julien is still away, so we could have a girls' night."

Julien is up in Leeds for business, which is part of the reason why we chose to have the bridal shower this weekend.

"Sure," Kensie says. "Shall we make a pitstop for wine?"

We stop in at a Tesco for a cheap bottle of white before getting on a bus to head toward Mel's place. Mel and I sit side by side with Kensie behind us, the garment bag draped over our laps.

"I cannot believe I am taking my wedding dress on a bus," she moans. We don't have a car with us, so it was either the bus, the tube, or a cab—and cabs are more expensive than buses. So here we are.

Once we get back to Mel's flat, we change into sweats. Kensie borrows a pair from Mel, groaning in relief when she removes the heels she chose to wear today.

"They went with the trousers!" she argues when Mel gives her a hard time. "I have no shoes besides those heels that go with those trousers. Linny, do you have any crystals that will help my feet?"

"The crystals can't erase poor decisions," I say, twisting the amethyst band I wear on my right ring finger. "I don't generally travel with ones I can't wear, anyway."

"Damn," Kensie exhales.

We all pile in front of the TV. Kensie suggests a romcom or some show called *Crestwater*, but Mel says, "No, no, let's watch *Buffy*."

So, we turn on *Buffy the Vampire Slayer*, a show all three of us have seen more than once all the way through. Mel's current rewatch has placed us in season two, so the debate of Angel versus Spike comes up, Mel arguing how Angel is good for Buffy and Spike is not, to which I counterargue that when Angel doesn't have a soul, he is *the worst*, and when Spike doesn't have a soul, he's annoying at best but capable of good and remorse, something soulless Angel is not. It's an argument we've had many times before.

Kensie laughs along, saying, "I'm only here for Daddy Giles."

Mel squirms in her seat. "I *hate* that you call him that."

"I love it," I say, sipping my wine. "Daddy Giles all the way."

Kensie cackles. "I will never not call him that. I may be a lesbian, but Daddy Giles can get it."

Mel shoves her lightly. "Shush, you."

I settle back into the couch. I love hanging out with Mel and Kensie, and miss them when I'm home, but I also love my life in Edinburgh. It's been my home for five years and I have no plans to leave, despite Mel's constant begs for me to move to London. My dad lives here, and it's where I was born, but it doesn't feel like home.

When Auntie Carolyn mentioned she was considering closing the shop, I knew I couldn't let that happen. So, I moved to Edinburgh from Syracuse, New York, where I grew up, and it instantly felt *right*.

It's just a shame I'm alone there.

...

The presents have all been opened and the games have all been played, so now I am sitting in the emptying event space where we held the bridal shower, nursing my drink. Mel is off handling the barrage of people coming up to her offering their best wishes for the fourth or fifth time, though I suspect all she wants to do is go home and look through her gifts. She hasn't given me the "Rescue me!" signal yet, so I assume she's fine.

I locate Kensie standing in a separate corner of the room in deep conversation with another one of the bridesmaids, Imani. I know Mel's other bridesmaids, but none of them as well as Kensie. Kensie, on the other hand, is friends with all of them, which makes sense. She's the one who is truly a part of this group. I'm the American cousin who lives up in Scotland.

My aunt Wendy, Mel's mum, slides into the seat next to me, pulling my attention away from the friends I should be trying to make. I noticed her carefully walking across the room, but was unsure if she was approaching me.

She pats my leg. "Hi, love. You alright?"

I sip from my drink. "Fine. The bridal shower came together nicely, don't you think?"

"It did. It did." She focuses on me, pushing her glasses back atop her auburn hair. "How are your eyes?"

My jaw tightens. "Functioning as best they can," I answer.

I don't want to talk about my eyes, but it's her favorite subject. Good for her, I suppose. Aunt Wendy and I share the same neurodegenerative eye disease, Retinitis Pigmentosa. Long story short: we're going blind. RP equals loss of night vision, peripheral vision, and eventual total loss of vision. I'm having a great time with it. I really enjoy having my world slowly shutter around me, degrading bit by bit as the years go by. Makes things interesting, all that impending darkness.

She uses the topic as a bonding method, which is fine, but I would appreciate it if we could talk about something else. *Anything* else. I was hoping her attention would be too ensnared by Mel and the wedding to bring it up today, but that does not appear to be the case.

"Same, same," she says. "I heard about a trial they're doing in the States…"

I try not to zone out as she talks, but she does this every time we see each other—asks me how my eyes are, then proceeds to tell me about a trial they're doing concerning RP that more often than not deals with a different type than we as a family even have. It's cool that there are people out there working on a cure, but it's hard to listen to when they're really nowhere close to having a solution. A fix. An end to this.

"That's cool," I say, trying to sound genuine and not constantly discouraged.

She tuts quietly, seeing through me. "It could always be worse, you know. I think we're lucky in the grand scheme."

The existence of other people's inarguably worse misfortunes does not diminish the impact of my own. However, I can't have this argument again, so I say, "Yeah, I suppose."

I think she finally senses that I am not an active participant in this conversation because she changes the subject to, "When are you venturing home?"

My shoulders sag in relief. "Early tomorrow morning. The shop is closed on Mondays, but since I was gone this weekend, I need to go in to work on a dining chair I'm reupholstering."

"Good, good. So, you'll be joining us for supper tonight? Shall I ask your father?"

"Yeah, we'll be there."

…

I slip out in the very early morning before Mel is awake to catch a train back to Edinburgh. I snooze a bit on the train, then pull into Haymarket Station and walk the twenty minutes back to my flat, dragging my suitcase behind me. I live above Better than

New Antiques in a nicely sized flat that Auntie Carolyn owns. She used to live here, but has trouble with the stairs—she can make it up and down them, but prefers not to on the daily. She rents a ground-floor flat a short stroll from the shop.

Dinner last night was…predictable. My father took it upon himself to one, bug me about never seeing him, and two, urge me to "get back out there." Time and time again, I have told him I am not ready for a relationship. I haven't told him I'll *never* be ready because I don't think he will accept that answer. He'll tell me I'm overreacting. Or rather, overcorrecting.

I can hear him now: "One bad relationship does not mean they will all be bad."

But the thing is, they *have* all been bad. Atti, my ex, may have been the worst, but each man I dated before him held a degree of the same negativity toward me.

I am perfectly capable and content on my own.

Mel tried to direct the conversation away from me every time my relationship status was brought up by my father or her mother, which I appreciated. She sympathizes with my stance on the whole relationship thing.

I try not to get angry with my dad. He means well, but sometimes he goes too far because he's worried about me. I understand why. I was an absolute wreck when Atti and I broke up. After telling my father everything that happened between us, he was about ready to spend life in prison for me. But it's because of that that he so badly wants me to try again.

I promised my dad I would see him soon, but I'm not sure when. Mel hasn't solidified the plans for her hen do, but I figure I will be heading back to London for that in a couple of weeks. I'll likely see him then.

But, for now, I am happy to be back in my own city.

My front door is securely closed when I get back, which is good. The door leading into my building has a very temperamental lock. I have to close the door in the exact right way for it to stay shut.

As I shove my key in the lock, I hear someone say, "Hey! Good morning!" *Grunt.* "Getting back from a trip?"

I pick my head up to see a petite blonde woman. Rachel, the American girlfriend to the owner of the new café next door to my shop. She's the only person who says this peppy of a good morning to me, not that I mind. I was raised in the States by an American mother, so I'm used to this.

"Hi," I say. "Yeah. I was in London over the weekend. What are you doing in the neighborhood?" The café isn't open officially until the end of the week, I believe.

"I told Ben I'd drop off this sack of flour that got delivered to Isla's place. Thankfully, it's not too far of a walk." I notice the sack she has clutched in her arms as she readjusts it without much avail. It's about the size of her, so I am not sure how she is managing.

"Ben is Isla's brother?" I confirm.

Isla is the owner of the café, whom I have met thousands of times by now, and Rachel about half as many, but I have never met Ben, Isla's brother and co-owner. They've been going through the opening process for six months now, so that's odd, but I don't dwell on it. I've seen the back of his head, or at least who I assume is him, once or twice. His hair is graying, so I wonder if he is a decent bit older than Isla.

"Right. Have you still not met?"

"Nope."

"He's been a bit of a recluse lately, so I'm not surprised." She adjusts the flour again, the sack seeming ready to escape her grasp. "Anyway, this is insanely heavy. I should get it inside."

"Good to see you," I say, twisting the key in my lock and heading upstairs.

CHAPTER THREE
Ben

"Hello, hello!" Rachel calls out as she enters the kitchen of the café by kicking the swinging door open with her foot. She's lugging a sack of flour that probably weighs more than her, so I am deeply impressed.

I take the sack off her hands with a grunt and drop it down on the metal counter behind me, causing a small cloud of white to float up around it.

"Thank you, flour queen," I say, bowing to her.

"Of course," she says, offering a half-hearted curtsy before brushing a bit of flour from her navy-blue jumper. "I was up early anyway. I'm heading to Loch Gelly to get some water samples. The last time I tested there, I found a smaller percentage of microplastics than in my initial sample, so I want to see if it's still going down or back up. Noting the rate of fluctuation is important when measuring how exactly this is affecting the marine life in those waters."

I nod with a squint, my attempt at a studious face. "Aye, well let me know what you find out."

She rolls her eyes. "Sorry. I could have just said I'm testing the water." Rachel is in the process of getting her Ph.D. in Marine Biodiversity, hence the water testing.

I wave her away. "Talk to me like I'm a fellow genius. I appreciate it."

Rachel slides up next to me and starts to shuffle through my handwritten recipes—likely searching for ones to steal, the little thief. Without looking at me, she says, "Oh, I ran into your neighbor outside."

I pluck the recipe for lemon curd from her fingers and place it back in the correct slot in my box. "Who? The elderly woman who owns the antique shop? She's nice."

"No, the one around our age with that gorgeous red hair. I don't know her name. She's told me, I know she has, so I'm scared to ask. It's been too long."

"Isla probably knows it." I close the recipe box on her, nearly snapping her fingers, because I need it kept in perfect order. Then I start to count my ingredients, ensuring I have everything I need. Flour, sugar, baking soda, baking powder, salt, cornstarch, the list goes on. It's too soon to start baking anything, but I need to make sure I have all the supplies I need before our grand opening at the end of this week.

Rachel leans against the counter, facing me. "I'm sure she does, but I never remember to ask. *You* could also ask for it."

"I will when I eventually meet her." I crouch down because I am not seeing bread flour. I have cake and bleached white, but…ah, there it is.

"You could meet her sooner rather than later. She's cute," she says in a sing-songy voice.

I stop my counting, scowling up at her. "Och, I knew you were up to something. I'm not interested. I'm sure she's very pretty and very nice. It doesn't matter." I stand up straight.

"Fine. I figured I'd give it a try." Rachel clears her throat and assesses me like she's running an experiment in her mind. "Ben, there's something I want to talk to you about."

I slap my hand over my heart. "If you're asking my permission to propose to my sister, the answer is an enthusiastic *yes*."

She holds her hands out in a halting motion. "Slow down, cowboy. I may be in love with her, but marriage is not on our minds yet. No, I mean something with you. Now, you can tell me to back off if I'm overstepping."

"Okay…?"

"I saw you a few weeks ago."

She pauses for so long that I think that's all she's going to say. "I saw you too? We see each other all the time. I saw you three days ago."

Her lips purse. "No, I mean, at night. I was heading to Isla's from Hoot and I took a wrong turn, as I do, and I saw you. In an alley. Making out with someone."

My eyes narrow at her as I'm still unsure of where she's going with this. "I do that from time to time. I'm no monk."

"I wasn't aware you did it with men." *Ah*. That's where she's going with this. She holds her hands up in surrender. "I'm just saying, as someone who also fancies multiple genders, I'm here to chat if you want."

I swerve away from the topic. "Look at you saying 'fancies.' British already, are ye?"

"Fine. It sounds like I'm overstepping. I won't bring it up again."

I sigh. "It's fine, Rach. I just don't want to make a thing out of it. The bloke you saw me snogging was just some bloke. There have been other blokes. There have been other lasses. I'm just having some fun." I look at her seriously. "Can we keep this between us, though? I mean, have you mentioned it to Isla?"

"We can keep this between us, sure, but I did technically tell Isla already. However, I did not specify the apparent gender of the person, nor did she ask. She only said she was glad you weren't holed up alone in your flat." She chews her lip. "I won't say anything else to her about it. I'm not trying to out you, Ben. It's yours to tell when you're ready, not mine. I just want to be sure that you're okay and to let you know I'm happy for you, no matter what."

I mumble, "Thanks," as I continue my count of supplies.

"David has been asking about you. I mean, he never stopped."

I freeze, numbers fading from my head. My voice is pitched too high as I say, "Oh. Strange change of subject."

"Is it?" I don't answer, so she moves on. "Are you still mad at him?"

I turn away, focusing on anything but her. "I'm not mad. We're just not speaking for reasons I wish not to divulge." I say carefully, "I don't want to talk about David."

Her tongue clicks. This is far from the first time we have had this discussion, so it's obvious she is beyond tired of me shutting it down. "Yeah, I know. I'm his friend, but I'm your friend too, Ben. I want you to be happy."

"You're not my friend," I say, earning a scoff, so I clarify, "You're my sister. Practically. And I love you, so I feel comfortable saying: *butt out* of my love life."

She bites the corner of her mouth. "Fine. Fine! I'm done. I should get going anyway. What are you up to for the rest of the day?"

"Heading up to Laggan Wolftrax. It's a nice day for once, so I figure this may be the last chance I have to get up there before Somewhere Special officially opens. I haven't been mountain biking since the summer." I'm not an extreme mountain biker, but I do like to hit the trails every now and then. I used to work at the café at Laggan Wolftrax Centre, a park in Newtonmore, before we agreed to open the café here.

"That sounds horribly dangerous. Have fun."

"Permission to hug?" I ask, holding my arms open. Rachel is not a fan of physical touch, but can be accepting of it depending on how close she is with someone or if she has warning.

"Permission granted." She pulls me into a quick, tight hug before she pivots and leaves the café.

I'm not far behind her. I dressed in long, fitted pants and a windbreaker this morning in preparation for the chill on the trail. As I take a left, I notice the door beside my café slightly open. It leads to a flat above the antique shop that neighbors us. I often see it ajar and figure it doesn't close all the way easily. I pull it shut, as I always do, keeping whoever is inside safe upstairs.

...

Before I get on the trail, I park my bike outside the café. I poke my head in to say hiya to my former boss, Angus, who is standing behind the counter.

His eyebrows lift when he sees me. "Ben, what the hell are you doing here?"

I scoff dramatically. "That counts as hello, does it? I'm here to ride the trails, figured it'd be rude not to stop by."

"You just want me to set aside a banana muffin for you when you get back," he accuses with narrowed eyes.

"You caught me," I yield. "If you don't mind. I can prepay."

He waves me aside, already grabbing the muffin out of the case and wrapping it in paper. "I'll save it for you. Today won't be that busy, though. It'll likely be here when you get back."

I tilt my head seriously. "Better safe than sorry when it comes to baked goods."

"They're not the same without you, you know."

"Are you still using my recipe?"

"Of course."

"Then I'm sure they're grand."

I leave him at that, hopping on my bike and starting my ride. I travel up and down bumpy hills and trails until I reach my favorite spot: a cliff overlooking high peaks and waters. I pause, chest heaving, holding on to the handles of my bike as I balance and set my feet on the ground. I wheel closer to the ledge. This is a good place to come when I need to think. The only problem is, now I'm at a stage where there's nothing I want to do less than think. Thinking is what got me into this mess.

Though, on the bright side, Rachel knows I'm bi, even if I didn't specifically say the word. Her knowing is a small weight off my shoulders. I mean, *I* know it. I've been playing around with it. I just haven't done the whole coming out bit yet.

Do I have to do that? I mean, I'm nearly thirty. I figured this out rather late, by some's terms. I'm aware there's no preset timeline for learning things about oneself, but I wish I had learnt this sooner. Do I have to make it a thing, or can I just *be*? Like, there's no way in hell I'll do a grand announcement on social media, because no one who doesn't know me well enough to be told in person cares. I should tell my family and friends, yeah? It's a rite of passage.

I sigh. The reason I haven't said anything yet is because when I had imagined sharing this tidbit, I was holding the hand of the man I loved, with him grinning at me while I said the words. Then all of our friends were going to be like, "Aha, we knew you guys were meant for each other." And then we'd kiss and celebrate and—

My hand drags down my face. I am so sick of being sad. So sick of moping over David. But every time I get a moment to think, or someone or something reminds me of him, a wave of something akin to grief crashes over me, leaving me to thrash and struggle until I can heave myself up and away from that darkness. Which is so *dramatic*. Everyone always says I'm dramatic. They're right. He's not dead. The only reason our friendship died is because I killed it.

These thoughts are the reason I've been forcing myself to go to therapy for the past three months. Haven't told anyone about that either. Not sure why I'm keeping these secrets from the ones I love. They're not shameful. However, even the non-shameful secrets will find their way back to the utter embarrassment of my failed love confession.

I hear bike tires crunching the ground behind me, turning me around and pulling me out of my head. The person pauses and undoes their helmet.

"Ben," they call. "Is that you?"

I squint, taking a moment for the recognition to hit. *Shite*. Molly. My ex. We dated for three years but broke up last May.

The thing is, I'm the kind of person who others prefer in low doses—too much of me can be excessive. In the end, I was too much for Molly.

It's not like our breakup was traumatic or anything, but…she stopped laughing at my jokes. She would roll her eyes at me, and not in a you're-silly-but-I-still-love-you way. We fell out of love. It happens.

It takes great effort to not throw myself off this cliff.

"Molls? Hiya." I walk my bike closer to her.

She looks gorgeous, though she always did whilst sweaty. However, no pangs of longing make an appearance. Which is too bad—she'd be an easy way to get over David.

That was a horrible thing to think. Never mind. I hope she has moved on from me as well and won't let me ever attempt to use her. *Jesus.*

She comes in for a hug. "How are you?"

"Good, fine." *Bad, terrible* would have led to some follow-up questions. "Isla and I are finally opening our café. End of this week, in fact. So, if you're ever in Edinburgh…" She won't ever be in Edinburgh. She hates the city.

"Yeah, for sure," she lies. "Congrats on that." She crosses her arms. "I wasn't expecting to catch you out here."

"It's a nice day."

Her mouth quirks, the same thought likely on her mind. Which is one of the reasons we used to work so well. We had a similar thought process a lot of the time.

"How are you doing?" I inquire, more out of politeness than anything else.

"Oh, good. I'm seeing someone."

I smile genuinely, even though that wasn't at all what I asked. "Happy to hear. I'm not, but that's okay."

She gives a pitying look. "That *is* okay."

"That's why I said it." I buckle my helmet, wheeling my bike back onto the path. "Listen, it was good to see you. I've got to get going."

She waves goodbye, then stations herself at the lookout spot.

That's actually where we first met, so it's not like it was *my* spot. It was my spot, her spot, then it became *our* spot, especially after we repeatedly lost a few items of clothing here, and now it's my spot, and her spot again. That's how life works sometimes.

I finish the trail and head back to the trailhead, stopping in the café to get my muffin and chat with Angus for a while. I eventually head back to Edinburgh, feeling refreshed and lighter.

Though by the time I get back, the heavy feeling that lives inside of me has returned. I can hardly make it up the singular step into my flat, the weight nearly too much to bear.

CHAPTER FOUR
Linny

I squint up from the candelabra I'm cataloging as the bell over the door of the antique shop jingles. My shoulders sag when I realize it's only my Auntie Carolyn. We haven't had a single customer today. There are a lot of days like this, but we still manage to do fine overall due to frequent sales of big-ticket items. However, the days pass by much quicker when people actually come into the store.

"The café next door is really coming along," Carolyn notes as she sets a box of bronze picture frames on my counter. Carolyn is sporting burgundy pants with a matching burgundy blouse, white permed hair holding a red clip-in flower. She owns one of those flower clips in every color.

"They're supposed to open in a couple of days," I comment, glancing at the box of frames.

We've had this conversation before. We've had this conversation practically every day since the café started to move in next door. Auntie Carolyn will walk by it on her way into the store, remark on the progress they've made, and I will offer their opening date, which has been posted on their light blue front door for the past three months.

"When is Melanie's wedding?" Carolyn asks me, another question that has been posed to me before.

"Six-ish weeks," I answer. Mel's wedding in Edinburgh is fast approaching. And yes, Carolyn has received an invite, so she does know the date of the wedding.

Mel and her fiancé Julien met in Edinburgh about three years ago. Mel was visiting me, and Julien was visiting Atti. Julien and Atticus are cousins as well, which means, yes, my ex-fiancé will indeed be in the same wedding as me. They asked him to be a groomsman before we broke up—otherwise, Mel may have fought against it, family or not. Mel has already promised we will not be paired to walk down the aisle.

Anyway, since this is where they met, it's where they want to get married. I support it. Edinburgh is a magical city.

Carolyn taps her pink pearl fingernails on the counter. "Aye, right. I can't keep track of the schedules of you youngins. I've a few more loads in the car," she says, gesturing at the box of picture frames. I do hope she means loads of general stuff and not loads of picture frames. They do sell, but they also take up room. She pivots on her heel, giving a wave to an invisible someone in the corner, and exits through the jingling front door. I swear, Carolyn enjoys collecting ghosts almost as much as antiques.

With a black pen, I write a price down on a paper price-tag, then loop the string around one arm of the candelabra, setting it aside as I move on to the first picture frame in the box.

We end up getting one customer soon after Carolyn comes back in with her loads of picture frames. A regular. Evelyn is an elderly woman who lives across the street and often putters into the shop when she's looking to fill her day. I'll take it, especially because I am convinced that little old Evelyn's dearly departed husband tags along with her everywhere she goes. Whenever she enters the shop, it sounds like two people entering instead of one.

Carolyn claims to have seen the husband, and I believe her. Auntie Carolyn has always considered herself somewhat of a medium, so who am I to argue? Can't judge anyone's sight but my own.

Frankly, I'm not entirely positive Evelyn isn't a ghost herself.

Soon enough, Evelyn wanders back out the door without buying anything, which is to be expected. Carolyn follows shortly after, always leaving the shop a half hour after we close for the evening. I'll likely be here for another couple of hours in an attempt to dwindle down my task list. So many picture frames to catalog and price, along with some polishing of silver and another chair to gently reupholster.

I turn on a table lamp to give me extra light. This shop can get pretty dark once the sun stops shining through the windows. Or on rainy days. Or always. It's a pretty dark shop. We've added light where we can, lamps around the store and brighter overhead lights, but an antique store tends to get so filled with *things* that those things start to absorb the light. It's alright. I make do since I'm used to it.

It's past 10 p.m. by the time I finally decide to be done for the night. Carolyn has long given up on scolding me for staying so late. What else have I got to do? I live just upstairs, so it's not like I have a long commute in the dark streets waiting for me.

I pull on my coat before setting the alarm system and exiting the front door, locking it behind me. Before opening the door to my flat, I glance at the café next door. It's dark inside—unsurprisingly, considering the time of night. I stare for a moment longer, unsure of why it's drawing my attention, before I shake my head at myself. It's a great time to go to bed. I push open my door as my warm bed, a cup of tea, and my cat are all calling my name from upstairs.

...

The next day, I'm in the back of the shop while Carolyn is up front dealing with customers. I need to be working on our finances, but I've been distracted by the slowly growing box of chipped and broken teacups I keep back here on the shelf. I keep meaning to price down the intact ones to sell them off and trash the ones beyond repair, but haven't gotten around to it.

I force myself away from the teacups and settle down in front of the computer, pulling up that dreaded spreadsheet. A few rows in, the bell above the door jingles, alerting me of someone's entrance. My focus remains on the numbers I'm inputting. Carolyn's got them.

That is, until I hear her call, "Melinda!"

Ugh. She is the only one who calls me Melinda. Nothing against the name, I've just gone so long not using it that I don't know how to respond to it.

I make sure my spreadsheet is saved before I push myself up from the desk.

"What's up?" I ask, brushing aside the curtains that separate the back from the front. I spot Carolyn before I notice the man standing behind her on the other side of the counter. When I do, I stop in my tracks. He's tall and lean with light brown skin, wearing a soft gray sweatshirt and black trousers. Striking streaks of silver disrupt his black hair, and his dark eyes are familiar.

"You," I say, tone accusatory.

He cocks his head to the side for a moment of confusion before those familiar eyes light up. "You," he mimics.

It's the man from six months ago. From the bench. What is he doing here? How did he find me?

Carolyn, utterly oblivious as always, looks between us, her smile lines crinkling. "Melinda, this is the owner of the café next door. He's brought us some pastries. Though he almost let Fergus out when he came in."

What? *He* owns the café?

I deal with Carolyn's ending comment first. "Fergus can leave whenever he wants—he always comes back."

Carolyn's mouth pinches. Fergus is her favorite ghost who frequents our shop. She doesn't want to lose him—I think he reminds her of her late husband. And she is a sucker for a kilt, which he supposedly wears.

The man from the bench's smile tightens. "Is Fergus a cat?"

"No," Carolyn and I answer together.

He waits for a moment before he understands that's all the information he's going to get. He shifts uncomfortably. "Erm, I brought pastries *and* an invitation to our soft opening." He holds out a paper that I gingerly accept, eyeing a flyer of the same light blue as the door to his café, Somewhere Special.

"You're Isla's brother?" I ask incredulously, still not willing to believe that this meeting is an instance of perfect chance. I knew the co-owner of the café's name was Ben, but that is a perfectly common name. When I saw the back of his head, I had no idea I'd recognize his face. His hair is graying, so I figured he was older, but he's got to be late twenties, early thirties. I hadn't noticed his hair when we first met in the dark.

"That I am."

"Did you know I worked here?" I question, keeping my line of suspicion.

He beams widely. "I did not. I only knew a bonnie ginger-haired lass worked here. Couldn't have guessed it was you."

Carolyn—finally taking a bit of a hint—says, "I need to retrieve something from the back. Excuse me. It was a pleasure, Bennett."

As she slips through the curtain, I ask, "Bennett?"

"Full name. Bennett Pyeon."

"She'll never call you Ben now."

"That's okay." He regards me with half a smirk as he adds, "Melinda."

"Linny. Jenkins."

"I like Melinda." He looks me over. "But you do seem like more of a Linny."

"Thanks."

He smiles again, then gestures to the flyer I still hold in my hand. "You really should come. It's tonight before the real opening tomorrow. My sister is going to sing. She's good enough that strangers often pay her. There will be free pastries, coffee, tea, and wine. Whatever takes your fancy."

I analyze the flyer. "Did you make the pastries?"

"Aye. That's my role in the café. Isla takes care of the rest. Not that I don't try to unsuccessfully assist. She continuously tells me how hopeless I am at the business side of it all. And I agree. I'm better in the kitchen."

"The perfect house-spouse."

"Yes!" he cackles. "I've said the same thing!"

That gets a smile out of me. "Well, this is a really weird coincidence, but it's nice to see you again."

"You too." He gnaws his lip for a second before saying, "I'd like to thank you for that night. It's ridiculous, but I really needed to snog a random woman on a bench."

I huff out a laugh. "Yeah, well, I needed it too." We observe each other for a moment—his eyes are too intense, too focused on me. I need to break this. "I've got to get back to work."

He nods, penetrating gaze shifting away. "Right. I've a few more places to stop by on my invitation tour…that was meant to be done a week ago." He goes to leave, but halts before he gets to the door. "I'm so happy I ran into you, Linny. Stop by the café anytime. Coffee's on me."

With that, he exits.

Bennett Pyeon. The man who helped me swim out of the deep end six months ago works next door. I mindlessly twist the amethyst ring around my finger. I didn't think I would ever see him again.

…

I consider not going to the soft opening for a very long time, mostly because non-family social settings and I have not been getting along lately. I try on five different outfits, which is absurd. Eventually, I settle on a long, black floral skirt with a white, cropped tank under a cream cardigan—something I would wear on a regular day. I slip on a delicate gold necklace, gold hoop earrings, and all my normal rings. At the last minute, I grab a small sodalite stone and slip it into the pocket of my sweater—to promote calm and dispel internal negativity—before I force myself to venture downstairs to Somewhere Special.

I know, I know. I should not have to force myself to go somewhere with free alcohol and baked goods, but here we are. I don't know what happened to me.

No. I do. What and who.

The café is pretty full when I enter. I recognize a few of the other business folk on the street in attendance, but I assume everyone else is friends or family of the owners.

Isla, Ben's sister, is on a makeshift stage providing music for the night via her guitar and a beautiful voice. Her curly hair is pulled into a bun atop her head and her arms are exposed to display a sleeve of black, floral tattoos.

I don't see Ben, but that's okay. I'll see him when I see him. I inch forward into the space, the lights dimmer than I assume they normally will be, then take a step too confident and run into a chair.

Sigh. This is why I need to walk with my eyes on the floor. Oh well. Where's the wine? I search for a moment, then spot it. Next to the girlfriend of Isla.

Forcing myself to be social, I approach with my best air of pleasantness. "Hi," I say. "Rachel, right?"

She grins back at me, fingers absently twisting a long strand of golden hair. "Right. And you're Linny?"

"I am."

"Ben said you guys know each other?"

I wrinkle my nose. "Sort of. We met once, like six months ago." Wanting the subject off of myself, I direct it toward Isla, still singing on the makeshift stage. "She's amazing."

Rachel grins even wider as she refocuses on her girlfriend. "Yeah, she is."

The front door opens and a tall Black man in a mustard yellow puffer enters, unzipping the coat and hanging it on the rack by the door.

Rachel gestures him over as soon as he catches her eye, calling, "David!"

He scans the café before he approaches, a look of disappointment, perhaps, etched on his face.

"No Callum?" Rachel inquires.

"No. We figured it wouldn't be…He's busy."

"Oh, okay. Well,"—she gestures to me—"this is Linny. She owns the antique shop next door."

I lift my wine in acknowledgment. "My great aunt owns it, but I do run it."

His eyebrows perk up. "Ah, another one of us."

"Hm?"

"American accented," he clarifies.

I laugh. "Right. My dad's actually English, but my parents are divorced, so I grew up in both upstate New York with my mom and London with my dad."

David hums. "I get that. My mom is American and my dad is Nigerian. I was born here, but grew up mostly in Massachusetts. Came back here for uni and then stayed."

"And never left school," Rachel adds into her glass.

"You're one to talk," David teases. "I doubt you'll stop at one Ph.D."

"I don't need more than one! I'm not a Marvel superhero." She explains, "David and I are both Ph.D. candidates at Heriot-Watt. Me for Marine Biodiversity and him for computer crap."

"Computer *Engineering*," he lightly corrects.

"Oh, wow," I say sincerely. "That's impressive."

They both shrug off the compliment like two people who are very used to getting it. I smile politely, glancing around to see if there is anyone else I know in this room.

David starts looking around as well. "Have you seen Ben?" he asks, making my ears perk up. I too am wondering where he is. I'd like to say hello and thank him for the invite.

Rachel purses her lips as she cranes her head in an attempt to see around the room. "He was here earlier."

David sighs. "I'm sure he saw me coming and ran away as fast as he could. Has he said anything to you?"

Rachel clicks her tongue, making a face that implies this question has been asked and answered before. "Still no. I can't believe you haven't spoken to him. It's been six months, my guy."

"I've *tried*, Rach. Many times. He *won't* talk to me. Every call ignored. Every text unanswered. Every DM unread." Desperately, he adds, "I just want to speak to him. I just want to *see* him."

I take that as my cue to slip away, both seeming to have forgotten my presence as they discuss what seems like a touchy subject. I move to a corner of the room, a bit out of the way, and stand there sipping my wine and watching Isla sing. Isla's gaze is locked on Rachel, even when Rachel is not looking her way.

My heart twitches in my chest, a sting of jealousy along with appreciation of that kind of happiness. Many months apart and months in therapy have made me acknowledge that I never loved Atti that much. So much so that he was the only person in the room for me. I'm not sure I even believed that was possible. However, I'm still not sure it's possible—for everyone at least. It's possible for Rachel and Isla, for Mel and Julien, but not for me.

"Melinda." I turn quickly to see the woman who said my name. Ah, the only person besides Auntie Carolyn who calls me Melinda. Gladys, who owns the beauty parlor down the street.

"Oh, hi, Gladys," I say, plastering a smile on my face. "Nice to see you."

She harrumphs. "I waved, but you didn't acknowledge me."

"Just now? I was watching Isla sing, sorry."

"No. This morning."

My smile drops. "Oh. Well, I didn't see you."

"You young people, always so distracted by your phones that the outside world means nothing to you," she scolds.

"I wasn't on my phone." I make it a habit to not stare at my phone and walk. Far too many accidents have been caused by me doing that. "I just didn't see you, Gladys. I swear I would never purposely ignore you." After this conversation, I might.

She harrumphs again, but continues to talk at me. This time about how late the light in our shop was on the other night. "I thought you were being burgled."

"Just doing a little work."

Once Gladys finishes her list of grievances against me, she continues on with her grievances against everyone else on the block. I finish my wine. God, that's upsetting. I nod along, anxiously searching for a moment to escape.

I finally catch one when she takes a breath.

"I need to go find a restroom," I say, slipping away before she can comment on my departure.

I turn down a little hallway, figuring that even if I don't have to use the restroom, I wouldn't mind a breath. I spot the small WC at the end of the hall, but find myself distracted by the swinging door to my right. Mostly because of the loud clanging coming from behind it. I push my way in to witness a tall man in a white apron whacking pastry dough with a rolling pin.

"Is that the best method?" I ask, leaning against the door frame.

Ben swivels around swiftly, rolling pin held up like a defensive weapon. He lowers it when he sees me.

"No. Probably not." He sets the rolling pin beside the dough he was assaulting. "Hi. What are you doing back here?"

I look pointedly at the dough. "Call me curious—I wanted to see what the banging was about." I step closer, narrowing the large gap between us. "Also, I was wondering where you were."

"Hiding," he says frankly.

"From David?"

His eyebrows shoot up. "How do *you* know David?" He looks around nervously, then in a low whisper says, "Bench girl, are you a spy? Was this a long-winded heist to steal my bread and butter?"

At a normal volume, I answer, "I just met him like five minutes ago. He was talking to Rachel about how you guys haven't spoken in six months."

Ben fidgets with the tie of his apron. "Well, we haven't. And we're going to keep not talking for longer."

"Why?" I ask. Then add as an afterthought, "If you don't mind me prying."

Ben looks away. "I'm…but he doesn't…I thought distance would…but it hasn't…" He sighs, dragging a hand down his face. "It's a long story," he settles on.

I nod, understanding that it is not my business. However, I can't help but ask one more question. "Are you okay?"

"Honestly? Never." He chuckles, but it comes out ingenuine.

"I get that," I say quietly, hating to agree but knowing that I do recognize what he means.

We look at each other, an understanding passing between us. Then a round of applause from outside the kitchen doors breaks the thread. Isla must have finished another song.

Ben clears his throat. "Well, I'm going to keep being a coward and sneak out the back." He whips off his apron and hangs it on a hook by the door. "Thanks for coming tonight." Then he's gone with the swinging door closing behind him, and the back door slamming shut moments later.

Okay, then. My attention falls back to the dough he left on the counter. That needs to go in the fridge. I find plastic wrap, wrap it up, and place it in the gigantic stainless-steel fridge before going back out to join the party, avoiding Gladys like the plague and eavesdropping on the conversation Rachel is having with a wild-haired middle-aged woman in a lavender vest and black wide-legged trousers.

I sip through another glass of wine, then slip out, heading my short distance back home.

CHAPTER FIVE
Ben

I'm still in love with him. But he doesn't love me back. I thought distance would help me fall out of love, but it has not.

I release a small groan, shoving my hands in my jacket pockets as I run away again. Well, one could argue I am *strolling* away. Strolling away to avoid an uncomfortable situation.

My life sucks. And it's my own damn fault.

I knew David was going to be there tonight. I did, and I thought I would be okay. I mean, I've hardly seen more than a glance of him here and there over the past six months, but tonight was supposed to be fine because it was in *my* café. We were finally supposed to speak. Be normal. Be friends again.

But I'm a coward. I overheard Rachel tell Isla he was on his way and instantly ran to hide in the kitchen.

Isla is going to kill me tomorrow for ditching her. Nothing new. She's been plotting my demise for months now. I moved here to be closer to her, to start the café, to be a part of the life of everyone I love in this city, but I'm not. I've distanced myself. Of course, I still spend time with her—and with Rachel—but the purpose always has the safety net of the café. Every time she's asked me to do something social, something David could potentially show up to, I've declined.

What I'm doing isn't healthy. I know it, but I can't stop. I keep waiting for something to happen, something to come in and change the way I am and make me better. I'm *trying*.

Don't get me wrong, it's not like I've spent the last six months sitting fully clothed in my bathtub crying over how the man I love doesn't love me back. Some of my time was spent that way, but I have been out there trying to get over him. Actively, if you know what I mean. Seriously, sexing it up all over Edinburgh (and getting tested regularly). I've met a lot of great people, some of whom I've really liked, but I am not *there* yet, despite my desperate craving to be.

Even Linny. Linny, the woman with hair the color of a bourbon sugar glaze drizzled over an orange pound cake. Beautiful, gorgeous, inquisitive, mysterious Linny is not enough to get me off this ledge of pining.

Not that she's even offering. Sorry, being a man here, aren't I? Beautiful woman is nice to you, must mean she fancies you, right? Wrong. I know that's wrong. My mind is all over the place—more than it was before. I feel like a shell of who I used to be, but also someone completely different. New. How is that possible?

I enter my empty flat, the ringing silence all-consuming. I should get a pet. A dog is too much work, but maybe a cat? I mean, I can manage to feed and love the thing, but I don't think I can manage to take it outside to have a wee on a regular schedule. Cats wee indoors, right? Though it would be fun to have one of those cats who will walk on a lead outdoors.

I need a drink. Or a cup of tea.

Actually, yeah. A cup of tea sounds nice.

I flip on the kettle, leaning full-bodied against the counter as

I wait for it to heat. I pull out my phone as I do so, scrolling through social media. It instantly overwhelms me, so I toss my phone away, letting it slide to the end of the counter.

The kettle whistles, and I prep my tea. My mobile vibrates from afar, signaling an incoming call, but I don't answer. Likely Isla phoning to have a go at me. I'll deal with her tomorrow. I mean, I have to, right? I have to get to the café bright and early to start baking, and she'll be there when it's time to open.

Tomorrow will be busy, which I'm looking forward to. Tomorrow will be fine. Tomorrow, *I* will be fine.

...

I am not fine. I am *not* fine. Why the hell is it so busy? I figured it would be busy, but not *this* busy. We've hired two additional employees beyond Isla and myself, but today it's just the two of us.

"Where did all these people come from?" I ask Isla through the side of my mouth.

She shrugs, smiling at the woman whose order she just took. "I've told everyone I know about our opening day, and I know a lot of people." A man steps up from the queue. "Hiya, you alright?"

With a grumble, I head back to the kitchen. It's been non-stop customers since we opened. It's only noon. We'll be open until three in the afternoon, but we've run out of the cranberry scones I allocated for today, so I'm already working on another batch. They should be ready any moment.

As if on cue, the oven dings. I pull on an oven mitt, yanking open the door and pulling out the tray. I place it on the cooling rack and rotate immediately back to the croissant dough I'm prepping for tomorrow. Once the scones are cool enough to handle, I transfer them to a tray and bring them out to slide into the glass counter where the rest of the goods are kept.

I expect people to cheer upon my and my scones arrival, but they do not. Oh well. I'm used to my expectations being stomped on with spike-bottom wellies.

The day-long rush ends at 2:30 p.m., only a half hour before we are set to close. The café empties out, leaving Isla and me alone.

She grins widely, tucking loose strands of her black, curly hair behind a silver-hoop-lined ear. "Successful first day, huh?"

I nudge her with my elbow. "Aye. Hooray for us."

"And now that the café is empty, I can yell at you." She smacks me hard on the arm.

"*Ow*," I emphasize, rubbing the spot where she hit me.

"Where did you go last night?"

"Home?"

"*Why?*"

"Because I had to get here at 5 a.m. to bake shit."

Her hands perch on her hips. "It had nothing to do with David?"

"David who?"

Her eyes are flames. "Bog off."

I hang my head. "Fine, I know David who."

She tsks, picking at crumbs on the counter. "I don't understand what happened. Would you just tell me what the hell your disagreement was about?"

Disagreement. That's what David called it, so that's the term I too picked up. "Nothing. It was nothing. Sometimes people grow apart. It happens."

"Actively avoiding is not the same as growing apart, Bennett."

"Well, not minding your business can lead to avoiding, Islington. I'd watch it if I were you."

She sighs, resigned, and starts to fiddle with the espresso

machine.

Same as with Rachel, this is not the first time Isla has broached this subject. Far from it. She brings it up nearly every time we see each other. I know it's coming from a place of concern, but it's bloody annoying.

One would likely think: Well, just tell her. She'll understand. And to that I say a resounding *no*. Will she? Sure. Will that save my humiliation about the whole damn situation? Fuck no. So, as a result, I will be keeping this to myself until I can confidently say that I am over him. Heh.

Considering our discussion complete, I aim for the hallway to return to the safe haven that is my kitchen when the over-the-door bell jingles. A ginger head enters the space. I smile upon seeing who that head belongs to. Linny.

She looks to Isla first and says, "Hey. Been pretty busy today, huh?"

"Extraordinarily. Sending customers your way, perhaps?"

She hums in confirmation. "Mainly browsers, but a few 'oh, that's cool' buyers. So that's something. Sold a few of the picture frames Carolyn's been hoarding."

"Good. I'm a personal fan of those picture frames, if you couldn't tell by my wall decor." She taps the tablet on the counter. "What can I get you?"

"An americano, please."

"Great. That'll be—"

I cut her off, "No, no. Coffee's on me. I promised."

Linny appears surprised to see me. "Looming in the shadows, aren't you? But no, I will be paying for my coffee."

"I am a professional loom-er. And no, you will not."

"I'd like to support your business."

"One free americano is not going to break us."

Linny looks to Isla for help.

Isla cancels the transaction, on my side in this argument. "Aye, on the house. But only cause we like ya." Isla turns away to make the coffee, flashing her eyes at me as she does so, though I'm not sure what she's trying to communicate.

I offer a tip of my head to Linny before I continue my retreat to the kitchen.

Though a moment later, Isla comes in and says, "Mind if I pop out real quick? I promised Josie I'd bring her a scone, but we got so busy I forgot. I'll be back to help you finish closing. Can you man the counter?"

I sigh dramatically, but say, "Sure. Rude of Josie to not show up for our opening day to get her own scone." Josie is somewhat of an aunt figure to Isla and me, who gave us a chunk of the funds we needed to start our café.

"She came to the soft opening—not that you were still here to see her."

I set my jaw. "Touché."

When I return up front, I'm surprised to see Linny still out there, a takeaway cup of coffee now in hand. She glances at me. "I'll be gone before closing; I wanted a look around while no one else was in here. I really like all the pictures you've hung on the walls."

"Isla found those at charity shops for the most part. Though most of the frames are from you." As I scoop up a fork and knife abandoned on a vacant table, I add, "Stay as long as you like."

I am so distracted by Linny as she takes her time observing the space that I don't notice the door opening until it's too late. And at 2:57 p.m. as well. I go to plaster on a well-mannered expression as I move behind the counter, but instead my expression drops.

David.

"Hey," he says. He's wearing a dark blue T-shirt and gray jeans with a light jacket layered over, doing nothing to hide those goddamn biceps. His face is clean-shaven, making his dimples even more prominent as he offers a tentative smile.

I look around, panicked, longing for an escape, but find I have none. Finally, I spit out a somewhat high-pitched, "Hi." Almost involuntarily, I back up, spine connecting with the wall.

"I'm not trying to ambush you," he says, hands out in front of himself like he's approaching a timid animal.

"Okay." My fist clutches the silverware still in my hand so tightly that it digs into my palm. I'm aware I should unclench, but I don't. The pain is helping me focus.

"I just want to talk." His hands wring together as he composes what he wants to say. I've seen this gesture before. He's nervous. "It's been six months. You've been avoiding me for *six months.*"

Why does *everyone* keep throwing that timeline at me? My hand stays clenched. Somewhere in the back of my brain, pain sensors are going off, but I don't listen to them.

"Right," I manage to say.

He regards me, eyes big and soft. "Six months is a long time. *Why* are we still doing this?"

Because I love you and you don't love me. The answer is simple to me. I don't understand why it isn't simple to him.

I don't respond, so he says quietly, "I miss you, Ben. I miss my friend."

I still don't reply, like my jaw is wired shut. What is wrong with me? I have never been one with nothing to say.

"Ben."

But it's not David saying my name. It's Linny. David seems just as surprised to see her as I am. I forgot she was here.

She's beside me. Where did she come from? She's taking my

hand, prying my fingers open to remove the silverware, letting it clatter down on the front counter.

"You're going to hurt yourself," she scolds softly, massaging my hand open as it still attempts to clench closed.

The pain radiates through me. How tightly was I holding the cutlery?

David's shoulders sag as he looks at my hand. "Ben," he says quietly, so much pity in that voice. Or perhaps it's caring. He *does* care about me. I know he does, which is what has made this so difficult to get through. Maybe if he hated me, it would be easier to get over him. Maybe that's what I've been trying to cause by avoiding him.

"How long are you going to stay angry with me?" His eyes find mine again.

That shocks me back to reality. "I'm not *angry* with you."

David cocks his head. "Then why…?"

Linny's hand removes from mine. "I should go," she says gently, as though trying not to disturb us. But I snatch her hand before she can leave. I need something to hold on to. Desperately. Someone to ground me.

"I'm trying…" I groan, dragging my free hand down my face. "Because I'm stupid, mate. Why else? Stupid and mortified. And I thought…well, figured you wouldn't want anything to do with me. To keep yourself safe from my…lustful thoughts."

He cracks a small smile. "Eloquently put. No, Ben. No. I still want to be your friend. I still *am* your friend. I miss you." He glances at Linny, holding tightly to my hand. I'm not looking at her, but I can feel her eyes on me. "You're not still…?"

"No," I lie. "Of course not. I mean, it's been six months, like you said. I've opened a whole café in that time. All the time in the world." I squeeze Linny's hand to remind me that she's there—

and to remind myself that I'm here. "I've moved on."

David gawks between Linny and me, a realization in his eyes. "Right. Okay. Wow." Relief crosses his face. "Good for you, man."

I should correct him since he has the wrong idea. I don't. Linny must not have seen what David saw, so she doesn't go to correct him either.

"So, friends again?" he asks hopefully.

I force a smile. "Yeah. Yeah, of course. Sorry I've been so… so *me*."

He tips his head sympathetically. "I love when you're you, Ben."

That guts me, but I don't let it show. The smile stays plastered on my face even though everything inside me is crying out in pain. Why does it still feel like this? Why is my heart still crumbling in his presence?

I suggest, "Can we get dinner soon?"

I'm trying. See, I'm *trying*.

David lights up. "Yeah. Yeah, good idea." He looks like he wants to hug me, but I am still pressed against the wall on the other side of the counter, so he can't. "I'll text you."

"I promise I'll answer." My eyes skirt around the café. "I-I have to close."

"Right. Sorry. I'll get out of your hair."

Old me would have made a joke about how I wanted him in my hair, not really knowing what I meant by that. This me just asks, "Did you want anything before you go?"

He points to the glass case. "Scone?"

"Sure." I finally push myself away from the wall to reach inside the case and grab the pastry. In doing so, I let go of Linny's hand. The calm air she spread over me vanishes. With my hand visibly shaking, I pass the scone to David. "On the house."

"Thanks," he says, offering one last smile. "I'll see you later?"

"Aye. Later."

David exits, and I sprint to twist the bolt behind him. Once the door is locked, I keel over with my hands on my knees, heaving like I just raced across town, not to the door. My vision is blurry as I suck in a staggered breath.

"Ben," Linny says, coming up to me and placing a small hand on my back. "Are you okay?"

I shake my head. "No. No, I am not okay. *Fuck*." I stand up straight, her hand losing its place on my back. "I'm a fucking mess." I swing my arm out in the direction of the street. "I am desperately in love with the man who just walked out that door, and I *lied* to him about it because I have spent *so much* time trying to get over him but failing over and over again." I aggressively shove a hand through my hair. "Sorry. I don't need to be dumping this on you."

"I don't mind," she says.

"Well, you should. I'm just the madman who owns the café next to your shop." I exhale, eyes closing in defeat. "Who may have implied to my best mate that you and I are dating."

She reels back. "What? I missed that."

"I figured."

"We're not dating, though."

"I know that," I snap. I huff out a sharp sigh. "Sorry. Lin, I need to close up."

"Right. I'll leave." She swiftly unlocks the front door and departs before I can say another word.

The sight of her abandoned coffee on the front counter makes my head hang. It's fine. I'll apologize tomorrow.

…

52

I slip away as soon as the café gets less busy and Isla gives me permission to leave, coffee in hand. Carolyn is behind the counter when I enter the antique shop. Her eyes crinkle. "Bennett. Hello."

"Carolyn, just the woman I was looking for." I hand over one of the coffees. "Same order as yesterday, so I hope you liked it."

She simpers as she accepts the drink. "Oh, sweet boy. Thank you. Aye, yes. It was lovely." She eyes the cup still in my hand. "Though, I assume I'm not the only woman you're hoping to find in this shop."

My expression drops in faux guilt. "You caught me. Is Linny here?"

"In the back, dear."

I take that as permission enough to push through the curtains to the office. When I do, I see Linny with her back to me, hair pulled into two French plaits behind her head. She's organizing items on a shelf while talking on her wireless headphones. She scoots a cardboard box of teacups to the side to make room for a few vases, arranging them in a straight line.

"No, it's fine," she says. "I mean, of course I don't want to see him, but I can be an adult about it…Yes…Yes…Yes…Okay…I know…*Mel.*" She sighs. "What are you going to do? Uninvite him? He's Julien's cousin…You can't do that…I know. Thanks."

The call must end because she groans loudly as she drops her forehead to the shelf in front of her.

Well, shite. It's weird that I'm standing here watching her. I have two options. One, hope those headphones started playing music so she won't hear as I retreat as fast as I possibly can. Or two, clear my throat.

Old Ben would choose option two, so I choose option two: I clear my throat. She whips around quickly to face me, hand on her heart.

"What are you doing back here?"

I hold out the coffee in a gesture. "Apologizing?"

She removes her headphones and stomps over to me, snatching the takeaway cup from my hand. "For?" From her tone, I can tell she knows what for.

"Snapping at you yesterday after you were very kind to me. And for not thanking you for keeping me from spiraling. I'm sorry. I'm an arsehole. Everyone says so."

Her expression softens. "I don't think you're an asshole."

"*Arse*hole."

"Arsehole," she repeats, a smile pulling at her lips.

"Correct," I commend. I peer at her seriously. "Today it seems my turn to ask: you alright?"

"Oh, grand. My cousin has informed me that her hen do next weekend will actually be a joint hen and stag do."

"Oh?"

"My ex-fiancé is one of the groomsmen."

"Oh. The tall one." I purse my lips. "Still not his biggest fan?"

"*He* is an asshole. And now I have to spend the entire weekend with him. Which would be fine if I knew someone besides my cousin and her maid of honor, but I don't really know her other friends. I've met some before, and they're nice and all, but they don't get it. Even Kensie doesn't really understand. I mean, why would any of them? But, if it wasn't her hen do, it'd be fine and she could be with me and help me if I needed it, but for this, I don't want to be a distraction. I don't want Mel to worry about me. But she will even though I'm an adult who can take care of myself. The bars we'll be bouncing between will be dark and Atti'll be an absolute *dick* every time I bump into something and I can't *fucking* handle—"

I hold my hands out in a halting gesture. "Whoa, whoa, whoa.

Ginger Spice, take a breath."

There is fire in her eyes as she glares up at me. But she forces herself to take a deep breath in through her nostrils, her lips pinched in a tight line.

Calmly, I say, "I'm missing something. Why are dark bars a concern? Do you think he's going to try and hurt you in one of them?"

Her brow furrows. "What? Oh. No. He's an asshole, but not that kind." She sighs. "Sorry. Uh, I'm night blind."

Understanding dawns on me. "Not the kind that eating a bunch of carrots would help, I guess?"

She snorts. "No. The kind where the cones in my eyes are mutating and killing the rods."

"Non-technical speak, please."

She narrows her eyes. "Didn't we all learn about rods and cones in school? Rods help you see in the dark, cones help you see colors. So, no rods, or limited rods in my case, equals poor sight in the dark."

"Got it. That sucks."

"It does suck," she agrees.

"So, how's your vision in the daylight?"

"Not terrible. Yet. However, my eye doctor advised me to stop driving a few years ago. I only started to listen after I got in a minor car accident. I hit a car I should have seen." She waves that away like it doesn't upset her. I can tell it does. "Um, in addition to the night blindness, it starts with loss of peripheral vision and moves inward. So, as my vision gets worse, it's like the world is shrinking around me. It's called Retinitis Pigmentosa."

I blow out a puff of air. "Damn. I'm sorry, Linny. That really sucks."

She grimaces. "Nah, it's great. I'm having a real fun time with it." She shakes her head. "Anyway, that's what I mean. I want Mel to have a good time, so I don't want to need her to hold my hand when I can't see. I don't think I'd even care as much if my ex wasn't going to be there. He's just going to make it worse. He's always so…so *mean* about it." She covers her face with both hands. "And Mel told me he's bringing his current girlfriend, so that'll be even better."

My ears perk up at that. "You're allowed to bring partners?"

Face still covered, she confirms, "Yeah, since it's combined, they're good with a giant group terrorizing the streets of London."

"I'll come with."

Her hands drop. "Excuse me?"

"If you want. I mean, you know me."

"Sort of," she interrupts.

I plow on. "I know the deal now. I'll hold your hand. It's only fair because you held mine yesterday."

"You don't want to come to London with me next weekend."

"I do."

"You literally just opened a café. Isla will not be pleased if you leave."

"The café will be fine." With my fingers, I tick off all the reasons this is true. "I don't work on Saturdays. I'll make up Isla's missed day off on Sunday some day during the week. We have two other employees. One of them, Scott, is my backup baker. And it'll be a weekend, so Rachel can lend a hand if need be." Linny still looks doubtful, so I add, "I'm sure she was already planning to hang about. Rachel can bake too. I'll need to prep the dough and anything, but she's a good baker. She's been bugging me to help out in the kitchen, anyway."

She shakes her head. "Ben, we hardly know each other. And,

to be clear, I am not looking to date you. Or anyone."

"Neither am I. This would be strictly platonic." I won't let her deter me. "Do you need references? I can give you references. Or, one reference, but I can find more if I need to."

"What references?"

"Can you leave the shop for a sec?"

"I don't know…"

I crane my head around and call, "Carolyn? May I borrow our dear Melinda for a half hour?"

Carolyn calls back, "Sure, love. Just make sure to not let Fergus out when you leave. I've been waiting for him to come see me all day."

This is the second time I've heard her reference that name. I mouth to Linny, "*Who* is Fergus?"

She says, "Fergus is a kilt-clad ghost. Ignore it." I'm not sure I want to ignore that. "Fine. Where are we going?"

"Josie's Music Shop."

Linny and I exit the shop, careful of said ghost, and walk the way to Josie's shop. Josie and my mum were good mates in childhood, more so acquaintances now. But Josie was always around when I was growing up, so she's still in my life even if she's less so in my mum's. It's been a while since I've seen her, so I'm anticipating a tight hug and a light knock on the head.

The door jingles as we enter, causing her to look up with a scowl. "Well, look who the cat dragged in. Didn't see you at your soft opening the other night." She's sporting a red scarf in her hair and a tan, floor-length dress.

I lift my chin and say, "I was hiding in the kitchen."

"Never known you to be one to hide from a party."

I raise my shoulders, attempting nonchalance. "Aye, well, people change." I grab Linny by the arm and pull her in front of me. "I'm here so you can tell her I'm nice."

Linny waves awkwardly. "Hi. Nice to meet you. I'm Linny."

Josie gets up, walking around the counter. "Nice to meet you, too. Linny, huh? Now, are you Carolyn Jenkins's niece?"

Linny's surprised. "I am."

"Hmm, she's a fun one." She fixes her attention on me, holding her arms wide. "Come here then, you wee shite."

I move easily into her embrace, murmuring, "Hi, Josie." I pull away, fingers finding a tub of guitar picks that I rummage through absently.

Josie turns her focus back to Linny. "So, you need me to tell you Ben is nice? He'll be nice to you, pet."

I pull away from the guitar picks as I request, "Tell her I'm safe, too." I wander a bit, my fingers brushing over a red electric guitar hung on the wall.

Josie glances at me out of the corner of her eye. "He'll keep you safe. Won't do anything to harm you. I won't make promises about what he'll do to himself, though. Not sure I ever saw him without a broken bone when he was wee."

I beam proudly, shoving my hands in my pockets to keep them to myself. "I was adventurous."

Josie puts her hands on her hips. "Still are, love. Is that all you needed me for?"

"Yes, Josie." I wander back to where Linny stands by the front door.

She points a finger at me. "I expect another visit soon. Next one a bit longer, yeah?"

"Aye, of course."

"Alright, off you pop."

I swivel Linny and myself out of the shop. "She loves me," I confide, "but she sure does love to kick me out of the shop."

"Is it because you mess with her things?"

"Yes." I keep pace beside her. "So, what do you say? Can I come to London with you?"

She crosses her arms as we walk. "I feel like that's a really bad idea. It would be weird for me to bring my platonic male friend, whom I hardly know—despite his glowing reference. What are we going to do, pretend you're my boyfriend?"

We pause before crossing the road. "We don't have to put any labels on it, but if someone calls me your boyfriend or you my girlfriend, we won't deny it."

She chews her lip and says again, "This is a really bad idea."

CHAPTER SIX
Linny

This is a really bad idea. A foolish one. But here we are. On a train to London. Me and Ben Pyeon. A man I hardly know. I know him well enough to have coffee or a drink with him, sure. But to go to London and share a hotel room with him? No. Not at all.

Too late. We're already in England. We'll be in London soon enough.

I lean back in my seat with a sigh, staring out the window at the long stretch of grassy land. "If we're going to pretend to date, we should go over the basics."

He mimics my lean. "Well, I already know you like it when I pay particular attention to your left nipple."

I whip my head toward him. "*Not* that. I meant my parents' names. My cat's name. My favorite color. Those kinds of things."

"You didn't say I was wrong," he sings under his breath.

"Harold and Emily. Oscar Wilde is my cat. And I like purple."

"What kind of purple?"

"All purple."

"So, you go horny for plum in the same way you do lavender?"

"That is *such* an odd way to put it. But yes."

"Got it. Well, not that I think anyone will be quizzing us on this, but my parents are named William and Jane. Mum is white, Da is Korean. If I had a cat, I would name them Pâte à Choux—Choux for short, Choux Pastry when they're especially cute. And I like orange. But specifically a soft sunset orange."

I bite the corner of my mouth. "How Peeta Mellark of you."

"Ta. But I don't think I will ever reach his level of cake-decorating skill."

"One always needs something to strive for." I move on to my next question. "Did you go to uni?"

"Aye."

"What for?"

"Sport and Exercise Science."

I furrow my brow. "Using that degree for all it's worth."

"I also did an eighteen-week course in culinary arts, post-grad." He shifts in his seat. "What about you?"

"That makes more sense." I point to myself. "Art History."

His lips purse. "What age were you diagnosed with RP?"

"Nineteen or twenty. I remember how it happened—my regular eye doctor noticed, sent me to an ophthalmologist, I got diagnosed. After, I sat in my car with my mom and shed a few tears, then we got froyo—but I've also sort of blocked it from my memory and have never really taken the time to fully process it."

"Healthy."

"The healthiest. My therapist tells me that all the time. Linny, wow, you are my healthiest patient. So good at processing your emotions and trauma."

He laughs. "Hey, me as well! Next question, a doozy. How old are you?"

"Twenty-eight. You?"

"Thirty."

"My god, you're old. No wonder you've got that sexy salt and pepper thing going on."

We keep going through the basics. He has one sister, Isla. I have two sisters, Chelsea and Sarah, both older and both of whom still reside in the U.S. Chelsea is married with two kids, and Sarah is a proud dog mom. I also have Mel, of course, who is less a cousin and more like another older sister.

"Oh," I add as we near London. "I like crystals. I'm not like a diehard believer of every potential benefit, but I enjoy having them around my flat or on my person." I show him the amethyst ring I wear on my right ring finger as evidence. "For stress relief."

"Really?" he asks, eyeing the ring.

"Yeah," I respond tentatively, prepared to go on the defense.

"Interesting. I don't know anything about crystals, but I can do a bit of research."

Huh. "You don't have to. Just because I like them doesn't mean you would too."

"A good boyfriend would at least take a general interest in something his girlfriend likes, even if just to converse about it."

Double *huh.* "Oh. Yeah, well. Thanks." I twist the ring. "Anything I should look up about you?"

"Erm, general know-how of mountain biking? I'm less into it than I used to be, but I do enjoy it. And nature in general. I spent a gap year before uni traveling around the States to visit different national parks. Just so you don't look completely lost if it gets brought up."

"Got it. Mountain biking and big parks. Easy enough."

By the time we pull into King's Cross Station, we know enough about one another to get through the weekend. Ben pulls my suitcase down from above head for me, then fetches his own. He's the perfect height. For grabbing things, I mean. I'm not that short, but short enough to have to stand on my tiptoes for a lot of things. It's nice to have someone who can reach up and get things for me, no tiptoes needed.

I shake myself out of that ridiculous thought. I don't need anyone to grab things for me. That's what stepstools are for.

"Come on," I say, pushing my suitcase down the aisle of the train and out the doors. "We need to catch the Victoria line so we can get to Soho."

...

There is only one bed in our hotel room. This circumstance should not be surprising, but here we are. Mel booked the room, but I figured (hoped) it would be a two twin-bed situation. But, no. One bed.

Mel was surprised when I asked if I could bring Ben. "Well, now that we're allowed to bring partners," I explained. But that, of course, did not explain why I had never mentioned him to her. "It's new," I said, which is technically true. "I mean, we met back in September, but just started seeing each other." Also true. We did meet in September, and we did just start seeing each other, only as in literally seeing and not as much in the dating sense. "I swear I have mentioned him to you before." Lie. "You've been so busy with wedding planning, you probably forgot." A little bit of gaslighting never hurt anyone, right? *Ugh.*

"Right," she had said slowly. "You know, maybe I do remember you mentioning him, now that you say that. No matter. I'm so excited to meet him!"

And now, here we are, standing awkwardly in our shared hotel room staring at the one and only bed in silence.

Ben breaks that silence with, "Looks like we're going to be doing some snuggling tonight."

"We will not be *snuggling*," I shoot back, amused by the

suggestion.

"Sharing a bed is a great way to get to know someone," he teases gently. "I've gotten to know several almost-strangers such as yourself through the act of sharing a bed."

"I'm willing to bet it wasn't the sharing of the bed but rather what you were doing in the bed that gave you a nice introduction to those strangers."

He scoffs. "Excuse me. I was talking about the morning cuppa. Get your mind out of the gutter."

I roll my eyes. "Sorry. I don't ever spend the night with my strangers I'm 'getting to know.'" I squat down to open my suitcase. "I'm going to change. And then we're supposed to meet them at the first bar."

The plan for tonight is to hit a couple bars, then end at a club (it's been years since I've been to a club, so I'm a mixture of excited for dancing and dreading the crowds). Then tomorrow, the ladies are doing a mini spa day, and the men are playing soccer or something. I told Ben he is invited to the stag activity, but he is under no obligation to go.

In the bathroom, I change into a dark green dress with a short skirt that I'll pair with tall boots. My legs are going to be freezing, but that is the expectation on nights out such as these.

I exit the bathroom, sensing Ben's eyes on me, but he doesn't say anything. He changed into a light blue button-down, collar open at the top and sleeves rolled up, but is wearing the same pants he wore on the train. *Men.*

I sit down on the bed to zip up my boots. Finally, when I stand, I witness Ben give me a dramatic once-over, head literally moving down and back up with his eyes.

"Yowza" is the word that comes out of his mouth. I have never heard that word in a Scottish accent before.

I push him away. "Shut up."

He groans, "Those *boots*, buttercup. What are you trying to do to me?"

I decline to answer that question as I grab my purse and exit our hotel room. "Come on, Ben."

He laughs as he exits behind me. "You look amazing, Linny."

"Yeah, yeah. Not so bad yourself."

"I clean up good." He tries and fails to fix a rogue lock of hair falling over his forehead before he hits the button for the elevator. "You have a nasty bruise on your leg." He's referring to the quarter-sized yellow and purple discoloration on my lower left thigh.

"Thank you for noticing. I have a tendency to bump into shit."

We make our way back down to the lobby, then take a right once we exit the hotel.

"Oh," I say on our walk. "Touching rules. Hand-holding is somewhat necessary. I'm okay if you touch me anywhere that's appropriate to touch in public. This isn't a romcom, so there will not be a moment where we are forced to kiss on the mouth to prove our relationship is real, but a kiss on the cheek is fine."

"Works for me," Ben agrees.

By the end of the ten-minute walk, I am regretting my choice of footwear. I wasn't planning on drinking much tonight, but I'll have to at least drink enough to numb the pain in my feet.

Ben grasps my hand as we arrive at the pub, already doing his part. I appreciate it as this pub is seemingly trying to cut costs on their electricity bill, but it's well enough lit that I spot Mel and Julien sitting at a large table consisting of three tables pushed together in the back. They're joined by most of the wedding party and a couple of their partners. My ex is not yet present. Naturally. He was always late.

Mel waves widely, as though I may not see her. I smile back, tugging Ben along behind me.

"Hi. Happy hen do," I say, giving Mel a tight hug. Mel is wearing a white mini-dress, her blonde hair wavy. Julien wears a maroon shirt that nearly matches the smudge of Mel's maroon lipstick on his neck.

"Happy hen do to you too." She eyes Ben. "This is the boyfriend?"

"This is Ben," I say, avoiding the term *boyfriend*.

Ben goes to shake her hand, but she pulls him into a hug instead. As she does, I say a quick hello to Julien, whose brown cheeks heat when I tip him off about the lipstick, and Kensie, who jokingly chides me for telling him, then smile around the table. As we take our seats, Mel does a quick round of introductions.

"Everyone, this is my cousin Linny and her boyfriend, Ben. Linny, you know all my bridesmaids, Kensie, Amber, and Imani. And this is Kensie's girlfriend, Jen. Then on Julien's side, we have Darren, Gregory and his wife Claire, and Paul, the best man." She looks up at someone behind me, and I can only guess who is approaching based on the darkening of her eyes. Her joyful expression drops as she says, "Ah, and here is Atti and his girlfriend, Bridget."

Ben's hand lands on the small of my back as Atti takes the seat across from me. He's donned on a casual gray suit that probably cost more than I earn in a month. When he's settled in his seat, he pretends to notice me for the first time, having the nerve to act shocked. "Linny? Hey. How are you?"

"Fine."

"Good. You look great."

"Okay."

His eyes shift around the table like he's looking for backup, but he receives none. He adds, "I'm a bit surprised to see you."

My eyes lift to the ceiling. "I'm a bridesmaid. Mel is my cousin, remember?"

"You hate to leave Carolyn alone with the shop, is all I mean. How is she, by the way?"

"Alive."

"Good. Great."

His focus flickers to the man beside me—Ben, whose hand stays on my back, touch radiating comfort through me.

"This is Ben," I offer, knowing the correct thing to do would be to look lovingly into his eyes, but my attention stays on Atti. He stiffens at the introduction, sparking a feeling of triumph.

He recovers quickly and reaches a hand across the table for Ben to shake. "You look familiar," he says. "Have we met before?"

"Likely not," Ben replies, voice cool and casual as he shakes Atti's hand. "Andy, Mel said your name was?"

Atti's jaw tightens at Ben's obvious snub. "Atti," he corrects. "Short for Atticus."

I introduce myself to Atti's girlfriend, Bridget. She's tall and brunette, with long hair falling in gentle curls down her back. Atti did always say he wished I were taller. Craning down to kiss me hurt his neck.

Bridget offers a civil smile. "It's nice to meet you. I've heard a lot about you. All great things."

Dammit. She seems nice. Or at the very least, polite.

We get dinner, and I avoid talking to Atti. Also, Ben's arm stays casually around the back of my chair the entire time, even as he becomes immersed in conversation with Paul, who is sitting beside him. Once we finish our meals, Melanie decides it's time to move on to the bar.

This bar is a step closer to the club we will end the night at. Ben takes my hand as we walk in. "Stairs," he warns in a quiet voice after we pass through the threshold. I appreciate the warning, squeezing his hand tightly as I descend the two steps. I didn't expect them.

The group of us is sat in a U-shaped booth, three small tables set up in the middle, hitting me at knee height. It's a tight squeeze, fourteen of us trying to fit. Kensie has already moved onto Jen's lap, and it looks like Claire is about to do the same with Gregory. Even then, it's compact.

"You could sit on my lap," Ben says in my ear.

Every thought in my head tells me no, that is an absurd idea. But aloud, I say, "Okay."

I pick up my drink and settle on Ben's lap. He grips my thigh, keeping me steady and in place. My skin prickles under his touch. I look at him, our faces so close, lips just a breath away, really. Air catches in my throat as the memory of our kiss all those months ago crashes into me like a powerful wave, yanking me under.

I'll be honest, I have hardly thought about it since. The kiss was great, don't get me wrong, but it happened on a night when I was in a really bad place, so it's not something I particularly like to think about. I was in a bad place for several months. But sitting here right now with his hand hot against my bare leg and his breath skimming my lips, all I want to do is kiss him again.

So, I do. On the cheek. I press a light kiss to stubbly skin then whisper in his ear, "Thanks again for this."

His lips move to my ear next, us performing perfectly as a couple exchanging sweet nothings. "A beautiful woman is sat on my lap. I'm thanked enough."

I lightly bite my lip. He's not shy with his compliments. I tease,

"Well, if you get too excited, I'll be able to tell."

"What would you do if I did get too excited?" His voice is low, taunting in a way that makes me clench my thighs together.

That microscopic movement was enough of an answer for Ben. His hand gently strokes my thigh as he takes a slow sip of his drink, eyes on me the entire time. I gulp, turning away from him. This is not why he's here. Obviously, yeah, Ben is a very attractive man. But I won't let myself be distracted by that.

I refocus on the group, finding it difficult to hear what anyone is saying over the loudness of the music, but I do manage to engage with those in my immediate surroundings. Ben starts talking to Paul again, and I strike up a conversation with Kensie and Jen.

I finish my drink, and the waitress is almost immediately by to ask if I want another. My feet still hurt, so I say yes, handing her my empty glass.

Once she brings me my next drink, Ben says in my ear, "You're too stiff. Lean back into me."

I do as he suggests without question, settling back into his chest, his grip on my thigh still firm. It's so natural to be at ease around him, his entire aura calming. As I settle in, the scent of pine fills my nostrils—that must be him. Like a cozy candle.

The night continues with chatting and laughing. I peep at Mel every now and then to make sure she's having a good time. Each time I do, she's smiling, which is a good sign.

Once I finish my drink, I lean forward so I can set the empty glass on the table. In doing so, however, I knock another glass off. Shards explode as it hits the ground. I didn't see the other glass.

"Shit," I say, hopping up from Ben's lap to go after the shattered glass. I reach out to start picking up the broken remains, but a hand closes around my wrist, halting me.

"Don't," Ben says in my ear. "You'll hurt yourself."

I pull back as a chorus of chatter erupts around me, but only one voice stands out.

"Nice one, Linny," Atti says, voice dripping with venomous annoyance. I freeze at the familiar tone.

I stand there, immobile, with Ben still holding onto my wrist. Someone must have flagged down our waitress because she comes over with a broom to sweep up the glass.

"Sorry," we all say, as though we *all* have something to apologize for. As though they should all be regretful on my behalf.

I turn away as she cleans, unable to watch. My eyes moisten, getting ready to become heavy streams, but all I will allow to fall is one tear. I shouldn't be crying over this.

Ben lets go of my wrist to loop an arm around my waist, pulling me closer, but doesn't say anything. His thumb gently strokes my side, offering a private comfort.

Bridget must also see the tear, because she says, "I break things all the time. I'm so clumsy, especially if I've had a few."

I smile politely. She's being nice, but she doesn't understand. I'm not upset because I broke a glass. I'm upset because I broke a glass I did not see. A glass I *should* have seen. A glass everyone else in our little group would have seen. And I didn't break it because I was drinking.

As the waitress sweeps up the last bit of glass, I offer again, "I'm so sorry."

The waitress shakes her head. "No bother at all. It happens when people are having fun."

Atti snorts distastefully. "She needs to be more careful."

Ben snaps, "It was an accident, mate," as his grip tightens.

Atti's lip curls as the waitress walks away. "All I'm saying is this isn't the first time I'll have to tip a waitress because Linny broke a glass."

Ben scoffs. "*You* don't have to do anything."

"It's fine, Ben," I say. "I'll add a tip. It's fine."

His hold remains on me and his eyes maintain the glare for Atti, but he doesn't say anything more. Everyone else settles back down, so Ben and I sit, me retaking my place on his lap. I lean back into him again, but no longer feel like talking. Tears are still threatening to escape.

It's ridiculous. It is so embarrassing when I do things like this and people assume it's because I'm drunk. It would be less embarrassing if they knew I was night blind, but there is no need to announce that every time I make a little mistake. I need to get a sparkly button that declares VISUALLY IMPAIRED PERSON whenever I go out in public, I suppose. I wish I had seen the glass.

If I keep sitting here, the tears will fall. I push myself up, saying, "I'm going to the bathroom."

"Do you need me to go with?" Mel asks, moving to stand.

But I'm already walking away—too fast. I bump into someone and apologize. I force myself to walk slower, eyes darting around the dark room in an attempt to see as much as I can. Thankfully, we have been here for a while, so I have had time to map out the path to the bathroom if I needed it. That's what I do, take in a less-than-light space for as long as I can before I have to move independently in it. It helps. However, it's never a perfect system because there is one factor that never stays consistent: people. They have a very annoying tendency to move.

I bump into a few other people, apologizing over and over, but I do eventually make it to the restroom. There's a small line that I'm fine to wait in. Finally, I get in and close the stall, covering the seat in toilet paper before I sit down heavily and let myself cry. I hate feeling like this. It's just a broken glass, but *no one gets it*. It's so hard to explain how much this frustrates me—how I feel like an inconvenience wherever I go.

Once I get the tears to stop, I emerge and wash my hands. My eyes are red and my makeup is smeared. I do what I can to fix the makeup with a wet paper towel, but not much can be done about the redness. Hopefully, no one will notice.

When I exit, a hand stops me. Ben is waiting for me in the hallway.

"Hi?" I say curiously.

"Hiya, I figured I could walk you back to the table."

My heart swells. "Thank you."

"Are you alright?"

I shake my head. "Not really."

His mouth turns down. "I'm sorry you broke the glass."

"Me too." I push into him, circling my arms around his waist and leaning my head against his chest. His arms wrap tightly around me in return, cheek resting against my head. He is warm and comfortable and consuming in the best way—and a part of me senses that he needs this hug as much as I do.

I'm not sure how long we stand there, but a few people have to push past us with annoyed grumblings to get to the restroom. Ben holds me until I pull away.

"We should get back," I say, crossing my arms over myself. "We've been gone a while."

"I have a good explanation for that," Ben says. He licks his thumb before dragging it across my lower lip. My body flushes at the contact, instinctively craving more. I shove that feeling aside because I don't understand what he's doing—until he presses that thumb to the corner of his mouth, smearing a bit of my lipstick. Ah.

He takes my hand and leads me back to the table. We sit down as we have been sitting, with me on his lap.

Mel catches my eye and mouths, "You okay?"

I nod with a shrug. I look down at Ben and laugh, ready to go back to maintaining our ruse. "Oh, Benny, you got a little lipstick on you," I say loud enough for at least Atti to hear. I lick my thumb and wipe it off with a smile on my face. He grins back at me.

Everyone else orders another round, but I refrain. Two was my plan for tonight anyway. Once they're all done, we move on to the club, our last stop of the night.

As we walk there, Mel takes my arm and ushers me away from Ben. "You good?" she asks again.

"Fine. Generally. Annoyed with myself."

She hums. "Sorry."

"Yeah."

She veers me away from one of those metal roadblocks that line the pavement.

I say, "God, I hate those things. It's like they purposely put them out of my sightline."

"Well, the whole world *is* against you."

"I agree," I grumble, only half-meaning it.

We wait in line for a bit before we get in, and once we do, we head to the second floor. I look longingly at the dance floor, excited to let loose and dance off the shitty parts of tonight.

Over the loud music, Ben says in my ear, "Want anything to drink?"

"No!" I yell back. "I'm fine!"

"I'll be right back, then. You okay?"

"Good!" I yell.

Mel grabs my hand and pulls me onto the dance floor with her.

She throws her arms around my shoulders as we dance. Soon enough, Ben comes back and hands me a glass.

"I said I didn't want anything!"

"It's water!"

"Oh! Thank you!" I take a swallow of the water, not realizing until now how much I needed it. I gulp the rest of it down.

Mel gives me a wink and lets Ben move into her place. His hands land on my hips as his eyes ask, *This okay?*

I bob my head as I throw my arms around him so we can dance together. We continue to dance through a couple of songs, staying close and moving with one another. This is fun. This is what I was looking forward to. After another song finishes, Ben says in my ear, "I have to use the toilet. You need a pitstop?"

"I'm okay!"

"Alright. Stay here. I'll find you when I'm back."

I look around for Mel and the others until I spot them a little bit away, faces aglow by the pink and blue lights of the club. I'll stay where I am so Ben can find me. A really good song starts next, so I keep dancing with my whole body. I bump into someone and apologize, but I don't even care because everyone is bumping into everyone here.

But apparently, that is not the general consensus. A voice says in my ear, "You need a shield around you."

I flinch at Atti's sudden appearance. I search for a moment before I determine his girlfriend is not there and ask, "Where's Bridget?"

"Toilet. Where's that guy?"

"Ben," I say flatly. "Also in the bathroom." I look away from him, continuing to dance. I am not in the mood for this. As I move, I hit someone very lightly with my hand.

"Seriously, Linny?" Atti admonishes.

I spin on him. "*What* is your deal?"

He peers down at me, his tone the height of condescension. "You need to be more careful. It'll make things easier for everyone else."

I groan, head falling backward. "Why is everything I do so embarrassing for you?! We are not together anymore, Atticus. You are no longer obligated to be embarrassed by me!"

A hand touches my back. I know without looking that it's Ben.

"Why don't you go find your girlfriend?" he suggests to Atti in a way that does not sound like a suggestion.

"Whatever," Atti spits before stomping away.

Ben does not remove his hand from me as he rotates me toward him, pulling me back into the dance. I appreciate that he does not ask me if I'm alright. I've been asked that enough for tonight.

We keep dancing until my feet start to kill me and I need to go sit. Ben and I find a little couch to rest on, me leaning against him. Soon enough, Amber and Imani join us, followed shortly by Paul, cheeks flushed and dark blond hair somewhat dampened by sweat. Ben lights up when he sees Paul, who sits down next to him—and I don't miss the way Ben's eyes drag over Paul's chest now that he's stripped down to a fitted T-shirt.

Ben wraps his arm around me as he and Paul pick up a conversation from earlier. I'm happy to just lean against him, feeling safe beside him. My eyes are heavy as I drink more water.

The night eventually wraps up, so we head back to our respective hotels and residences. I did what I hoped to accomplish— my feet are so numb that they don't even hurt anymore, so the walk is not bad. Even though the streets are well-lit enough for me to make it to our hotel without assistance, Ben holds my hand the entire way. And I let him.

CHAPTER SEVEN
Ben

"I'm going to shower the club off of me," Linny says once we're in our hotel room. She sits down on the bed to yank off those boots. God, I love those boots.

"Okay," I say. "I'll shower too when you're done."

Once the bathroom door is closed, I sit down weightily on the bed, falling to my back with my feet still planted on the ground. Linny said Atti was an arsehole, but I'm not sure I understood the full extent of it until tonight. The way he speaks to her, that bastard. If he speaks to her like that now, he certainly spoke to her that way when they were together. How her cousin let him in the wedding party, I'll never know.

Soon enough, Linny steps out of the bathroom in pajama pants and a little tank clinging tightly to her breasts. It's an effort not to stare, but I am a gentleman.

We switch places so I can shower off the sweat of the night. I was planning on using the hotel-provided body wash, but I spy Linny's sitting on the tub's edge. She smells so good. I pour a little bit of it in my palm and rub it up and down my arms, the scent of her filling my nostrils. It was all I could smell as she spent so much of the evening sitting on my lap.

I finally let loose on something I have been resisting so strongly the entire night, growing hard at the thought of her. I shouldn't be having these thoughts. She said very clearly that she does not want to date me, and it would be incredibly unfair of me to pursue something with her while my heart is stuck on someone else.

Yet, the memory of her soft lips comes back to me. Her breast under my hand. Her ass pressing into my lap, her full body reclined on mine. I get a whiff again of her body wash and can't help it when my hand closes around my cock. She's just right outside the door, so I work myself as quietly as possible, mind on that fiery red hair and bright blue eyes the entire time.

I finish up in the shower soon after, getting out and toweling off. I dress and reenter the now lamp-lit hotel room to find Linny in bed, sitting up on her phone, gold-rimmed glasses on her face instead of contacts.

"You look cute in glasses," I comment as I drop my dirty clothes in my suitcase and pretend I didn't just wank off to her in the shower.

"Thanks," she says, hardly glancing up.

I pull my own glasses out of my bag and put them on. "'You look cute in glasses too, Ben,' is what you're supposed to say." I astutely push the tortoiseshell frames up my nose.

She finally looks up at me for real and says in a monotone voice, "You look cute in glasses too."

"I don't believe you," I say with a sigh, climbing in the bed beside her. "I only need to wear them when reading, or driving, or watching TV. Even so, I don't wear them as often as I should. Contacts and I don't agree, and these slip down my nose too much."

"Oh yeah, that's annoying. I hate when mine do that, which is why I prefer contacts if I'm leaving my house."

I turn on my side toward her, glasses askew under my palm. "So, how shall we do this? Put a barrier of pillows between us?"

"We're adults. I don't think that's necessary."

"Oh, so you *do* want to cuddle. Got it."

"Literally not even close to what I said. I'm not a cuddler."

"That's shocking. You cuddled pretty well on my lap tonight."

"Well, that was an extenuating circumstance." She puts her phone down on the nightstand. "Tomorrow morning we're doing the spa thing, and then afterward I should go see my dad since I'm in town. You can head back to Edinburgh whenever you feel like it."

"Okay," I say, flipping to my back. "I'm gonna go to the stag thing. It's been forever since I've played football. I mean, Andy's a prat, but the rest of the blokes were nice. Especially Paul."

She ignores my snub of her ex and raises her eyebrows. "Paul, huh? You mean Paul was nice or Paul was *nice?*"

I narrow my eyes at her. "A bit of both, to be fair. Not that I'm going to do anything about it since he thinks you and I are dating."

"Sorry to hold you back," she says, looking away.

"That is not what I meant," I protest, hearing what I said too late. "I just mean he's fit. And seems like a good guy."

She sucks her teeth. "Well, if you're really interested, we can break up in a week or so, and then you can pursue him. I mean, we'd have to break up before the wedding anyway so people don't ask where you are."

I'm not going to pursue Paul. I intend to tell Linny that, but instead I ask, "You don't want me with you at the wedding?"

"No? I just needed moral support tonight. I'll be fine at the wedding."

"Okay."

"Okay."

I switch off the lamp on my side. She follows suit, and I hear her set her glasses on the nightstand. I do the same with mine.

In the dark, I ask, "You sure you're not a cuddler?" I suggestively brush my foot against hers.

She kicks me back. "Bennett Pyeon, I swear to god if I wake up to you spooning me…"

I chuckle. "I swear I won't be!" I turn on my side, facing her. She shifts to face me as well.

I'm about to say goodnight, but she asks, "So, are you ever going to tell me about David?"

My breath catches in my throat. "I did tell you about David."

"Not really."

I grumble, "He's been my best mate since uni. I gave him a grand confession, and he turned me down." I squeeze my eyes shut as I say, "The night you and I met was the night I told him how I felt."

She sucks in a small gasp. "Oh, fuck. Really?"

"Aye. I can't tell you enough how grateful I am to you for that night." I silently groan before pressing my face into the pillow, muffling my voice. "I have a confession."

"What?"

"The last time you asked me if Andy was still watching us, he had gone, but I said he hadn't. I lied because I wanted to keep kissing you."

Linny doesn't hesitate as she washes away my guilt. "Well, I'm a good kisser, so no shame in that."

I huff out a laugh.

Gently, she says, "I'm sorry David doesn't love you, Ben. I honestly can say I don't understand how he couldn't."

I shift, shoving my arm under my pillow. "The problem is, he does love me. I know he does—it's just purely platonic. There's an invisible line that he is unable to cross. I find it highly unfair that I crossed that line alone."

She makes a sympathetic sound. "I'm not sure if this will make you feel better, but don't discount the blessing of platonic love. I am so sorry he doesn't love you the way you want him to, but platonic love is so important. It's so special, and it's something you should try to hold onto if you can."

Her words settle with me. She's right. That's the thing of it. That's why my head is all over the place when it comes to David, because even if all we are is friends, I want him as a friend. I *need* him as a friend. He is one of my favorite parts of life, and not having him at all is worse than not having him in the way I want.

"I know," I settle on saying. "Goodnight, frisky whisky."

"Night, Ben."

...

I blink awake as a crack of sunlight breaks through the gap in the blackout curtains and hits my face. I feel breath on the back of my neck and a body pressed against mine in the bed. After blinking a few more times to start my eyes, I peer down to see Linny's arm around me and my hand gripping hers.

I laugh silently. Oh, I get to tease her so hard about this. I'm about to flip over to wake her up when I realize…*shite*. I'm hard as a rock. Lord smite me. I stay as still as I can, pumping my thoughts full of egg salad and brown snow and other unsexy things to get him to calm the hell down.

Once I manage that, I turn in the bed, careful to keep Linny's arm around me.

I brush the hair out of her face gently, and she blinks awake, taking a moment to focus on me. I fully intend to tease her about spooning me in the night, but what comes out of my mouth instead is, "You're beautiful in the morning."

Because, goddamn, she is. The light that woke me is making her hair glimmer and burn. Those eyes are soft and sleepy and pure magic.

I expect her to remove her arm from me, or comment about how we are sharing a pillow and are chest to chest, but she mumbles, "You're a bit blurry in the morning."

"You're a liar," I say quietly.

She blinks, confused and not fully awake. "What?"

"You said you're not a cuddler, but I woke up to you cuddling the bloody hell out of me."

Her eyes widen, and I think she's finally awake. "Shit."

She rockets away, making me cackle.

"Don't be a dick," she scolds, throwing a pillow at me.

I brush the pillow off so it falls to the ground. "I'm not. It was nice! I slept great in your arms last night," I can't help but taunt.

She shoves me hard, almost pushing me off the bed as I continue to snicker. She sits up, grumbling. Then she twists back, "Did you use my body wash last night?"

I roll onto my back. "Yes."

"That explains why you smell good."

"Well, that and my natural pheromones. They say I have better pheromones than the rest."

"*Who* says that?"

I gesture widely. "They. All of them. Every them, along with everyone in the world. I swear, go to anyone I've ever even brushed past and they'll be like 'Oh, Ben Pyeon? The guy with the best pheromones on the market?' Try it. I dare you."

"You are such an odd person." She makes that sound like a compliment. She retrieves her glasses from the nightstand and sets them on her face. "So, when do you leave for the soccer thing?"

I check the time on my phone. "About an hour. Have to head to Stratford. It's where the pitch is, I guess. When do you leave?"

"About half an hour, so I'd better start getting ready."

She sits at the desk under a mirror, gathering a brush and hair ties with her. I watch as she splits her hair down the middle, then proceeds to plait one side, then the other. Her glasses are back off as she does this, so clearly she doesn't need to see to form these perfect plaits, her hands and muscle memory providing enough sight.

As she touches up her hair, pulling down strands to frame her face and the like, she says, "You can head back to Edinburgh after the stag thing. You don't have to wait around for me."

I sit up. "That's the second time you've told me to go home. Would you like me to leave? I know I'm a lot."

She faces me, putting her glasses back on as she does so. "You're the perfect amount. No. I just don't want you to think you have to stay."

"I don't think that. I think I'm going to go play football with some lads, then I'll wait for you here while you're at your da's. In the morning, we'll take the train back to Edinburgh together. That's my plan. I'm hoping it aligns with yours."

Linny's mouth twitches. "You can come to my dad's house if you'd like, so you're not spending the evening alone."

"I'd love to."

She lets that smile grow full. "Thanks for being here."

I wave her away. "Stop thanking me. Not doing this out of the kindness of my heart, you know."

Her eyebrows lift playfully. "You're not, are you? Then how come?"

"I want something in return."

"I can flash you my tits," she offers.

"While I would *love* that, I was thinking something a little less physical. A favor. Nothing specific yet, but when I need a favor, I have you to call on."

"That can be arranged." She sticks her hand out for me to shake. I crawl down the bed and extend my hand to meet hers, soft and delicate in my grip. We shake, and she says, "Deal."

"Deal."

...

I meet Paul at the tube station that will take us to Stratford. I'm wearing a T-shirt and joggers with trainers that I'll replace with boots on the pitch. Paul's lending me an extra pair. He grins when he sees me, and man, is he handsome. However, one look in his blue eyes reminds me of another pair I like a lot more.

The temptation is hanging in front of me like a carrot on a string, though, because if anything were to happen with Paul, it wouldn't mean anything. That's the difference. With Linny, taking it anywhere would mean *something*. I can feel that fact deep in my bones. But I can't give her everything she deserves yet—and she doesn't want it. Paul on the other hand...

No, no. I can control myself.

"You and Linny have a good night after we all left?" he asks as we wait for the tube.

"Aye," I say. "Just went back to the hotel, had a shower, and went to bed."

"That all?" he asks.

Oh, shite. If we were dating, the sexual energy I felt last night could have been directed toward Linny. We certainly could have done more. I cock a smile and lie, "Well, neither of us showered alone."

He gives a single nod. "Right. Nice."

That probably wasn't exactly what he was asking, was it? I quickly nudge the subject away from me. "How about you? You were talking to that one bloke at the club for a while."

"Yeah, nothing happened. Got his number."

The train comes and we step on, taking two free seats. I will say, I think the London Underground is pretty clean compared to other cities I've visited, but I have never understood why the seats have to be carpeted. That's not the case in New York City, say, and I can see how it provides for a much easier cleanup. I mean, can you imagine the amount of piss in these seats? Or simply just absorbed sweat?

We get off the train once we reach Stratford, and I let Paul guide the way. I have never been to this part of London before— not as if I'm a West Ham fan. Paul takes a turn, so we walk through a collection of shops and restaurants. As we reach a long stretch of road, Paul pauses, looking at his phone and then up at what's in the distance before him.

London Stadium. Where West Ham United plays.

He mumbles at his phone, "No bleeding way."

"What?" I ask, trying to see what he's googling.

He sighs, then starts typing a furious text. When his phone buzzes, he sighs again and then pockets the phone.

"Sodding bastard. He only gave the address, I guess to make it more of a surprise? Or pretend to be humble, I'd wager. I figured we were headed to a pitch by West Ham."

"Are we not?"

"No. The bastard booked our match at London Stadium."

Paul starts walking with determination toward the stadium. I follow after him, feeling incredibly confused. Who the hell has the money to do this? "Who? Julien?"

"No. Atti." I cringe at the name. "His father is a very well-compensated sport agent, and is from a distantly noble family, so he has a lot of connections. Apparently, this is one of them. I cannot imagine how much he paid for this." Paul shakes his head. "Atti's fine and all." I doubt he means that. "But he tends to wave his money around like a shield. Or a prize, if you're lucky enough to be chosen. It's exhausting."

"I can see that," I agree. Linny vaguely implied Atti came from money, but she did not imply it was *this* kind of wealth. "From what I saw last night, Atti seems like an exhausting person." I swallow. "He's not very nice to Linny."

Paul nods. "Yeah, from what little Mel has said about their breakup, I've gathered that. Mel made it sound like it was something he said more so than did to pull that final straw. Which, more power to her. You and Linny seem like you're much better suited. For one, you're nice to her."

"I always plan to be," I say. It's simple, really, though many people act like it's not. Be nice to your partner. Be kind to them. If you have a slip-up, apologize. Not that Linny is my real partner, but the same idea applies.

Paul is grumbling at his phone. "We have to enter through bridge two," he says. I trail along beside him.

A worker immediately meets us as we walk in. Once we explain we're here for a stag party, said worker leads us through a concrete tunnel that eventually opens out onto the pitch.

I pause as soon as I step out onto the turf. Wow. I mean, these pitches look massive when you're watching matches on the telly and sitting in the seats of the stadium, but on the ground, it's even larger. I suddenly feel so very small. We are not worthy of playing on a pitch like this.

Paul practically has to drag me along to meet up with the rest of the lads who have stationed themselves near the middle of the grass. It's the other groomsmen and some blokes I haven't met before. When we reach them, Paul gives Julien a big hug and says, "Sure this is not what you expected, is it?"

He laughs. "Not a bit. But you know Atti."

"I do indeed."

"Speaking of," I cut in, "where is that tall fella?"

"Right here," a deep voice says behind me. I try not to jump.

I turn to see him carrying a carton of plastic waters. Sure, he can rent out London Stadium, but can't spend the extra few pounds on reusable water bottles. That would be a great party favor. Reusable water bottles with Julien's face.

Paul hands over the extra pair of boots he brought me, so I take to the ground to lace them up. Once they're on, I pop back up and count. There are enough people here for a good match of six on six, ten on the pitch, two on the goals. They've been kind enough to pull the goals inward so we're not playing across the entire stadium.

"Suppose we'll pick teams," Atti proposes, arms crossed over his broad chest.

Julien claps his cousin on the shoulder. "I'll be team captain for blue and you, red?" he suggests.

I notice the box between them, shirts of red and blue mixed together.

Atti nods. "You're first pick."

"Paul," Julien says without pause.

Atti picks Darren. Julien picks some guy named Trevor. Atti some bloke named Wes. Julien, Gregory. Atti, Alfie. Julien, Kip. Atti, Holland. Now it's down to me and a lad named Mark. I'd be insulted if I weren't the odd man out. Though Julien better pick me, as I would much rather play against Atti than with him.

And he does.

Mark heads over to Atti's team, mumbling, "Always picked last."

"You've got a bum knee. You're of no use anymore," one of the blokes taunts.

"Mark almost went pro," Paul says quietly, "but tore his ACL at uni. Knee hasn't been the same since. Right shame."

"That's shite," I comment, catching the T-shirt Paul tosses at me. I pull off the one I wore and throw on the new one. Paul does the same, and I can't help but glance his way. Though I will admit, it was more of a linger than a glance. My cheeks burn as he catches that linger, but he just smiles.

Atti asks obnoxiously, "You know how to play football, Ben?"

"I have an understanding," I state.

We separate into two sides, and a referee comes out of no-where to toss the ball in the air. Julien steals it, passing it to Paul, I follow alongside, ready for it. Atti comes and steals the ball, tak-ing it back toward our goal. I run up beside him, sliding in there and kicking the ball from his path.

The death glare he gives me is enough to make me want to have a doctor check my years.

Paul catches the ball I kicked, running it back toward the goal. He gets boxed in, and I wave my arms to signal I'm free. He kicks the ball over to me, so I run it down the pitch, taking aim and shooting. It glides into the goal, right past Mark, who swears like a sailor. I give him a shrug and jog back over to my team.

"An understanding?" Paul asks incredulously.

"I mean, I played at school. Then on a club squad at uni," I say loud enough for Atti to hear. He grumbles, but gets back in line, ready for the ref to toss the ball back into play.

We play through the game, ending on a three-to-three tie. Afterward, the plan is to head to a pub in the area.

"You coming?" Paul asks as he unlaces his boots to throw back in his bag.

"Can't," I say, handing him my borrowed boots. "Linny and I are going to see her Dad."

"Is this your first time meeting him?"

"Aye, so I need a shower beforehand."

Paul nods as though I am truly a boyfriend trying to make a good impression on his girlfriend's dad.

I pull out my phone to give Linny an update on my timeline. There's a text waiting for me, but it's not from Linny. It's from David.

> So, for dinner this week, I was thinking I could bring Callum and you could bring Linny? I met her briefly at the soft opening, but I'd love to get to know her better. I didn't realize then you were dating

Yeah, me neither. "Fuck," I murmur.

"Something wrong?" Paul asks.

I sigh. "Naw. Nothing."

Nothing except that David has clearly invited Callum and Linny to our supper because he's afraid to be alone with me— using our partners as a shield.

Paul stands up, and I follow suit. We trail behind the other guys as we leave the stadium.

I text Linny as we catch up.

What time are you thinking for your dad's?

I'm heading over there at 6

Then I won't be far behind

CHAPTER EIGHT
Linny

I admire my lavender nails as I wait for my dad to open the door. This is a great color. Well chosen, me. I ring the bell again. Then again. Come on.

My finger is poised on the bell as he swings the door open with a huff. Thin, wire-frame glasses rest on his nose as he peers down at me. "Impatient today, aren't we?"

I move in for a hug. "It's cold out here."

He gives me a tight squeeze and ushers me in as I shove a hand in my cardigan pocket, pulling out a tiny, clear quartz crystal. I place it in his palm and say, "It can help with your headaches."

"I'll sleep with it taped to my forehead." He doesn't give me a chance to explain that that is not what he should do before he inquires, "I thought you were bringing a boy?"

I groan as I close the door behind myself and follow him toward the front room. "I told you I *might* be bringing my friend, who is a *man*. We're not dating. We're only pretending for this weekend." I take a seat on the couch. "Ben's on his way."

"Hmm," my dad muses as he takes the seat opposite me. "Lying is never a good idea, Linny."

"It's only a fib to keep Atti off my back. It's fine. It'll be over before the wedding."

"Atti. Uck. Never liked that Atti." He's lying. He loved Atti. Until I told him why we broke up. Hasn't been a fan since. "You see him last night, then? Hope you showed off that old right hook of yours."

"We both know I am not coordinated enough to get in a good punch. Anyway, I don't need to hit him." I lean back. "Even if he deserves it. He was an ass for the entire night. I broke a glass because of course I did, and he commented that it wouldn't be the first time he had to tip a waitress on my behalf."

"What a prick. Well, as I've offered, my fists are open for commission."

"The answer is still no on the physical violence."

He seems disappointed by that, but moves on. "Want a drink? I've a whole bar. Or wine. You like wine."

"I do like wine. What are we having for dinner? You think red or white?"

"White, for sure. We're having salmon. I've a great chardonnay you'll love." The doorbell rings the moment he stands. "That'll be your boy. Excuse me—*man*. I'll let you get it."

He heads toward the kitchen as I push myself up from the couch, stressing again that, "He's just a friend."

I open the door to find Ben in nice slacks and a forest green sweater under his open jacket. He looks good. He always looks good.

"You used my body wash again," I say in greeting. The citrus scent hit me as soon as I opened the door.

He smiles, and I can't help but match it. His genuine smile is contagious. "You smell so good, orange blossom. I want to smell like you." He looks pointedly at the foyer. "May I come in?"

"Oh. Right. Yeah, come on." I point to where he can hang his jacket, then lead him into the front room where my dad is waiting with two glasses of wine.

He sets them down on the coffee table, saying, "You must be Ben."

Ben stands up straighter and says, "Yes, sir. Pleasure to meet you." He holds out a hand for my father to shake. My father does not take it, which makes Ben grow even stiffer. I swear, sweat forms on his brow.

Part of me wants to see how long Ben will hold his hand out, but I figure I'll be nice. Especially because my dad isn't being a jerk by not shaking Ben's hand—it's because he doesn't see his hand. "Dad, Ben's trying to shake your hand. Don't be rude," I joke.

Other people might be embarrassed by the personal flub (me, I mean me), but Dad, as always, takes it in stride. He sighs loudly and says, "Well, if you insist." His eyes take an extended moment to locate Ben's still outstretched hand before he slaps his own into it. "Pleasure's mine. And you can call me Harold." Still gripping Ben's hand, he tugs him forward and says quietly, "If I like you well enough by the end of the night, Harry." He releases Ben and places his eyes on me. "My Linny seems to really like you. She was just saying she may be in love."

"*Dad!*" I scold, my cheeks heating. I explain to Ben, "He knows we're not dating."

My dad cackles, his jokes only funny to himself. "Ben, you fancy a white wine?"

"Yes, sir," Ben says, still a bit rigid. "I mean, Harold." A flush climbs his neck.

"I'll go fetch you some." My dad heads back to the kitchen.

I swipe my glass from the coffee table and sit back on the

couch, pulling Ben with me. "He thinks he's funny," I say. "Don't let him psych you out. He's being overprotective."

Ben relaxes into the couch. "Does he have RP as well?"

"Yeah, it's genetic. Had to come from somewhere." I sigh. "He didn't see your hand—it was in a blind spot. Though most of his spots are blind. He doesn't have a lot of vision left, but it's less obvious in his own home."

"I figured." He angles his head toward me. "You told him we're not really seeing each other?"

"Are you surprised? Of course, I did. Can't have him getting his hopes up. I told my mom, too."

"Where is your mum? She here?"

"She's in Syracuse, New York."

"Oh, right. Sorry. You mentioned they were divorced."

My dad comes out with a third glass of wine for Ben. He hands it to him and says, "It's been a happy divorce." He sits back down, running a hand over his bald head. "Food should be ready in ten. So, Ben, Linny tells me you're a baker?"

"Aye—I own a café with my sister. She handles the business. I handle the sugar."

My dad continues to grill him with much protest from me while dinner finishes up. As he does, I fear he already has his hopes up. I've told him I'm not looking for anyone. I don't need anyone. If he can do this, *life*, by himself, so can I. I *can*.

Once dinner is ready, my dad plates it, then we join him at the table.

"Oven-roasted salmon?" Ben asks, observing the plate of pink fish as we take our seats.

"Yes, indeed," my dad confirms. "You're not allergic?"

"Not at all. It smells amazing. Roasted over lemons and brushed with butter, garlic, thyme"—he sniffs as he studies the plate—"oregano, and honey?"

Dad lifts his chin. "You've got a good nose."

"I've got an amazing nose. It's good at picking up scent, too."

I snort at the joke and examine his nose. It is a nice nose.

Dad's eyes glimmer as he says, "It tastes even better than it smells. Serve yourselves."

As Ben places some salmon and roasted potatoes on both our plates, I ask him, "How'd the match go?"

"Pretty good," he answers. "Ended in a tie, but that's alright. I got to show off some of my moves." He adds quieter, "Which pissed Atti off."

"Good," my dad comments loudly, shoving his fork into his mouth.

I ignore my dad and ask, "Moves?"

He shrugs, taking a bite. Once he swallows, he says, "I've been playing all my life. Some would say I'm quite good." He points to his plate. "Like this. This is amazing, Harold."

I did not know this. It's not a surprising fact—I can tell he's athletic just by looking at him. And he mentioned something about mountain biking and an enjoyment of nature.

"Where was the match again? A field in Stratford?"

Ben lets out a sharp laugh. "Yeah. At London Stadium."

"London Stadium?" I question. "Wait, you mean where West Ham plays? *The* West Ham?"

"The very one."

"How did you guys…?" I trail off when the realization hits me. *Oh.* "Never mind. I know the answer to that. Atti."

Ben nods, taking another bite. "Yeah."

"Prick," Dad mutters into his wine, which makes me burst out laughing. My dad is the best.

We finish up dinner, then Dad insists on pouring us all another glass of wine. I try to refuse, but quickly give in. By the time we finish the second glass, it's getting late.

"Sorry this was such a quick visit, same as the last," I say to my dad as I slip on my coat. "I'll come down for an actual visit soon. I promise."

He gives me a tight hug once my coat is on. "I'll hold you to that. But I'll see you for sure at the wedding, love." He extends his hand for Ben to shake. "Good to meet you, son. Hopefully, we'll meet again soon."

"Yes, hopefully," Ben replies. "Thank you again, Harold. The meal was wonderful."

"You can call me Harry. You've earned it." My dad offers me a head tilt as Ben's eyebrows shoot up in surprise. "I like him. He's good at sucking up."

"Jesus, Dad. We're leaving." I grab Ben by the arm and yank him with me out the door. "Love you!" I call behind me.

"Love you too," Dad says. "Get home safe, please."

"I always try," I respond.

Ben and I take off down the street, heading toward the tube station. I shove my hands in my pockets as we walk.

"You don't need a hand out here?" Ben asks.

I shake my head, glancing upward. "Nah. Street lights. My eyes do better in the dark outside than they do inside. I'm not sure why. Light fills the space in a different way? Who knows."

"Okay," he says. "Good to know." As we stop at a street crossing, waiting for cars to pass, he clears his throat. "So, what would you think about extending this little fake dating thing we have going on?"

Oh no. I blow out a puff of air. "I don't think so, Ben. I mean, don't get me wrong, I like you a lot. But that's why I can't. I really am not interested in being in a relationship."

A walk sign pops up, so we cross the street. Ben laughs lightly. "No, Lin, I literally meant the *fake* dating. I'm needing to call in my favor sooner than I expected."

I angle my head toward him. "Oh?"

"Oh. David has invited his boyfriend to our dinner, and you as well."

"Why would he…? Oh, right. Because you accidentally implied we're dating." I swallow. "In that case, sure. I like dinner. But, Ben, are you sure you want to lie to him?"

We arrive at the tube station and enter through the gates. More people are milling around this station than I expected, speed walking in every direction. I grab Ben's arm as an extra precaution, my eyes darting around in an attempt to see everyone all at once.

"No, but I think I have to," he finally replies. "I believe the only reason David invited you and Callum was as a barrier. He doesn't want to be alone with me."

I scoff. "I doubt that's the case. He probably wants to get to know me better. I'm great."

Ben smiles, but not his real one. "I'm sure that's it." He sighs. "Either way, I'd like to have you there—just to prove that I've moved on." He clears his throat. "Even though, as much as I've tried, I haven't."

"Got it. Well, I'm happy to go." I squeeze his arm in reassurance.

"Thanks," he says gratefully as we descend the stairs. Once we get to the platform, I release him.

The train comes, so we board, huddling in side by side. We arrive back at the hotel and run into Kensie and Jen. They both wave and say hi.

"You headed out?" I ask.

"Yeah," Kensie says. "There's a spot around the corner we want to check out. You both are welcome to tag along."

I shake my head. "I am actually really excited to go to bed."

"Me too," Ben says quietly, causing my face to flush. He's too good at this.

There's mischief in Kensie's eyes. "Got it. Well, I guess we'll see you both at the welcome dinner?"

"Yeah," I say, accepting the hug she's offering. I don't bother to explain that Ben won't be with me for either the rehearsal dinner or the wedding. "See you soon."

We get up to our room, and I immediately kick a trash can upon entering. "That's in a different spot," I grumble as I nudge it back to its rightful place. "I'm going to shower."

Ben nods, kicking off his shoes and flopping back onto the bed. He grabs the remote and flips on the TV as I close the bathroom door.

I turn on the shower to let it heat up as I get undressed. I climb in, standing under the warm water. I wash my face and body, then nudge the water a little hotter before shaving my legs since I've developed goosebumps that will not be conducive to shaving. The water gets hot, but not hot enough. I turn it all the way so it's practically boiling.

The scorching water pelts my skin, the momentary sting of pain feeling good. I close my eyes and take a deep breath. This is something I do occasionally—take a moment under the heat. Once my skin gets used to the temperature, I prop my leg up on the lip of the bathtub so I can shave. When I'm done, I turn off the shower and step out, seeing my pinked skin in the steamed mirror as I secure the thin, white hotel towel around my chest.

At the counter, I take one contact out and pop it in my case. I move on to the next, and it slips off my finger as soon as it's out of my eye.

"Shit," I swear, searching the counter and the ground from where I stand. I don't see it. Annoying thing is, yes, I've got the whole deteriorating eye thing going on, but my correctable vision is quite poor as well—which is mostly unrelated. I kneel to get a better look, but still cannot find it. *Ugh.* How stereotypical. I snatch my glasses from where I had left them on the counter this morning. They're a thin gold, metal frame with thick lenses. As soon as I put them on, they fog up. I take them off, wipe them on the towel around me, and then try again. Again, they fog. I grunt and stand to crack open the door in an attempt to level out the steam.

My glasses go back on my face as I decide to just wait for them to unfog. I bend over to continue hunting for my lost contact, but misjudge the counter's edge. The corner of my glasses connects with the counter, slamming them back into my skull.

"Fuck!" I exclaim loudly, hand going to my face as I drop to the floor, eyebrow stinging in pain.

"Linny?" Ben calls out, his voice getting louder as he approaches the bathroom. "Are you okay?"

"Yes," I reply, voice cracking. Tears are streaming out of my eyes.

"You're crying," Ben says as he pushes his way into the humid bathroom, feet bare and now just in an undershirt and his trousers, eyes widening when he sees me sitting on the floor, wrapped in only my towel, tears freely flowing.

"I'm fine," I say, voice still strained. "That just really hurt." He steps toward me, but I say, "Wait!" He pauses, regarding me curiously. "I dropped my contact."

"You're bleeding," he says in response. Of course I am. He nods as he thinks. "Okay. Don't move. I'll find your contact first." He searches for a moment, making a sound of triumph when he sees it. "It's stuck to the side of the counter." He scoops it up, balancing it on his finger.

Finger extended, he holds it out to me, passing it to my outstretched finger like children passing a bug. Without getting up, I grab my contact case from the edge of the counter and place the contact inside with the solution. I screw the top on and make to stand, but Ben shakes his head at me.

"Stay there."

He kneels in front of me, removing my glasses and setting them up on the counter. He snatches a tissue and gently dabs above my eye where I injured myself. Pain stings where the tissue touches.

"A lot of blood," he comments, "but not too deep." He grabs a fresh tissue and presses it to the cut. "Hold this here," he directs. "I'm going to see if the front desk has a first aid kit. Don't move."

I take the tissue from him, applying pressure to the spot. "Not even to put on clothes?" I ask, painfully cognizant of the fact that I am only in a towel.

"Especially not to put on clothes," he says seriously. "I'll be right back." He leaves the room while I stay in that spot, sitting on the bathroom floor.

The tears stopped already, but they nearly start again when I'm hit with how annoyed I am at myself. When things like this happen, I never know if I should blame my eyes or my knack for clumsiness. I hold the tears in. There have been far too many on this trip.

Ben soon returns, supplied with antibacterial cream and bandages. He kneels back before me, gently guiding my hand away from the injury. "It's already stopped bleeding," he observes. He dabs on the cream, smoothing it into the cut with the pad of his thumb. He then places the bandage on the spot, concealing half of my eyebrow in the process. "Cute."

I glare.

He responds with a laugh. "I'm serious!" He brushes a loose strand of my damp hair behind my ear, then presses his lips against the bandage. I feel myself anchoring toward his mouth. He pulls away only slightly to say softly, "Kiss and make it better, right?"

"Right," I whisper back, eyes trained on a light bruise on my bare knee. "I'm not usually *this* much of a mess," I promise, even though I'm not sure that's true.

"I like a bit of a mess." As if suddenly aware of how close we are, he pulls back and stands. "I'll leave you to get dressed." He exits, closing the door behind himself.

I pull myself back to my feet, finish my skincare routine, glare at the bandage affixed to my face, then put on my PJs. By the time I exit, Ben has changed into shorts and is wearing his glasses as he watches TV. When he sees I'm out, we switch places in the bathroom. I climb into my side of the bed, pulling out my phone but not really looking at anything.

He comes back out, teeth brushed and face washed. Before he climbs in with me, he grabs two pillows and puts them in the middle of the bed. He then snatches one of the pillows from behind my head, causing me to slam back into the wall, and puts that in the middle as well.

"What the hell are you doing?" I demand, sitting up.

"Building a barrier," he says, "since you clearly can't keep your hands to yourself in the night."

"Oh my god," I say, snatching back my pillow and tossing it behind my shoulders. "You're such an ass." I grab another pillow and chuck it at him.

He chuckles as he catches it, flopping down onto the bed and throwing it behind himself. "I told you, I liked it. I'm happy to cuddle anytime." He shoves his body under the sheets.

I cross my arms. "It won't happen again."

"I won't be upset if it does."

I sigh heavily and take off my glasses, tossing them on the side table, then switch off the lamp. I slide down lower into the sheets and lie on my back.

Ben follows suit, turning off his light and settling into the bed. "So," he says into the dark room. "I realized you know why I was on the bench, but I don't know what led you there. Why were you in Grassmarket? Not trailing Atti, right?"

"*No*," I snip. "I was just…" I huff out air through my nose. "I was taking a walk. I know that sounds weird because it was eleven o'clock at night, but I do that sometimes. Not as often anymore, but it's, like, proof that I can. Taking a walk in the dark by myself reminds me that I have agency."

"Hmm," he muses. "That makes sense. Can I make one request, though, for when you do that?"

"What?"

"Take some form of weapon with you. Protect yourself."

My heart hums at the concern. "I have mace."

"Good."

I shift on my side toward him. "I was happy to have you here this weekend. I hope you had an okay time."

"I had a great time." He flips on his side as well. "I was happy to be here."

I don't say anything to that, but I extend my leg so my foot can touch his.

"Your toes are freezing," he whispers.

"That sucks for you," I whisper back.

He lifts his feet up to encompass mine, rubbing like he's attempting to create heat.

I laugh loudly. "Ben!" I try to yank my foot back to my side of the bed, but he has trapped it. I keep giggling, my hand on his chest in a poor effort to push him away. Once I get my foot free, I kick him lightly. "You're ridiculous."

"I've been called worse," he says through a smirk I can hear.

"Good*night*," I say assertively, flipping onto my other side.

"'Night," he responds, his foot hitting mine one last time.

...

I wake to light on my face. I blink my eyes open and find myself face-to-face with Ben. His eyes are closed—he is clearly still asleep. Neither one of us is spooning the other, but we are sharing a pillow. As I come to and assess my surroundings, I realize it is me sharing his. *Damn.* I'm the cuddler once again. Very closely, at that. My arms are gathered in front and pressed into his chest. One of his arms is shoved under the pillow—and the other is resting on my waist. Our legs are gently intertwined.

I should move away, but every instinct is telling me to move closer. I don't.

I carefully pull away, untangling our limbs, and twist to get out of the bed, not wanting Ben to wake up to us like this. I'll keep this morning to myself. If I keep it for myself, it makes it less real.

And that's better.

CHAPTER NINE
Ben

After we arrive back in Edinburgh, Linny and I walk together from Waverly. She's heading home, and I'm heading to the café. Once we reach the doors to her flat and Somewhere Special, we stop and look at each other. I'd like to hug her goodbye, but she crosses her arms, shutting that down.

"Want a coffee or anything?" I ask, shoving my hands in my trouser pockets.

"I'm okay."

I give a jerk of my head. "Well, this has been fun. I'll let you know about dinner."

"Please do."

"Text me when you get home?"

Her face falls flat, eyes flashing to her front door. "You mean, when I get up the stairs?"

"Yes."

"Okay."

We go our separate directions. I walk into the café to see a few people sitting at tables engaging in light chatter, and Rachel behind the counter. She smiles as I drag my suitcase inside.

"Shouldn't Gemma be behind the counter?" Gemma is one of the two employees Isla and I hired, who is supposed to be working today.

"Isla let her leave about twenty minutes ago. Did you walk here from the station?" she asks as she messes with the espresso machine.

"Yeah." I guide my suitcase behind the counter as I join her. On the counter are notebooks with scribbles of things I likely won't be able to make sense of, but I think I see the words "microplastic" and "algae" about a dozen times.

"That's a gross amount of energy you have. How was London?" She turns around, handing a cup of hot coffee to me. I accept it with a mutter of thanks.

"Good. Expensive. London." I take a sip. "You make a good coffee for someone who hates it."

"Everyone I love has an aggressive caffeine addiction," she says gravely.

Isla pushes out of the swinging door to the kitchen. "And how was Linny?"

I attempt to hide the shock on my face. I did not tell them who I was going to London with. "She's wonderful," I answer, eyes narrowed. "Who told you?"

Isla smirks, leaning back against the wall as she assesses me. "David said something about you and her dating. Also, Linny's aunt came in yesterday and mentioned she was in London for a joint hen and stag do. You said you were going for a last-minute stag do. Doesn't take a genius."

"That's a lot of conclusions to jump to," I gripe into my mug.

"Aye, and you confirmed them when you answered how Linny was." She whacks me on the arm. "So, are you seeing each other?"

I consider telling them the truth because I am not looking for more people to lie to, but I can't tell them the truth, then lie to David. Especially because it would come out that I lied rather quickly. David and Rachel are close. And once they discovered I lied to him, I would have to explain why. So, I do lie and say, "Sort of."

Rachel snorts. "You went away together for a weekend. Feels like more than sort of. Why haven't you said anything about her?"

I try to tell as much truth as I can. "Because it's new."

Isla and Rachel exchange a look. I hate when they do that.

Isla asks, "So you decided to take a spontaneous trip to London for a hen and stag do of a couple you don't know with a woman you just started seeing? That's weirder than when you were driving here from Newtonmore practically every other day."

I groan. Okay. Fine. So, when I was figuring out the David of it all, I was coming to Edinburgh a lot to visit him. And Isla. I dispersed my time. But Newtonmore is a two-hour drive one way on a good day. Yes, it was mad. But driving all that way gave me a lot of time to think. I needed a lot of time to think.

I ignore the comment about the drive and say, "Her ex-fiancé is in the bridal party. He's a proper arse. Partners were allowed to attend, so I offered to go as support. I like her, so why would I not?"

Isla groans back at me. "You are always doing nice things. It's bloody annoying."

Rachel makes a face. "You say that like *you're* not constantly doing nice things for people."

"Yeah, but I do it more quietly." She loops an arm around Rachel's waist.

"Sure."

My phone buzzes in my pocket, so I pull it out, grateful to have a distraction from this conversation. I smile when I see that the message is from Linny.

She included a picture of a cat sitting on her chest. Most of the photo is overtaken by gray fur, but I can see her crystal blues peeking out from behind the cat.

Isla distracts herself from her girlfriend long enough to glimpse over my shoulder at my phone. "Who's that?"

"Oscar Wilde," I say, remembering the name of her cat.

Isla nods in approval. "Dead queer icon texting you. That's cool."

I let out half a laugh. "I just came to check on my kitchen and get a head start on tomorrow."

I pivot around the counter, heading to the back and taking my coffee and suitcase with me, feeling thoroughly done with the conversation about Linny. The café will be closing soon, so I put in my headphones and pull out flour, butter, and sugar, more than ready to lose myself in this bake.

•••

A few days later, Linny and I are set to meet at the restaurant where we're having dinner with David and Callum. I have not seen her since we separated after the train station. I kept meaning to run over and bring her a cup of coffee or a muffin or something, but the café has been busy. Thankfully, I suppose. She hasn't stopped by either, so there's that.

I arrive at the restaurant and take a peek inside to see David and Callum already seated. I pull back from the window, figuring I'll wait for Linny out here. She approaches a little while later and smiles when she spots me.

"Are we waiting for David and his boyfriend still?" she asks.

"No. They're in there. I was waiting for you."

She narrows her eyes at me. "Are you being a chicken?"

"*No*," I emphasize. Honestly, I noticed it's a little dark in the restaurant, but I figure if I say that aloud, she may get annoyed with me for thinking she can't do it by herself. Which, fair. I know she can. Maybe I am being a chicken. I change the subject when I look at the plaster affixed under her right brow. I reach out, causing her to flinch back.

"What are you doing?" she asks, her full body angled away from me as her eyes find my hand, still hovering near her face.

I chuckle. "Looking at your injury." I reach for her face again and gently press my thumb above her brow, brushing downward toward the bandage. She settles back into me, angling her head up so I can see as I lean forward, just a breath away now. "How's it doing?"

"Fine," she grumbles. "Mostly healed. It's just a big, ugly, red, crusty line now. The band-aid is less noticeable, so that's why I still have it on."

"Think it'll scar?"

"No."

"Damn. That would be cute."

She rolls her eyes and pulls away from my hand. "Should we go in or are you still being a chicken?"

"You're a chicken," I mumble, reaching for her hand as I open the door with my other, letting her go in first, but then leading the way to the table. They don't see us right away, so I clear my throat. "David," I say, immediately wishing it came out better than the slight squeak that exited my mouth.

He turns around quickly. "Hey, man." He gets up and gives me a hug, which I accept with one arm, my hand still holding tightly to Linny's. He releases me and gives Linny a quick hello as we round the table to sit down.

I introduce Linny and Callum since this is their first time meeting. Callum's curly hair is longer than when I last saw him—long enough to pull into a bun atop his head.

Linny says, "Hi. Nice to meet you," but does so while taking a very long time to remove her coat and hang it over the back of her chair. Since I know better, I know she is doing this as a way to avoid shaking Callum's hand, which he has not had the chance to extend while she is preoccupied. Or, rather, to avoid missing an extended hand with the intention to shake.

Once her coat is off, I place a hand on her back, more of a reassurance for me than for her. She pats my leg, then says to David and Callum, "Ben said you all met at uni?"

Callum corrects, "Ben and I actually met in sixth form. I transferred to his school after GCSEs."

I hum in confirmation, having a hard time meeting Callum's eye. He's my friend as well, and I feel incredibly guilty for my attempt at ruining what he and David have. It wasn't like I did it with mal intent—it was a poor judgment call. I was being selfish, thinking only of myself and *my* feelings.

David smiles, glancing at Callum. "Ben and I met first term of uni when I was freshly moved back here from the States. We had one class together, and during the first week, Ben sat next to me, started talking my ear off, then asked me to get lunch. The rest was history."

I give a stiff nod, repeating, "The rest was history."

The night continues, and I am embarrassed to admit that I let Linny lead most of the conversation, keeping to myself. I mean, she's doing amazingly by asking knowledgeable questions about David's Ph.D. and Callum's work. I have no idea what a micro-controller is, but she seems to. *Fuck*, she's beautiful *and* smart. I'm so happy to have her by my side tonight.

I'm not moping, I'm not, but I don't know what to say. We get our food and continue the light conversation throughout, but I cannot help but note how surface-level it all is. I hate it. I hate that I did this to us.

After I finish my meal, I excuse myself to the toilet. I use the facilities, wash my hands, then run into David as I'm leaving. I step back, retreating into the WC with him following me. God, like I'm running away.

"You okay?" he asks, eyeing me worriedly.

"Fine," I grit out.

"Ben. You've been quiet all evening. You haven't been you."

I swallow. "I haven't felt like me," I admit. "Not for a while."

David looks around, like he's making sure we're alone in here. "Because of me?"

"No," I say quickly, then sigh. "No, not only you. I mean, not really. I'm sorry."

"Don't apologize. Ben, let's talk about this."

"In the toilet?"

"Yes, in the toilet," he says. "Have you talked to anyone about this? I mean, what's going on with you?"

"You mean me falling in love with my best mate and him rejecting me?"

Guilt flashes across his features. It's not my intention to make him feel bad, but I have trouble keeping my mouth shut. "Yeah. But also you figuring out your sexuality. Normally, I'd be the person you spoke to about that. But I'm not."

"Well, I sort of dumped it all on the first man I had sex with."

David's mouth drops open, but he recovers quickly. "Sure. And how did that go?"

"The sex? Great." I clear my throat. "I have a therapist. I've been going for about three months now."

"That's awesome," he says, looking relieved that I haven't exclusively been using my hookups as cheap and ineffective therapy. It was just the one time, I swear.

"Linny knows," I add.

His eyebrows lift. "She does?"

I nod, throat tight. "She knows everything."

His face softens. "You really like her, then?"

I can't help the small smile that grows on my face. "She's great." I let out an exhale. "David, I…I'm still trying to move past this. With us. My…my *feelings*. I'm sorry I had them." *Have*, I correct in my mind.

His lips purse, clearly agreeing with me but not wanting to say that. Instead, he asks, "Is there anything I can do to help?"

I huff humorlessly. "Get ugly? Become a horrible person? I don't know." I shake my head, offering a real answer. "Just keep being my friend. Keep pushing me. You know that's what I need sometimes. To be pushed."

"What you need is to be shoved."

I snort in response.

"But okay," he adds.

"Okay."

Turns out David only came to the toilet to find me, so we return to the table together. When we do, I place a hand on Linny's shoulder for a moment, hoping my silent thank you is communicated. She's mid-conversation with Callum, but she grabs my hand and squeezes it tightly, her rings digging in. I think she's asking if I'm okay. I squeeze back, letting her know I am.

...

The two pairs of us head in separate directions after dinner. I say to Linny, "I'm walking you home."

"Fine," she agrees.

As soon as we're out of sight from David and Callum, she drops my hand. I'm surprised by the chill that spreads over me when she does. We soon walk up on the door between my café and her shop.

"This is me," she says unnecessarily.

"Can I come up?" I find myself asking.

She narrows her eyes. "Why?"

I propose, "To meet Oscar Wilde."

She nods, shoving her key into the front door and escorting me up to her first-floor flat. She opens the door and leads me in, flipping on all the lights. "Oscar," she calls, wandering down the hall as I stay in the entryway, taking in her flat.

The walls are a cream color, and the couch that centers her living room is a sage green. Dark wooden furniture accents the room. Everything besides the couch looks like an antique. Well, considering she runs an antique shop, I figure it is. There are little ghosts set up in random spots around her flat, all the same shape but varying in color and size. They're two different sizes, one about nine centimeters tall and the other about five centimeters. They're shaped like a typical ghost under a sheet, with oblong eyes at the tops of their head. I pinpoint one that is black with rainbow speckles, then a little lavender one with darker purple marbling.

She comes back, a gray cat flung over her shoulder, clinging to her around the neck. She sets him down. I crouch as the cat spots me and quickly approaches. I notice something I failed to notice in the picture she sent me.

"He only has three legs." Oscar is sporting his front two legs and a back left leg, but appears to be missing the back right leg.

"Damn," Linny says flatly. "Must have left that one behind. Be right back." She rotates and pretends to walk back to what I assume is her bedroom, but twists around to me with a smirk.

"Yeah. He broke his leg when he was a kitten. It was so bad, it had to be amputated. Second most traumatic day of my life." She kneels with us.

I scratch Oscar Wilde's head as he rubs up against me. "What was the first?"

She leans across and strokes him down the back. "He manages just fine with three. Right, handsome?"

I duly note the obvious avoidance of my question as the cat moves to lend his attention to her before quickly coming back to me.

"He loves strangers," she says.

"Well, I love him too," I say, gazing down at the cat like he truly is the only source of light in the world. Well, maybe one of two. I peek back up at Linny, who is watching us interact. "So, when shall we break up?"

She chews her lip. "I was planning to talk to you about that. Would you mind, maybe, keeping this going until the wedding?"

I raise my eyebrows, surprised. "Sure. Of course. Why'd you change your mind?"

She sighs. "Mel texted and told me she'd given me a plus one for you. To both the wedding and the rehearsal dinner. I think she had to do some rearranging to fit you in, so I'll feel bad if I have to tell her you're not coming." She then adds with a grumble, "And it'll be nice to have you there."

I cup my hand around my ear. "What was that?"

More clearly, she says, "It'll be nice having you there. If you can go, that is."

"Of course. Happy to. Maybe I can break out the ol' kilt."

"You own a kilt?"

"I'm Scottish, of course I own a kilt. Though I haven't worn it since I was wee. Baws may be swinging below the hem if I tried it on."

"That's quite the picture you've just painted."

"You're welcome." Oscar Wilde has moved on, leaving us to go sit on his cat tree in the corner and stare out the dark window. Yet, we remain where we are on the floor. "If we're going to continue this charade until the wedding, we'll need to spend some time with Isla and Rachel. They'll get suspicious if I keep you all to myself."

"Are you sure you're okay lying to them?"

"I don't love it, but I wouldn't mind them thinking I'm in a happy relationship for a bit longer." Isla was insulted when I told her Linny and I were getting dinner with David and Callum, asking if she and Rachel could tag along. I told her no, and that made her angry. "Maybe we could have them over to my place sometime and I could make supper? Something casual."

"I mean, is dinner your only idea of fun?"

"Dinner is great! Especially if I make it."

"Fine, we'll continue to make the dinner rounds with everyone in our lives."

"Just need to go to Saratoga for your mum."

"Syracuse, and no, we don't. She'll be in town for the wedding. You can meet her then. What about your parents?"

"We can FaceTime them."

"Sure."

I reach out a hand, saying, "Shall we shake on it?"

She finds my hand with her eyes, then her hand. "Fine. We'll keep this going for another month or so?"

"Then we can have a very dramatic and tragic break-up. It'll be great."

"Deal."

CHAPTER TEN

Linny

"Melinda?"

I search for Carolyn but don't see her amongst the clutter of our store. I'm in the rear where the furniture can be stacked high. It doesn't help that she probably does not clear five feet anymore.

"Yes?" I call back, hoping for a bit of echolocation.

"Melinda?" she says again.

"Marco," I respond.

"No, it's me, Carolyn," she says in her normal songbird voice.

"No, you're supposed to say...never mind. Meet at the register." I set down the picture frames I have been carefully placing in various locations around the store since Carolyn brought in that hoard. I find her standing by the front counter with her hand on her hip. "Yes?" I ask.

"The shop is very dusty."

"I just dusted last night." Last night, it was dusty. I could hardly enter the store without sneezing. I take full responsibility for that. However, I did clean.

Her lips wrinkle. "Maybe the evening hours are not the best for dusting." *For you* is the unfinished end of that sentence.

I grumble and survey the shop, scanning the surfaces caught by the streaming light. Fine. It's still dusty.

"Point taken. However, I will argue that this stuff seems to generate dust. I think it's perfectly possible the store was spotless last night."

"I suppose it is."

"I'll start dusting."

I go to the back to grab a duster, pausing to check my phone. Nothing. My shoulders fall. I'm not sure why I expected something. From Mel, I mean. Something about the wedding. I don't know. I've gotten used to a notification-lacking phone. Not sure why it's bothering me now.

I grab the duster and proceed to swipe every inch of the shop until Carolyn is happy.

...

I make myself leave the shop as soon as we're closed today. I've spent too many late nights here when I should be spending them watching TV or going to yoga or reading smutty romance novels (all Carolyn's suggestions). As I'm locking the door behind me, I notice the light in the café is still on. They close before we do, so this piques my interest. I peer into the café to see a group of people sitting at the tables, all facing Ben, who stands defensively behind the counter.

I don't think before I knock on the locked front door.

Ben's eyes dart to me and grow grateful. Isla beats him to the door and says, "Linny! The perfect person for this. Tell Ben he has to celebrate his birthday."

I step inside, but don't get too far beyond the threshold. I look at him with wide eyes and ask, "Birthday? When's your birthday?"

"Never," Ben says.

"Tomorrow," Isla corrects, falling back into the seat beside

Rachel.

I step in a little farther, crossing my arms in front of myself. "What birthday is this? Thirty-one?"

Rachel pipes in, "Thirty."

I furrow my brow, still looking at Ben. "You told me you were thirty already."

"I'm close enough," he states.

David sighs from where he sits in a chair facing away from a table, Callum on the other side. "Ben, you love your birthday. And thirty is a big one. We want to celebrate it with you. Please let us."

Callum hums in agreement. "Yeah. Your last birthday was a week-long celebration spanning multiple cities."

"Right," David agrees. "We did that nice hike in the Highlands, went out with your buddies from work, wandered around Edinburgh for two nights. We're just asking you to do *one* thing this year to celebrate."

Ben's palms splay flat on the counter. "Well, you lot are free to make a party out of it. I'll be hiding away with Oscar Wilde, patiently awaiting thousands of pounds in bank transfers."

Callum questions, "Oscar Wilde?"

"My cat," I clarify.

Ben shakes his head. "Nope. I meant the real deal. I'll be in Ireland drinking a Guinness by his grave and reading *The Picture of Dorian Gray*. My flight's tonight. Or maybe I'll take a boat, spice it up a bit."

"Hate to break it to you," Isla says, "but Oscar Wilde is buried in France."

He squints at her. "Then what am I thinking of?"

"That memorial statue of him in Dublin?"

Ben just frowns in response.

I make my way behind the counter with him, setting a tentative hand on his arm. "Thirty is a big one, Ben. You should celebrate."

He looks at me, aghast. "You're supposed to be on my side, butterscotch."

"I *am* on your side. You should spend your thirtieth birthday with the people you love."

His eyes quickly flash to David, making me feel an unwelcome pinch in my gut.

Isla calls out, "Listen to your girlfriend, Ben."

"Fine," he laments. Everyone cheers, but he focuses his attention on me. "You'll come?"

"If you want me there."

"I do, but…"

"But what?"

"It's bowling."

"That's extremely lame. I see why you'd want to spare me."

His mouth quirks. "That's a good point, and a good pun, but that wasn't the but. It's dark in the bowling alley. Maybe we could do something else?"

"I'll be fine."

"Are you sure? If I'm saying it's dark, it's dark."

I squeeze him on the arm. "You don't get to decide my limitations." Understanding crosses his eyes. Louder I say, "So, bowling tomorrow night. Do we have a cake?"

Rachel raises her hand. "I'm making one. Unless you want to, Linny? I don't want to take that from you if that's something you'd like to do."

"No, no. Please. Bake away. I commend your bravery to bake for a baker."

Ben laughs. "She's going to steal my recipe, so it'll be good."

"Damn right," Rachel agrees.

•••

The next evening, Ben picks me up at my door so we can walk to the bowling alley together. He's wearing a green and blue bowling shirt with his initials "BP" stitched into the spot on his right chest.

I eye the shirt. "So, like, you *like* bowling. You are into bowling."

"I do like bowling."

"Why bowling?" I ask as we set off.

He smiles shyly. "They were trying to plan an activity that would mean something to me. I had been saving for years and years because I wanted to travel during that gap year I took before uni. As you know, I went to the States for the national parks, but I didn't want that to be the only thing I did while there. So, in each new city I visited, I went bowling."

"Because?" I prompt.

"It was a cheap option, and I like the atmosphere. Old men and stale beer. Glow-in-the-dark floors. Half-broken arcade games."

"And screaming children," I add.

"Naw, I'd go while they were in school. It was silly, and random, and made me feel like I actually took the time to visit these new places."

"Huh," I muse. "That's a good idea. Unique. I like that you did that. So, you're good at bowling?"

He laughs. "I'm much worse than you'd expect."

"Well, I'm much better than you'd expect."

"Then, game on, Jenkins."

We arrive at the bowling alley, but he pauses outside it.

"Ben?" I ask. "Are we going in?"

"Yeah."

He doesn't move.

I nudge him with my elbow. "What is it? Why don't you want

to celebrate your birthday?"

"I don't deserve it," he says simply.

"A birthday party?"

"Aye. I mean, I've been a shite friend. A shite brother. The only good thing I've been lately is a business partner. Also…" he trails off.

"Also?"

He kicks the ground absently. "I still don't feel like myself. Everything feels different and it feels wrong celebrating this big milestone birthday when I don't feel like me."

I purse my lips before throwing out, "Have you ever considered that you actually feel more like yourself than ever? That you *should* be celebrating this milestone because of that?"

"I…no?"

"You're adding layers, Ben. That's what life is. Layers and layers that make up a whole person. Not every layer is a warm blanket—most probably aren't, but these layers are *you*."

He considers this for a moment, letting my words spread over him. He gives a slight indication of his head before he takes my hand casually, leading me inside.

The space *is* dark, but it's also bright, lit with that weird mix of black, glow-in-the-dark carpet floors and neon light fixtures. This lighting is mostly fine for me. After we collect our bowling shoes, I could easily make my way to the table where his friends are gathered in front of our reserved lane without his assistance. However, I keep hold of his hand. For myself or because of the nerves radiating off of him, I'm not sure.

We join Rachel, Isla, David, and Callum where they're sitting. I take a seat next to Isla to tie my bowling shoes and try not to think about all the other feet they have been on.

Rachel plugs Ben's name into the computer first, but instead of "BEN" she types "BIRTHDAY BOY."

"Rach, I'm not turning ten," he admonishes, but the smile hinting at the corners of his lips tells me he's enjoying this.

Rachel confirms, "Linny with a y?" as she types my name in below Ben's.

"Yep."

Once Ben's shoes are on, he offers his hand to me again. "Let's go pick out our balls. Find you a purple one."

I let him lead me to where the balls are lined up for our choosing. "Think we can find you one the color of sunset?"

He laughs loudly as he locates a pink-and-orange-hued ball. "Looks like the birthday boy is in luck!"

Next to it, a deep purple one sits.

I grab it, holding it with both hands as I trail behind Ben on our way back to his friends.

Ben is up first. First bowl is a gutter ball. The next, he manages to hit one pin. When he does, he pumps his arms in the air and shouts, "Yes!"

"Amazing," I say as we swap places. I bring my ball back, then swing forward, releasing it. It rolls down the center of the lane, striking the pins and…

Ben shouts, "Strike! Damn. You *are* good."

"I told you!" I revel in the compliment as I walk back to the table, passing Rachel as she goes up for her turn.

We progress through all of our turns until it's Ben's again. He manages to hit two pins this time—and again, he celebrates like he got a strike.

As I go to take my turn, I say, "You *are* bad at bowling."

He chuckles. "I know."

"Why do you like it so much?"

"You don't have to be good at something to like it."

I suppose that's true. I take my turn and get another strike. I beam at Ben as I walk back to the table.

"Bowling empress," he says as he does a little bow in his seat.

"'Empress' is quite the title."

We continue to go through our rotation. I'm winning with Callum close behind. Ben is losing. Badly. He is in such a good mood despite it.

"You know," David says, "we have been sitting here for nearly an hour with no drinks and no food in front of us. Maybe it's the American in me, but what's the point of bowling as an adult if you're not going to drink crappy beer and eat crappy food? Ben, you want to help?"

Ben's mouth opens, but no response comes, his eyes growing wide with panic. I jump in, "How about I help? The birthday boy shouldn't be fetching drinks."

Ben's mouth closes, and he nods before saying, "I do like to be serviced."

"Say that a different way," I advise with a pat on his arm.

His focus falls on me, eyes deep, and in a low, growling voice, he says, "I do like to be serviced."

My cheeks grow hot as I clear my throat, standing up from the table. "I meant, use different phrasing."

Isla chuckles. "He's lucky it's his birthday."

David leads the way up to the bar. As we wait in the short queue, he asks quietly, "How is he? Really?"

"Getting better." I purse my lips before I ask, "How are you?"

He laughs humorlessly. "Getting better." He shakes his head. "Ben said you know everything?"

"I do."

"I'm glad he…well, I'm glad he found you. I…Linny, I hope you know how much I love Ben. He's my best friend. I never wanted to hurt him."

I frown. "I know. He knows that, too. You can't help your feelings any more than he can help his."

"Yeah," David says. "I hate…I hate that we didn't talk about everything sooner. I wish he had told me sooner. If we would have just had a conversation after we kissed last June, maybe we could have worked through this before—" He cuts himself off when he notices my eyes bugging out of my head. One hand covers his face. "You didn't know we kissed, did you?"

I keep my voice steady. "He failed to mention that. Ben always made it seem one hundred percent on his end and zero percent on yours."

And, because timing has always been the universe's strong suit, it's our turn in line. David choppily orders for everyone, then spins to me. "Fuck, it's not what you think. I shouldn't have brought it up—I just have not talked to anyone but Callum about this because I knew Ben did not want anyone to know and you are the first person who *knows* on Ben's side and *dammit*. I am so sorry."

I hold my hands out in an attempt to calm him. "David, listen. It's okay. You can talk to me." I am *desperate* to know more information. Maybe because I'm nosy, but mostly because Ben is an enigma that I am eager to learn all about. "So, you kissed?"

He makes a frenzied sound somewhat close to a whimper. "Last June. Ben showed up at my door unannounced, talking about fate and the universe and a necklace and electric cars. I don't know. He was excited and upset. We ended up going out and getting a drink. Then another drink. And another drink. We got pretty drunk that night, so I let him sleep on my couch because he was still living in Newtonmore at the time. After we walked into my flat, I don't even know how it happened, but he kissed me. And I kissed him back. When I realized what was happening, I cut it off. Said we were drunk. He agreed. Apologized. Mentioned something about his ex. I figured we would talk about it in the morning, but he was gone by the time I woke up. I never brought it up. Neither did he."

"Oh, wow," I say as the bartender sets beers in plastic cups before us. "And, after that, you didn't think…?"

"Ben was *straight*," David says, distraught. "I thought he was straight. He always *said* he was straight. And he acted like nothing happened. I figured he was embarrassed. I never thought…" He loads the six cups of beer onto a plastic tray, balancing it with the skill of someone who works in food service. His voice is thick as he says, "He would flirt, but jokingly. It's what we did. Always, since uni." His voice cracks, "I didn't mean to lead him on."

I shake my head, grabbing the fries we ordered and putting them on another tray. "This isn't your fault. This is no one's fault. Ben isn't upset with you. He's just…"

"Heartbroken," David finishes. "I'm heartbroken too. I know it's not the same, but…"

"Friends can break your heart." I would know. My heart has been broken a time or two. I glance to where Ben is sitting at the table, hands thrown up in the air, while Isla is pointing aggressively at him. I bet he tried to mess up her bowl. "This is such an inappropriate question, but can I ask, *how*? I mean, how can you not love him like that?"

David follows my eyeline, but his focus locks in on someone else. "My number one reason is the man who…" He trails off with a surprised laugh. Callum has just pulled a brick of a book out of his bag, handing it over to Rachel. "The man who is lending Rachel yet another book he will never get back."

God, the way he gazes at him. Everyone wants to be looked at like that. I carefully choose condiments for the fries. "And?"

He shifts uncomfortably. "I'm not going to say I haven't thought about the reasons why, even though honestly, my number one reason is the only one I need. But…it's not that I don't find him attractive. I mean, he's gorgeous. And he fucking knows it. There's…there's this thick line between romantic and non-romantic feelings, and I can't cross it. It's not possible for me with him."

"That's reason enough. Sometimes there doesn't have to be a big reason." I finally pick up my tray. "You know, have you ever seen *Gilmore Girls*?"

"Yeah?"

"You know Max Medina? Great guy. Good-looking. Kind. Loved Lorelei. Wanted the best for Rory. Overall, a catch. Nothing wrong with him. But he wasn't the one. It's a simple reason, but it's a *good* reason."

"Well, would you say *you're* the one for him?"

I blink hard. I forgot Ben and I are supposed to be dating. "I…it's too soon to know that."

David smiles. "We should head back to the table. Keep this game going."

"You lead the way," I say, gesturing with my head. I like to follow in low-light places, have someone else establish the safest pathway.

We make it back to the table, David putting on a happy face that Callum immediately catches is amiss. Callum whispers something in his ear, David shaking his head slightly, as Ben returns to the table from bowling his turn.

Ben looks between David and me, but doesn't say anything about it, only, "You're up, Strawberry Shortcake."

CHAPTER ELEVEN
Ben

We're back at Isla's. Rachel carefully brings a cake out from the kitchen and places it on the table, lighting a *3* and a *0* candle with a lighter. She starts the song, and I squirm as everyone joins in. When it finishes, I blow out the candles.

Linny squeezes my knee. "Happy Birthday, Benny." She's only done it twice or so, but I like it when she calls me Benny.

I don't say thank you, but rather dip my finger in the cake frosting and plop it in my mouth. "Fair go of it," I remark, the consistency and the sugar-to-butter ratio actually perfect. I go back and scoop up more, holding my finger out to Linny. "Try."

She lifts an eyebrow at my finger, and only then do I realize what I'm doing. Oh. This is not normal behavior for people who aren't really dating. This isn't normal behavior for people who *are* dating when they are surrounded by their friends and family. Too late to back down now. My heart is pounding in my ears. I feel everyone's eyes on us.

What seems like a century later, she opens her mouth and accepts my finger, carefully licking the frosting off. My cock pulses at the sensation of her wet tongue. When I pull my finger from her mouth with a small *pop,* she releases a tiny moan.

Fucking hell. I'm half-hard already, tadger pushing against the zipper of my jeans. *Do not* put that finger in your mouth, Benny.

Too late. I quickly lick off the last bit of frosting.

Linny's face goes pink as she covers her mouth with her hand, licking the rogue frosting from her lips, saying, "Very good, Rachel."

Rachel goes for a knife to cut the cake. "Ben's recipe. I followed it to a T."

After cake, David and Callum leave first. I walk them to the door where I give Callum a hug goodbye, thanking him for coming. I should hug David as well, but all I offer is an awkward pat on the arm before swiftly turning away, eyes finding Linny as soon as they can.

She seems to understand my silent plea as she stands and says, "I've got to get going too. Thank you for having me."

"Aye," Isla says, hand tangled in Rachel's. "Ben wouldn't have come himself without you."

"We like having you around, Linny," Rachel adds.

I grab her coat and help her slip it on. "We do like having you around," I agree, fixing her collar. "I'll walk you home." I pull my own coat on.

They each call out a final "Happy Birthday!" as the door closes behind us and we descend the blue carpeted stairs.

We walk side by side, hands shoved in our respective pockets. When we get a fair distance away, Linny says, "Just a thought… maybe don't stick your finger in my mouth in public anymore."

"Can I still do it in private?" I can't help but ask.

She clicks her tongue. "There is no private."

I chuckle. "Sorry—honestly wasn't thinking. Did you not like it?"

"That's not what I'm saying, I just…" She groans slightly.

I let her off with, "I promise I will keep my fingers out of you." *Until you tell me otherwise*, I add in my head, even though the likelihood of that scenario is slim.

She huffs through her nose, moving on. "Tonight was fun, though," she says. "Did you have a good time?"

"I did," I answer truthfully. "Thanks for encouraging me to do this."

"I can't believe you were going to skip out on your thirtieth birthday."

"I had solo plans, I told you."

"Fucking off to Ireland to drink with a dead man does not constitute as plans."

"What an American response," I admonish. "Anyway, sounds like I would have been fucking off to France."

She nudges me on the arm. "Your friends love you."

"Aye." Annoying of them.

"Despite you doing everything in your power to change that."

I sigh, head hanging as my pace morphs to trudging. "Yeah."

"I'm jealous," she admits.

My head rockets up in surprise. "Are you? You have Mel and Kensie and them."

"No, I have Mel," she corrects. "Kensie is *her* friend. I mean, we get along, don't get me wrong, but we would never spend time together one-on-one."

I purse my lips in a fine line.

Quietly, she confides, "I had friends. I did, but after things with Atti ended…I was depressed. Like clinically. I'm taking meds now. I mean, I think I had depression for a while before that, but everything with Atti kind of put me over the edge. Before I got myself to the doctor for help, I shut everyone out. I did what you are trying to do, Ben, but the difference is, my friends gave up on me."

My heart pinches in my chest. Before I can say something, she keeps speaking.

"I'm not saying it's completely their fault. It's hard not to give up on someone who's given up on themselves, but I wish they hadn't given up on me so quickly. My retreat into myself played a huge part in the fizzling of these relationships, but it also felt like…like they were glad to be rid of me. Glad to finally have an excuse." She blinks rapidly, trying to suppress a sudden onslaught of tears. "Your friends are refusing to give up on you, and I am immensely jealous because from what I've seen, you've given them every reason to."

"I…" I drag a hand down my face, chest aching. "You're right. Shite. I'm sorry, Linny."

She shakes her head. "*I'm* sorry. I didn't mean to make this about me."

"You're not. You're knocking some sense into me, is what you're doing. You're good at that, you know. My friends *are* the best," I agree. "They're my family and I'm glad they haven't given up on me." As we pause for a street crossing, I toe the pavement. "I would never give up on you, Linny."

"You can't say that for sure."

"I can," I say with a finality. She looks away, so I change the subject. "David seemed upset when you came back from getting drinks earlier."

She discloses, "He was. We were talking about you."

"All bad things, I hope."

The light changes, so we cross.

"Not exactly. He said you kissed. Last June."

"Oh." Nearly forgot about that.

"It slipped out. He thought I knew."

I sniff sharply. "I kissed him. He stopped it and called it a drunken mistake. I pretended to agree, then convinced myself that if I cooled it for a bit, I could try again. Less intoxicated."

"Did you?"

"Naw, but that didn't stop my brain from concocting all these scenarios where I would. I thought I'd kiss him again, and everything would be *right*." I clench and unclench my fists. "But I also knew deep down that wasn't true. It's why it took me so long to tell him. I *knew* he didn't feel the same way, but I had a fantasy that he did."

"I'm sorry, Ben."

"Me too." Quietly, I confess, "You know, I moved here for him."

"I thought you moved here for the café?"

"I did, but I also convinced myself that if I lived here, he would see me differently. That it was only distance keeping us apart. Not the fact that he wasn't interested in me. Not the fact that he was already with Callum." I chuckle to myself. "God, Callum. Callum is so nice. He's a total laugh, in the best and most surprising way. Quiet, but David likes quiet. Or, he likes quiet people who can be loud for him. And I know he knows, but he's not making me feel weird or bad—even though he should *hate* me."

"I like loud and gentle, personally. Like you."

I smile. "I like a little grumpy and devastatingly beautiful, like you."

She bumps her shoulder into me. "Oh, he's a sweet talker in his thirties."

"Well, I suppose I'm one of those grown-ups now."

We reach her door to find it propped open slightly. "I hate this damn thing," she says, kicking it open the rest of the way.

I let out a small sigh. I don't know what about her makes me want to be unabashedly truthful. She's a good listener, yeah, but I also have this desperate need for her to *know* me.

"Last August, I was in town and I went out with David and Callum. It was the first time I really saw them together. I mean, I had seen them together before, but it was less…I don't know. Less serious. They'd been flitting around each other for years, never quite making it official. This time, I realized how much David liked him. I was deeply jealous and so goddamn frustrated with myself. For waiting so long to tell David. For not talking to him about the kiss. For living far away. For not figuring out my sexuality as soon as I would have liked. I thought I needed more time. I thought I needed less time. I was so obsessed with time. But in the end, it didn't matter. Timing didn't matter. *Time* didn't matter. He was never meant to love me back."

Her mouth opens and closes like she doesn't know what to say. Understandable—I keep dumping things on her. She ends up grabbing my hand and squeezing it tightly.

"You will get through this," she says.

"I know."

Her hand drops. "Oh, shit. I almost forgot." She digs around her bag until she pulls out a smaller bag, sheer and pulled closed with a ribbon. "Here." She places the sachet in my outstretched palm.

"Crystals?" I observe.

"Yeah—sorry. This was last minute, so it was crystals or a doorknob Queen Victoria may have touched. I know you're not into them, but I wanted to get you something."

"I *could* be into them. What do they mean?"

She opens the bag and dumps them into my hand. She points to a small, smooth pink crystal first. "Rose quartz—that one is for your heart, emotionally speaking." Then one that is tinted yellow. "Citrine—attracts positivity." Next, a black stone. "Black obsidian, for protection and grounding." Lastly, the purple crystal. "And amethyst. Like my ring. Good for stress."

"Cool," I say genuinely. "Thanks, Lin." I scrunch my palm to move the crystals together before tipping them back into the bag.

"I won't be offended if you set them on a shelf and never look at them again."

I narrow my eyes. "You gave them to me—why would I do that?"

"Because it's silly."

"I don't think so."

Her eyes glow as she looks up at me. "Happy birthday."

"Thank you. It was a good one."

...

Several days later, as I'm unlocking the café, I'm startled by the door to Linny's flat opening. I haven't seen her since my birthday.

"Good morning, coffee bean."

She spins around to face me, hand on her heart. "Jesus, I didn't expect anyone to be out here this early."

"What're you doing up in the wee hours of the morning?"

"I couldn't sleep, so I figured I'd come down to get some work done. I'm heading to an estate sale later and won't be in the shop for most of today. I have spreadsheets to organize." As if evidence of her desire to spend the morning staring at a computer screen, she's wearing her glasses.

"That's ambitious."

"What else have I got to do?"

I suggest, "Drink coffee in bed with your furry ball of pure love and terror and watch the news?"

"I was with you until you said, 'watch the news.'"

"Eh, well, maybe you could come give me a hand in the kitchen instead?"

"You want me to ruin the food you sell to make a living?"

I nod.

"Sure. Why not?"

I open up the front doors, disable the alarm, then flip on the lights. I don't normally turn on all the lights up front this early, but Linny doesn't need to know that. I lead her toward the back to the kitchen, hanging my jacket on a hook next to the door and directing Linny to do the same. I put on a white pinny, then offer her the extra one I have hanging beside mine. I pull on plastic gloves, giving her a pair as well.

"What first?" she asks, pulling on her gloves.

"Croissants," I answer, opening up the fridge to retrieve the dough I prepped yesterday and let chill overnight. "We're going to roll it out, cut the dough, then roll the croissants up and let them sit for an hour or so before they bake."

I drop the dough on the counter, then hand her a rolling pin. She takes one step toward the dough, but I halt her. "Sorry. Wait. Have you a hair tie?" Her long hair is down and loose around her shoulders, fiery and bright, but I can't have those long strands making their way into my food.

Her fingers meet the ends of her hair. "Oh. No." She goes to leave, holding the rolling pin out to me and saying, "I'll go grab one."

I halt her again with, "No need."

I pop out of the kitchen, pulling off my gloves as I go, heading behind the counter to fetch a pink scrunchie from the bucket Isla keeps behind the counter.

I push back through the kitchen door. "Isla has an abundance of these. Mostly for Rachel."

Linny holds out her hand for me to give her the scrunchie, but I choose to stroll behind her to handle the hair myself. "You've still got those gloves on," I say as an explanation. I gather her soft hair in my hands, fingers brushing her neck as I collect all the loose strands.

This is normal fake dating behavior, *said no one ever.* I see a visible chill run down her spine from the contact, my cock twitching at the reaction. *Fuck,* there he goes again. I quickly slip the scrunchie around her gathered hair, tightening it at the base of her neck so I can step away.

She clears her throat. "Thanks."

Once again, my tadger is attempting to make himself known, but I am begging him to take it easy. It is far too early in the morning for this. In response, I say, "Your hair is wicked soft, Lin." I clear my throat. "So, let's roll the dough."

She presses the pin into the dough, stretching it into a long rectangle as she goes. I watch over her shoulder.

"You need to put even pressure on it so it can all be the same width," I say.

"Like this?" she asks, rolling again.

"More like"—I reach over her, caging her in as I place my hands over hers on the rolling pin—"this." I press gently so that she will do the same, rolling the dough together until it reaches the size I want. "There we are," I say, knowing I should retreat, but staying firmly put.

She angles her head up toward me, eyes radiant through her glasses and mouth so goddamn close to mine. "Are you making a move, Bennett Pyeon?" she teases. "Because it feels like you're trying to teach me to play pool or hit a baseball."

I bite the corner of my mouth as I release her and step back. "*No.* I'm just far too controlling when it comes to this stuff." I grab a rolling knife and step up next to her against the counter. "We need to cut the dough into equal-sized rectangles. I'll do it."

When I'm done, I pick up one rectangle and hold it up to her eye level. "Look at all those layers."

"Those are some nice layers."

"They are some *beautiful* layers."

I slice the rectangles into triangles, then we roll them up together, starting with the top of the triangle and rolling in. We set them on the baking sheet.

"Like I said, they have to sit for an hour before we bake. Now, I move on to muffins. Want to help with those?"

"Yeah, that's why I'm here. Free labor."

I snort. "Naw, you're here to keep me company." I open the fridge to take out the frozen blueberries, tossing them at her. She catches the bag in one swift motion. "And for your free labor."

"Can't believe you don't use fresh blueberries," she says in mock astonishment.

"They're more expensive than the frozen," I explain. "Isla won't let me buy fresh."

I hand her my recipe card for the blueberry muffins. "These are simple if you want to get started on them, just follow my recipe. I'll get to work on the double chocolate muffins." I know my recipes by heart, so no need for a card for myself.

We split into two mixers, she creating her muffins and I creating mine as the oven heats up. When the oven is ready and all muffin batter is in the appropriate pans, we slide them in, one pan at a time.

I switch on another row of the oven so I can get the croissants baking soon.

"Next, banana loaf and cranberry scones. You take the loaf and I take the scones."

"How about I do the scones?"

I open my mouth, shocked silent, trying to figure out how to say *hell no* nicely before she laughs and says, "I'm kidding, Ben. Jeez, you are a control freak about this."

"Oh, shush." I get out the ingredients and a recipe card for the banana bread.

Linny finishes the loaf before I finish the scones, so she pours it into the correct pans, then watches me while I work. I feel her eyes on me, and while I don't mind, I am buzzing under her gaze. I knead the dough for a moment, just to get it to stick together before rolling it out. When I'm done kneading, I give it a light slap on the top.

Linny snorts from behind me. "Who are you? Donut Daddy?"

I spin to her. "Now, *who* is Donut Daddy?"

"No one. Just a TikTok guy." Her burning cheeks indicate otherwise.

"Show me."

"No."

"*Lin.*"

She sighs, pulling out her phone. She pulls up a video of a striking man who is baking in a very sensual way.

"Jesus," I say. "That is wildly attractive."

"It is."

"I could be a Donut Daddy." I meet her eye. "I would thrive as a sexy baking influencer."

"Sure, you would. Go sexy-bake your scones."

The oven dings, signaling it's at the correct temperature.

I indicate my head toward that ding. "Can you put the croissants in the oven?"

"Sure."

She comes back and continues to watch me, baking perhaps a

bit more sexily than I was before, now that I know where her standards lie.

"You do this by yourself every day?"

"Aye—for the most part. Scott is my backup baker. He handles things on Saturdays when I'm off and can throw something together when he's here later in the day. But all this in the morning most mornings, is me. That's why I get here so early, so I can have all this ready to go. I mean, here's the thing, there are corners I could cut. Pre-made things I could buy and heat up, but what's the fun in that? I own a café, so I can bake whatever I want. I love it."

"I'm glad. And you change what you make every day?"

I shape the scones on a baking sheet while I say, "Yeah. I mean, I have the standards like the croissants, the blueberry muffins, and the banana loaf, but I like to add some change-ups every day. Sometimes depending on supplies, sometimes depending on my wild whims."

"I enjoy your wild whims." The timer goes off for the muffins. "I'll get them," she says, finding my oven-mitts and pulling the muffin tins out of the oven one by one, sliding them onto the metal cooling rack. I swap places with her, putting the scones in the oven.

She comes back over to me, checking the time on her phone. "I should probably get over to the shop soon."

"You don't open for another two and a half hours," I say, crossing my arms over my chest. It's half past seven. Her shop opens at 10 a.m.

"I told you, I have things to do. If Carolyn keeps buying every picture frame she sees, I will never get them all cataloged and priced. I also have to touch up the upholstery on this chair we bought in last week."

My shoulders sag, partially because that was a natural instinct and partially because I'm being dramatic. "Fine," I sigh. I stand up straight. "Thanks for giving me a hand this morning."

"It was fun," she says. We stand there regarding each other for a moment before the bell of the opening front door shakes us out of it.

"That'll be Isla," I say.

Linny grabs her jacket off the hook next to mine, slipping it on and pulling the scrunchie out of her hair. "Think she'll want this back?"

I shake my head. "You keep it." She slips it around her wrist. I swerve around Linny to grab a cooling muffin, handing it over. "Take this."

"Happily." She holds the warm muffin with the tips of her fingers. "I'll see you soon?"

"Count on it."

After she leaves, I check my phone to see a text from Paul. Paul, huh? Almost forgot we exchanged numbers.

I send him a few links to trails that I like, offering a few details about my favorites. Paul's a nice bloke. It's too bad he lives in London. I'm not saying I'd pursue anything with him, but he'd be a good friend to have. It seems like we have a lot in common.

Speaking of friends, I switch over to my text thread with Oscar Wilde's Mother.

> Do you fancy a hike?

> It's been so long since we've spoken. Oh, how I have missed you

> Don't be cheeky. Answer the question

> Sure. I like hiking

> I mean, nothing hardcore, but I don't mind a steep hill or having to weave around fallen trees. I like a nice hike on a nice day

> Why? You don't mean now, do you?

> Naw. Just curious

> What are your thoughts on mountain biking?

> I don't trust me on a bike, but the concept of it is fine

I snort as I type my response.

> Fair

> Do you wear those tight little numbers when you mountain bike or is that just normal cycling?

> That's more of a speed cycling thing. Why? You want me to?

No, I really don't. I'm not sure there's a single person, even you, who could pull off that outfit

I can pull off ANY outfit, thank you very much

But next nice day, maybe we should go on a hike?

I gnaw my lip as I await her reply. I'm asking her as a friend and not even specifically asking. Just throwing out an open-ended suggestion. An open-ended suggestion that is ignoring our fake dating plan. Should I unsend the text? Before I can even attempt that, she responds.

Not sure when that mythical nice day will come, but yeah. Why not?

I grin stupidly at my phone before I slide it aggressively down the counter. Enough of that for today.

CHAPTER TWELVE
Linny

On Friday, Carolyn comes out from the back, red rhinestone-decked purse clutched in her hand. "I'm meeting a friend for lunch, so I'll be closing the shop for an hour."

I hardly glance at her from where I'm organizing vases on top of an antique dresser. "I don't mind manning the store for an hour. Or, I guess if you do want to close, I can get some stuff done in the back."

"You need to have a rest every now and then, Melinda."

"What am I supposed to do?"

"Eat a meal. Go up to your flat to say a hello to that cat of yours. Walk over to the café and give that boy a good snog."

"Ben's not my real boyfriend," I remind her.

"A man doesn't have to be your boyfriend for you to snog him, love. Listen, I don't care what you do on your own time, but whatever it is, it will be done somewhere other than my shop."

With her hands, she shoos me out the front door, my feet stumbling beneath me, following behind me and locking the door. When I regain my balance, I fling an arm toward the now locked door. "My phone, keys, and wallet are all still in the back."

She clicks her tongue like that was my fault, and reluctantly removes one key from her keyring. It's the key she has to my flat. "Here you are."

"Thanks," I say dryly, taking the key. "See you in an hour."

She waves goodbye as I trudge up to my flat. I do as she suggested and eat a meal sitting down at my kitchen table. Then I say a hello to Oscar Wilde, who is too busy wreaking havoc by climbing to elevated surfaces he should not be able to access to give me the time of day.

If I had my phone, I would be content to slouch into the couch and scroll for the hour, but that is still locked in the store below. I stand with my hands on my hips as I assess my living space, searching for something to do.

On my mail table, I spot a box I have been meaning to put into a more secure location. This small, black velvet box holds Mel's wedding rings. She gave them to me to keep safe because it eased her anxiety by having them in the city where she's getting married. I wander over to the table and pick up the box gingerly, like I could break it. I crack it open and stare. This is admittedly not the first time I have done this—gazed at these wedding rings with a tiny inkling of envy. I don't do it a lot, and I'm really not *that* jealous.

I pick up the ring intended for Mel, pinching it between my fingers. It's a silver band, matching her elaborate engagement ring. It's simple, but elegant. I love it. It is perfect for her. I wonder...

Without even fully planning to do it, I slip the band on my left ring finger.

I immediately regret it.

This ring is tight. Too tight. I pull at the ring to remove it with no luck. *Shit.* I twist and turn the ring, but it won't budge. "Shit,"

I say aloud, still yanking at the metal band. It's stuck. "Shit, shit, shit."

I search around wildly, trying to figure out what to do. My finger is swelling around the ring. I run to the kitchen sink and douse my hand in dish soap, trying to wiggle it off—but my hands keep slipping and I can't get a good grip.

I don't know what to do. I don't have my phone. Carolyn is out.

But Ben is downstairs.

I'm out the front door of my apartment before I even finish the thought. I push into the café with a clatter. Gemma is behind the counter and says a confused hello to me as I rush past her, offering back little more than a grunt. I push through the swinging door to the kitchen so aggressively that it hits the wall beside it.

Ben whirls around from where he's working and drops his rolling pin. "Lin? What's wrong?"

I hold up my trembling hand. "I can't get it off," I whine.

He approaches me and gently takes my hand, twisting the ring and trying to pull it off. I squeak in pain as he is not having any more luck than me. He swears under his breath. "Muffin, we might have to take you to hospital and have this cut off."

I shake my head aggressively. "No, no. We can't do that. This is Mel's wedding band."

His eyebrows raise, but he thankfully does not question why my cousin's wedding ring is on my finger. He nods once and pivots around, walking away from me.

I let out a frustrated whimper before I realize what he's doing. He comes back with a bucket of butter. He sets the butter down on the counter beside us, scooping up two fingers full and slathering it all over my hand. He tries to work at the ring, but my hand is shaking too aggressively for him to get a solid grip.

"Let's sit," he suggests, keeping his voice calm. I fall to the ground without any more prompting. Ben sits more gently, moving to cage me in his legs. "Like this," he says, adjusting us so his one leg is propped up and acting like a backrest for me. My legs are bent over his other leg, skirt draping him like a blanket. We are incredibly close.

He takes my quaking hand in his and continues to spread the butter around it. As I watch, tears leak from my eyes. I need to get this ring off. It *needs* to be off of me.

Ben notices my tears and uses a buttery hand to wipe them from my face, effectively spreading the butter on my cheeks. "Sorry," he mutters.

He refocuses on the ring, twisting and turning. He pulls at the ring, and right as I think all hope is lost, it slips from my finger just as easily as it slipped on in the first place. My finger pulses and attempts to bring blood back to the correct places as I finally let myself breathe, relief rushing through me.

"Your cousin's fingers are freakishly small," Ben comments before he sets the ring up on the counter next to the tub of butter.

He wipes his hand on the apron he wears, then, using that apron, tries to clean my hand as best he can. We're both still slick and greasy. Tears gently escape my eyes, left over from the panic.

"We're good, Lin," he reassures me, wiping at the butter on my cheeks, clearing my tears as well. "I got it off."

"Thank you," I say, my voice small.

"Of course. Thank you for coming to me for help."

He doesn't make any attempt to move, so neither do I. We stay where we are, folded over one another and so close we can share breath.

Eventually, I admit, "I don't know why I put it on."

He nudges me with the leg behind my back. "Everyone does

things like that. No judgment from me."

"I guess I was wondering what it would feel like. I never... I never got to the wedding band part. Just the engagement ring part."

He regards me curiously. "How did it feel?"

"Well, I felt nothing. It's not my ring. The love of my life didn't put it on my finger. But that nothing was very quickly taken over by panic."

His leg bumps my back again. "Well, hard times are over now. Are you okay?"

"Yeah, yeah." I finally go to stand up, using his shoulder as leverage, then I help him up. I grab the buttery ring from where he set it. "I should get this back to a safe place."

"Maybe give it a little clean as well? Can you imagine if Julien tried to put it on Mel's finger and it slipped out of his hands because of the grease? That would be hilarious." He coughs as a smile perks my mouth. The image of Julien scrambling after a ring that won't stay in his hands flashes through my mind. "I mean, bad," Ben corrects. "That would be bad."

"Really bad," I agree. I squeeze him on the arm. "I'll see you later?"

"Of course. I'll see you at mine for supper with Isla and Rachel tomorrow?"

"I'll be there."

"Bye, ring thief."

...

The next day, Ben makes me leave the shop early to go grocery shopping with him for dinner, but I honestly think he just wants someone to trail after him with the cart. He grabs things off the shelves seemingly at random and throws them in the basket as I push.

I follow him through an aisle as he mutters, "Couscous," to himself over and over until he spots it on the shelf. He nudges his eyeglasses up his nose with a knuckle as he stares down at the grocery list typed on his phone. To me, he spouts off everything he's grabbed, then asks, "Anything else?"

"You haven't told me what you're making, so I don't know."

He wags a finger at me. "I told you, it's a surprise."

"Then garlic. We need garlic."

He throws his head back gleefully. "We *do* need garlic! Come on." He runs us back to the produce section, picking through cloves of garlic that all appear the same to me before he settles on one.

After we check out, Ben drives us back to his place, where I help him bring in all the groceries. His glasses get discarded on the kitchen table as soon as possible as he claims they're annoying. He only wore them because he was driving.

His flat is on the ground floor—small, but nice. Ben says it's about a twenty-minute walk from Somewhere Special, so unless it's pouring or bitterly cold, he likes to walk. It's clean and has private access to a back garden.

I give myself a little tour with his approval, poking my head into his bedroom and flipping on the light. He has a bedframe— thank god—as well as several cardboard boxes piled in the corner of the room. I'm about to switch off the light when I spot something that piques my interest. I wander closer to confirm what I already know it to be. The crystals I gave him sit on his nightstand in what looks like the lid to a jar of marinara sauce. I pick up the rose quartz, running my thumb over the smooth surface before dropping it back in his makeshift dish.

When I return to the kitchen, he asks, "Done going through my drawers?"

"I opened zero drawers, but yes. I like your place."

He shrugs as he turns on the tap, sticking his hand under the water to test the temperature. "It's a roof over my head."

"Need any help?"

"Naw."

"Then what am I supposed to do?"

"Keep me company."

So, I do just that, leaning against the counter and nursing the glass of wine he poured me as we chat and I watch him cook. I find his speaker and connect my phone so I can play music.

"What in the hell is this playlist?" he asks after the fifth song.

"Just my liked songs," I say defensively.

"We just went classic rock to showtunes to alt rock to Noah Kahan to 90s hip hop."

"And? Isn't everyone's general playlist like that?"

"Aye, but who just listens to their general playlist on shuffle? That's chaotic."

I laugh. "I thought you liked a little chaos." I boost myself up onto the counter behind me so I can sit.

Ben's lips purse. "Your arse on my counter is not very sanitary."

"You're not using this counter and your chairs are too far away." I drink my wine and keep my eyes on him to watch his smile grow as he shakes his head.

"Fine."

He keeps cooking, but eventually comes to stand in front of me.

"What?" I ask.

"Spread your legs."

"*Excuse* me?"

He chuckles. "I need a spoon. You're sitting over the utensil drawer."

I bite my lip. "There were other ways to say that, you know."

But I do as requested and open my legs wide enough for him to reach between them and pull open the drawer. Even with that, my long skirt falls over the open drawer. With a delicate hand, he lifts it, retrieving the spoon. He pushes the drawer closed, and I close my legs, feeling the need to squeeze them shut now. I cross my legs instead, hoping it a more natural gesture. Ben goes to stir his finished couscous, moving it off the burner.

"Let that sit," he mutters to himself, moving on to the chicken in the oven, peeking inside. "Few more minutes."

He turns back to me and says, "Drawer."

I uncross my legs and spread them again so he can open it. He pulls out another spoon, but accidentally brushes it against my bare leg. The sudden coolness sends a shiver up my spine. He notices, eyeing where the spoon touched me.

His voice low, he asks, "What was that?"

"It was cold," I explain.

"Yeah?"

He brushes the spoon over my skin again, and again I shiver. He smirks, moving it to my other leg. My body reacts again, but no longer to the cold, a trail of sensual hunger following the smooth metal. He grabs another spoon, setting it to the side before he crowds me, closing the drawer with his hip, and settling into the space between my legs.

"You like this?"

I swallow, admitting, "I don't hate it."

He runs the spoon down my cheek, dragging it over to my lips and across them. A dull ache pulses through my entire being. When he lets it leave my lips, I involuntarily dart my tongue out to wet them. His eyes catch on my mouth, focusing in.

Then he moves away so swiftly that I need a moment to catch my breath. That spoon gets discarded in the sink as he picks up the other one he set out. The new spoon dips into the saucepan, then he taps his finger into the spoon before putting that finger in his mouth for a taste. Ben muses over it, then plunges the spoon into the sauce again, but this time, he swivels toward me.

He places himself again in the space between my legs and whispers, "Try," before dipping the spoon into my mouth. I am hit with a bold lemon and herb flavor. Delicious.

The pleasure must show on my face because his mouth quirks up. "Good?"

"Yeah," I breathe.

"You've got a bit…" His thumb finds the corner of my mouth, swiping across it gently to rid any remnants of the sauce. However, instead of wiping his thumb on a napkin, he dips it into my mouth. My tongue brushes the pad and then I find myself sucking lightly. What did I say about him not putting his fingers in my mouth anymore? Glad I specified *in public*.

His eyes are fixated so heavily on my lips. Without even thinking about what I'm doing, I give him a subtle nod.

He accepts that nod and moves in, pulling his thumb to my cheek and finding my lips with his. I melt into him as his mouth opens on mine, our tongues meeting. *Fuck*. I knew I wasn't romanticizing our first kiss from all those months ago. My legs cage his waist, pulling him closer as his hands get trapped in my hair. His mouth is like lightning. Shocking, intense, shattering.

His lips move to my neck, skating kisses across my pulse.

"Ben," I heave.

"Hm?" he murmurs into my skin.

"What are we doing?"

He draws away, glancing up at me devilishly. "I'm kissing

your neck."

"Okay. Cool." I pull him back up to my lips, tongue plunging into his mouth as his grip glides down to my hips. I drag my fingers through his hair, grasping on tightly as he devours me. *God,* I'm obsessed with his hair, so thick, soft, and coarse.

His fingers find the base of my oversized sweater, moving underneath to brush against my bare skin. His hands are warm, sending fire through my body. I need his hands all over me. We separate so I can pull the sweater over my head and toss it to the side. Ben aims for my lips again, but pauses before reaching his destination.

"Is that a tattoo?"

I follow his eyes to the French script on the side of my ribs. "Clearly."

"I like it." His tender fingers brush over the inked skin, admiring. "What does it mean?"

I huff out a sigh, wondering if this is *really* the time to talk about my tattoo, as I say, "'Chacun voit midi à sa porte.' Literal translation: 'everyone sees noon at their door.' It means: everyone sees things in their own way."

I yank his lips back to mine as he smiles into the kiss. Eventually, his mouth trails away, moving to my neck again. This time, he travels down from my neck until he is kissing the top of my breast. Then his lips are tracing over the hard point fighting its way through the thin fabric of my bra. His hands skim over the lace, gently tugging it down so those lips can meet my tight and pinching nipple. His mouth is soft, tongue gliding over the peak, then he is gently sucking.

"*Fuck,* Ben," I breathe, hand lacing through his hair, holding him to my chest. His teeth lightly scrape over my nipple, making me whimper. Vaguely, I think I hear something, but I hardly acknowledge it, distracted by the overwhelming sensation of his mouth on my breast.

But then I hear it again. Knocking. And Isla's voice shouting, "Ben! We're here!" Knocking again.

"Ben," I say. Then more firmly, tugging his hair. "Ben." He pulls away, staring up at me in a daze. "Your sister is here."

"My sister?"

Isla knocks again.

Then he stands up straight and says, "Shite. My sister." He fixes my bra so it is again covering me, then fetches my sweater, tossing it my direction.

Isla continues to knock, yelling out Ben's name.

"Just a second!" he yells back.

I pull the sweater over my head, feeling flushed and a little dazed myself. "I'm going to the bathroom to fix myself up. Re-tuck my sweater."

His head bobs. "Okay. Okay."

Isla knocks again.

"Hold on!" Ben yells, looking around in a panic. I'm pretty sure he just doesn't want to open the door with the semi he has going on.

I slip away and into the bathroom. My hair is a mess. I run quick fingers through it in an attempt to calm it down. I re-tuck my sweater into my bra so it appears cropped. I need to buy one of those crop-tuck things. Oh hell, my underwear is soaked through.

I hear Ben open the door at last and Isla proclaim, "Finally! Jesus."

Ben clears his throat. "Sorry. Cooking."

Rachel laughs. "We saw you and Linny through the window very much not cooking."

Isla cackles. "We had agreed to keep that to ourselves, love!"

Well, no point in hiding now that I've put myself back together. Though there is still a pulsing in between my legs that I am begging to dull. I exit the bathroom at that moment, saying, "Well, that's embarrassing."

Rachel tips her head at me. "We didn't see anything. Just a lot of kissing and moving."

Isla shrugs off her coat, tossing it over a chair. "Aye. Still saw too much, in my opinion. Maybe invest in some curtains that close?"

I slip next to Ben, letting him put his arm around me and falling into our act of normalcy even though, *oh my god,* we were just making out, which is far from normal for us.

"Maybe don't go peeping in other people's windows? Feckin' pervs," he jokes. He presses a kiss to my head that causes a pang in my chest, then pivots to go take his chicken out of the oven. "Did you bring the wine I asked for?" he calls, setting the tray of chicken atop the stove.

"Naw," Isla says. "I saw a red I wanted instead." She pulls out the bottle as evidence.

Ben exits the kitchen, eyes wide. "That is not—I had asked you to get a Sauvignon Blanc. That won't go with the chicken."

Isla looks defiant, but Rachel immediately caves, pulling out another bottle of wine from her own bag. The Sauvignon Blanc. "I can't do this. Here you go."

Ben takes the wine gratefully, pressing a kiss to the stem. "I like you better than my sister," he says to Rachel. Or maybe to the bottle of wine.

Isla smirks. "Sorry, sorry. Couldn't help it. I bought the red for me for another time."

I take the bottle from him. "I'll open this."

I open the bottle to pour four glasses of wine as Ben finishes up dinner. I ask Rachel how her Ph.D. program is going, and don't understand a word, but she seems passionate about it. I like that. Also, the way Isla looks at her when she's talking about it is adorable. She loves her so much.

As per usual, a longing settles in as I mourn something I will never have.

"Linny," Rachel says, pulling me from my grief, "do you remember that night we ran into you all those months ago outside the café?"

I don't recall what she's talking about.

"In August," Isla adds, seeing the confusion on my face.

Ah. August. There's not much I remember about July and August, but if I said that, I'd have to explain why. I was going through the motions, but nothing was sticking in my brain. I think I vaguely know what they're talking about, so I say, "Oh. Right."

Rachel smiles. "You told us they were lowering the tenancy price on the café, which was Isla's sign to make the jump officially. We call you her café angel."

My eyebrows lift in surprise as Ben sweeps out of the kitchen, platter in hand. "If Linny is anyone's angel, she's mine."

"I'm no one's angel, but I'll take the compliment."

Ben sets the platter on the table, saying in a horrible French accent, "Dinner is served."

"Bon appétit," I respond as I take a seat at the set table. Then add, "Ce repas a l'air délicieux."

Ben pauses halfway down into his seat, eyes wide. "Melinda Barbara Jenkins, do you *speak* French? It's not just that saucy little tattoo?"

"First of all," I say with a laugh, "that is not my middle name. Second of all," I hold my fingers a centimeter apart, "Un peu."

He groans as he drops fully into his seat. "Linny, why would you do this to me?"

"*What?*"

"Speak French! That's so bloody sexy. Oh my god." He leans back in his seat, looking utterly devastated. I can't help the butterflies that flutter in my stomach.

"Jesus," Isla mutters, digging a fork into her salad, as Rachel jokes, "Get a room, you two."

He is putting his all into this evening. Or…he means it? I don't know. He's not *supposed* to mean it.

Ben sighs, still acting dramatic. "Dig in." He throws a wink my way.

Oh. Got it. He's putting on a show. I am not disappointed by that. I'm *not*. It doesn't matter that we kissed. That was just hormones at work.

Maybe I need to get back on the apps and find something casual. It's been two or so months since I've hooked up with anyone. I'm just getting a little frustrated, is all. And Ben is, you know, *Ben,* so he's tempting as hell.

I take my first bite and nearly curse. "This is amazing," I moan.

I swear Ben gulps. "Yeah?"

"Yeah."

"Umhm," Rachel agrees. "Wonderful, as per usual, Ben."

Isla hums. "Aye, really good." She takes another bite. She swallows and says, "So, I've been meaning to say, that new stripe of gray hair you've got going on makes you look like the bride of Frankenstein."

I snort into my wine, causing Ben to look at me, insulted that I would laugh. I squeeze his leg. "Sorry, sorry. That surprised me." I didn't even notice it. I mean, his hair has always had a bit of gray in it, but Isla is right. There's a thick stripe of silver on the left side of his head.

He lifts his chin and says, "The bride of Frankenstein is hot, so thank you."

Isla says to me, "He's impossible to insult. Every time I try to throw something at him, he turns it into a compliment."

I smile, suspecting he's doing that as a defense.

"I think it makes you look more like Mr. Fantastic," I say.

Ben beams hugely. "Oo, he's also hot. Thank you."

The rest of the night goes off without a hitch. As Rachel and Isla get ready to go, Ben says, "Rachel, lovely to have you. Islington, less lovely. You're mean."

She groans. "I'm *sorry* about the wine."

I ask, "Is your name really Islington?"

"No," she says as Ben says, "Yes."

I'm inclined to believe Isla. We offer hugs goodbye before we send them on their way with leftovers.

I help Ben wash the dishes, but we do so in silence. I'm comfortable with silence, but this one is heavy. I know what we're both thinking.

My mouth opens to speak, but Ben beats me to it.

"I think we're blurring the lines of our agreement," he says roughly.

I swallow. "Agreed. The kiss was probably a mistake, right?"

"Right. I mean, great kiss."

"Yeah," I concur. "Anything more like that will confuse things."

"Yeah."

And that's that. We continue to wash the dishes in silence. Once all the dishes are cleaned and dried, I bid him goodbye. It takes a little effort, but I get him to let me head back to my place alone. He offers to walk me back about a thousand times before

I finally make it out the door.

"Fine," he laments. "But I expect a 'home' text with a picture of Oscar Wilde." He opens the door for me and then adds, "Actually, while we're at it, I expect daily pictures of Oscar Wilde. I think I deserve it."

"You '*deserve*' it?"

"Yeah. For being so handsome. Handsome people get things like that all the time."

"Sure."

"I can send you daily pictures of something in return. I'm not sure what, though." I involuntarily glance at his crotch. My eyes shoot back up, but he catches me. "Oh ho! Is that what you want?"

"No!" I argue. "I don't want daily pictures of…of *that*."

"Well, if I were to send daily dick pics, I would expect daily pictures of a different kind of cat."

I wrinkle my nose. "Ew. Don't call it that."

He wrinkles his nose back at me. "Yeah, I regretted it as soon as I said it. Kitty?"

"Hell no."

"Honeypot?"

"*No.*"

"Fanny."

"Eh."

"Lady parts."

"Ben. Just say pussy or something normal."

He steps closer and says, "Pussy." He looks me up and down. "What are your feelings on the word that starts with C? I know Americans don't like that word."

"I don't have an issue with it."

He leans close and says, "Cunt," in my ear.

I angle back and cackle. "Okay, unprompted, I'm not sure how I feel about it."

"Would you like it if I said it to you in the bedroom?"

I gulp. "Ben, we literally just agreed to keep *out* of the bedroom. We were both a part of that conversation, were we not?"

"I'm only asking a simple question."

I raise my chin, determined to act normal in this conversation. "Then yeah. I think I'd like it if you said it to me in the bedroom."

"Just me or anyone?"

"Goodnight," I say purposefully, turning on my heel, hoping to hide my flushed cheeks.

"'Night!" he calls after me.

The cool air greets me, but does not cool me down enough. I need to go home and pull a little something out of my nightstand drawer. Well, a big something.

CHAPTER THIRTEEN
Ben

"All done here?" I ask the pair sitting at the table by the window. They give me yeses, so I clear their places and bring the dishes to the back, dropping them in the sink to be washed after we close.

Which—I glance at the large clock I have hung in the kitchen—will be in ten minutes. Normally, I get off at 2 p.m., but Scott had an appointment this afternoon, so he came in early like I normally do, and I agreed to work until close with Isla.

I love owning this café, I do, but my ideal would be if I could hide in the back and bake all day, coming out only when I feel like a chat. However, when it's just Isla and me, I have to be baker, runner, and busboy while Isla handles the front.

The bell over the door jingles, hopefully signaling our customers leaving and not new ones entering. I poke my head out of the kitchen door. Leaving, thank god.

I go back out front to wipe down the tables, getting a head start on closing procedures. I grab a lone mug sitting on a table as the clock hits 3 p.m. and Isla locks the door.

"You doing anything tonight?" she asks as she moves back behind the counter and to the register to start counting it out.

"I don't think so," I say, snatching a napkin from the floor and crumpling it to throw in the bin before I take the mug I'm holding to the back with the other dishes.

"Not seeing Linny?"

"Naw, she has a thing," I fib. I have no idea what Linny is doing tonight. I haven't seen her since Isla and Rachel came over for dinner. Since Linny and I snogged for a while and I asked how she'd like me to refer to her cunt in the bedroom. Aye, that *was* an odd conversation to have with someone I am not trying to date. Call it genuine curiosity—I had to know.

I snatch a discarded wooden stirrer from a table, tossing that in the bin as well, as Isla says, "Too bad. David's working at Hoot tonight, so Rachel and I are gonna spend our evening there if you want to come." She moves on to the next stack of bills in the drawer, counting one by one and entering the amount in the computer.

"Oh. Erm, you know. I am seeing Linny tonight. I forgot," I lie quickly.

"If she has a thing, maybe you can stop in for one drink? We'll probably be there a while." She continues to count another set of bills, not glancing up at me.

I swallow. "We're busy. I forgot," I say again. "Her thing is tomorrow. We're doing something tonight. As soon as we close and it'll go until late."

Isla moves on to the coins. "What are you doing?"

Why the hell is *parasailing* the first excuse that pops into my head? I can't say that. Oh, fuck. I can't think of anything else. My mind is blank.

Well, no, actually it's yelling: *Parasailing! Parasailing! Parasailing!*

Isla is regarding me curiously. I need to say *something*.

"Having sex," I finally say. Nice.

Isla props a hand on her hip and asks slowly, "You can't get one drink with us tonight because you're too busy having sex with your girlfriend?"

I raise my chin and say cheekily, "Aye. We're very passionate."

She rolls her eyes and goes back to the drawer. "Right. And this has nothing to do with the strange thing going on between you and David?"

"There's *no* strange thing."

Isla turns back to me. "What world are you living in? After avoiding him for months, you went to dinner with him like two weeks ago, then basically ignored him at your birthday, and now haven't seen him since." She shakes her head. "David may not have told Rachel exactly what's going on, but they still talk. He's heartbroken about whatever happened. And you? You get weird whenever I bring him up, all stiff and sweaty. I'm tired of it. I mean, you used to act like you were in love with him, and now you can hardly look at him."

The mug I'm holding slips from my hand, shattering on the floor. "Bollocks," I swear.

I quickly pivot away, Isla calling after me, "Ben!"

"I have to fetch a broom!" I call back. I retrieve the broom and then begin to sweep up the broken ceramic.

"Ben," Isla says again, softer.

I keep my focus on the broom, crouching over as I sweep the remnants of the mug into the dustpan. Isla crouches down with me, grabbing my wrist and saying one more time, "Ben."

I look up at her, panic alighting my eyes.

"Oh my god," she whispers, the realization dawning on her. "You're in love with him."

I shake my head and say, "I'm with Linny," like that removes David from the equation. Like that was even a true statement.

"Talk to me. Please."

I sigh, pushing the broom and the dustpan full of broken mug to the side, dropping fully onto the floor. I bring my knees up, resting my arms on them. Without looking at her, I say, "Seven months ago, I told him I was in love with him. He does not feel the same. If his heart was broken, mine was shattered." I glimpse up to see her shoulders sag.

"Shite."

"Tell me about it."

"Are you still…?"

"I'm trying to get past it."

"Any luck?"

"Hard to say." I offer a small smile that feels more like a grimace. "I guess this is as good a time as any to tell you I'm bi."

She stretches forward, pushing my legs to the side to wrap her arms around me. "I love you and I accept you," she says into my shoulder.

"Don't make this a thing," I groan, tolerating the hug.

She pulls away and meets my eye. "I love you and I accept you." Then she shoves me and says, "Also, I knew. I've seen the way you look at Orlando Bloom."

I throw my head back in a laugh that almost immediately dissolves into tears. When she came out to me back when she was a teenager, I told her I knew because I'd seen the way she looked at Keira Knightley. Goddamn her. "Orlando Bloom *and* Keira Knightley," I sob.

"Of course. The classic bisexual awakening."

"You're the first person I've told," I say through the tears.

She cocks her head to the side. "What about David?"

"I didn't come out really. I just told him about the love bit. You're the first person I've said the word to. Bisexual." I sniff loudly, so she snatches a stack of napkins from off the counter, chucking them at me. "Rachel knows too-ish. She saw me snogging some bloke behind a club."

She scoffs. "Are you taking the piss? Rachel knows?"

"I asked her not to tell you. Don't be cross."

She points an aggressive finger at me. "Stop telling my girlfriend to keep your secrets from me. She's too nice to betray your trust."

"Fine. Linny knows as well, I guess, but again, I never said the word."

She falls back to her arse on the ground, mirroring my position with her knees brought up and forearms resting on them. "Well, even though it sounds like I'm actually the last to know, thank you for saying the word to me. So, what about Linny? Are you sure you should be seeing her while you're trying to get over someone else?"

I exhale heavily. "I shouldn't be. Which is why I'm not."

"You broke up?"

"We were never dating in the first place." I give her a quick rundown of our agreement and why we made it. "You can't tell anyone, though. Please. Not even Rachel."

Her jaw stiffens. "I don't keep secrets from Rachel, Ben. Even for you. That's where she and I differ."

I look at her pleadingly. "I don't want this to get out to David. Please, Isla."

Her face grows soft. "Alright. But I can't keep this secret forever." Her fingers drum against her arm. "Okay, so you're not dating Linny, but you're snogging in the kitchen? Please tell me that was not for our benefit."

"Don't be a perv. No. It was an ill-advised moment of weakness. We agreed to not do that anymore."

"Okay. Next question. Do you fancy her?"

"Of course I fancy her. Have you fucking met her? But I *can't*. Not until this thing with David is through." I shake my head. "And even then, she does not want to be in a relationship. With anyone. Ever. I don't…I don't want to fall for someone else who will not feel the same."

She reaches out to squeeze my knee. "I get that. However, I will note, Rachel also convinced herself she was not looking to date. But then she met me and couldn't help herself."

I give half a smile. "Brag, why don't you? I think you and Rach are a special case. Not everyone is as lucky as you."

Isla weighs her head. "True." She stands up, grabbing both my hands to pull me up with her. "Come on. We have to close. Then you are coming with me to Hoot. If you want to get over this David thing and be normal with him again, you have to spend time with him. Think of it as exposure therapy."

I grip the broom tightly, knuckles turning white. "What if it has the opposite effect? What if I fall again?"

She tips her head sympathetically. "Then we'll reevaluate. But if you want me to spend tonight pointing out his flaws, I can."

"What flaws?"

"Well, for one, he talks about computers too much."

"He's getting a Ph.D. in Computer Engineering."

"Exactly! What a bore. Everyone knows getting your Ph.D. is only cool if you're a hot girl getting one in Marine Biodiversity."

"Aka, your girlfriend."

"Bingo."

...

It takes the entire hour we are closing to convince me, but I finally agree to go to Hoot with Isla. Though I still hesitate once we get to the red door leading down steep stairs to the bar. I focus on the sign beside it, wondering if I'll discover my fortune tonight: HOOT THE REDEEMER PSYCHIC PALM READINGS CRYSTAL BALL GAZERS WAITING FOR YOU INSIDE.

She gives me a considerate glance and says, "One drink, Ben. If you can't stand to be in the same room as him, you can leave, but if you want to move back into normalcy with him, you have to at least try."

My face falls. Goddamn her for being right.

I follow her down the stairs, letting her push through the door marked by a life-size psychic woman statue. When we walk in, my first thought is about how ridiculously dark it is in here. Linny would not be able to see very well, and I am annoyed on her behalf. To hell with ambiance, right?

Rachel is already here, sitting at the bar, sipping something bright green. She beams when she sees Isla, hopping up from her stool and planting a long kiss on her lips. So long, in fact, that I clear my throat loudly to remind them that they are not alone. Rachel pulls away quickly, throwing a smile of apology my way. Isla just looks annoyed with me as she uses a thumb to clean burgundy lipstick from the corner of Rachel's mouth.

David is not behind the bar. Someone else is, but that's okay. Gives me a second to settle in. I take the seat beside Rachel, Isla stealing the one on her other side, resting her foot on the bottom of Rachel's stool.

I pull out my phone, opening up my chat with Oscar Wilde's Mother as a reflex.

Hi

Hey. What's up? You okay?

Fine. Just thinking about you. And your cat

In response, she sends back a photo of Oscar Wilde on his back, clutching a toy mouse with his front paws.

You better mean this cat. You're sure you're ok?

I may have had a bit of a sob fest today. Isla knows about us now, btw

She sends back a new photo of Oscar, now curled in a ball on his cat tree.

Do you want to talk about it?

Yes, but I'm at Hoot. Isla is making me do 'exposure therapy.' Do you want to come by?

Probably best to not bring your emotional support fake girlfriend to exposure therapy

But text me later?

I frown at my phone, wishing she said yes, but understanding why she said no. I respond: **Will do. Thank you, Lin**

"Rachel, I've something to tell you," I declare as I place my mobile face down on the bar. She swivels toward me, curious. "I'm bi."

She grins like a maniac. "Are you? Welcome to the club!" She holds up her hand for a high-five, which I slap enthusiastically.

"What are we high-fiving about?" A deep voice asks. David walks behind the bar, setting a black serving tray down as he does. He's in a fitted, deep green T-shirt with black trousers. The new stubble on his face is shaped to perfection, as is the fade on the sides of his head, like he recently went to the barber. The other bartender changes places with him, heading into the back.

I twist toward David and give him a small smile. I can be normal. Lifting my chin, I say, "I'm doing the coming out rounds. I'm bi."

David looks thrilled, reaching across the bar to squeeze me on the shoulder. "Congrats, man. Thanks for telling me. Officially."

I nod, throat tight.

Isla must sense my oncoming emotional detriment, because she cuts in and says, "Well, our little group is slowly filling out the alphabet. Not that Ben is adding to it."

"Maybe I should start identifying as pan to add another letter?"

Rachel pokes my arm. "Only if that feels more right."

"Naw. I think the B is right."

"Bitch," Isla says as though in confirmation.

I snort. "Exactly."

David shakes his head at us, sticking a hand in his pocket to root around. He gestures for me to hold out my own hand, so I do, palm up. David drops two one-pound coins into my palm. "Go pick a flavor or two from the claw machine. Drinks on me."

Hoot has a claw machine in the back of the bar with various mystery flavors for a pound each. It's a fun thing to get if you want a random, cool drink.

"Thanks, sugar daddy," I say, pushing myself up from my stool. I pause at that, eyes widening as I acknowledge the words that fell from my mouth. That was a very old-Ben thing to say. The words didn't feel wrong coming out, but they do feel out of place. Forced, even though it was a slip.

However, David must not see it that way because he throws his head back in a laugh. "Wow, I missed you. Just go get your flavors."

And with that, I think I can manage this.

CHAPTER FOURTEEN

Linny

It's been nearly a week since I've seen Ben. We've texted a bit, but I haven't *seen* him. I consider going over to the café just to visit him a humiliating number of times. *Humiliating.* But I hold back. I don't need to go see him. It would be for no reason other than *just* to see him. Though I suppose if we're "dating," I would be going over to visit him, right? So maybe I should?

No. No, I don't need to. Isla knows we're not really together, so there's no point. We should be avoiding the one-on-one thing, anyway.

I check the time. It doesn't matter. I have to get to an appointment at my ophthalmologist's. I go every six months. It's not that big of a deal, just a task. Not one I love, but not one I hate. I mean, what are they going to tell me? I'm losing my vision? Fully aware.

I pop in the back to tell Carolyn I'm taking off, then head out the front door, careful not to bring any ghosts with me.

The eye doctor is within walking distance from the shop, so I'm over there in fifteen minutes. I wore my glasses today because I'd have to take my contacts out anyway, so it's easier to wear glasses that I can take on and off as necessary. I walk in, and the receptionist smiles at me. "Hi, Linny. We'll call you back in a sec."

"Thanks," I say, taking my seat. I don't believe I'm here often enough for the receptionist to recognize me on sight, but two visits a year for five years must be sufficient.

The tech calls me back and sits me down in front of a big gray machine, the one where you have to look in and stare at the hot air balloon. She explains how it works and what they're testing for, and I nod along like I haven't had to take this test at every eye doctor appointment since I was seven, when I got my first pair of glasses.

Then she drops two eye drops in my eyes, the first to dilate and the next to numb. The numbing drops are so they can touch my eyes with this tool to take the pressure. Gross, I know. My eyes are spread wide as they do so. Okay. Done.

After the pressure is taken, I am led to the back to sit while my eyes fully dilate. As my near vision gets blurrier, I still try to look at my phone. I have a few texts from Mel that I cannot make out. I lift my glasses off my eyes and find I can see better that way. Though texting is still a bit touch-and-go. I find myself thankful for autocorrect as I attempt to converse with my cousin.

Should I have invited more co-workers to my wedding?

No? Not if you don't like them

But I do like them. Or, a few of them. Some of my American colleagues

Why would you invite your American colleagues?

I guess so they can send presents

But because they're in the US, maybe they would think you only invited them to get presents

Yeah. But I have one colleague whose sister lives in Edinburgh. I should have at least invited him. He and his girlfriend probably would have liked the excuse to come visit his sister

They don't really need a wedding to do that. It's fine. Your day. Don't worry about random coworkers

Fine. Okay. You're right. Thanks

Doing okay beyond that?

Yeah. It's just getting so close! I'm anxious

Understandably. It'll all work out though. It will be a great day

The tech calls me back to do more tests. It's time to do a field vision test, which is basically the worst video game ever invented. I stare at a green cross in the middle of the screen as dots flash around it. Every time I see a flash, I press a button. There are gaps between me seeing flashes that last a little too long, so I know I'm missing some. The gaps get bigger every year. We do one eye at a time, and I have to keep a silly eye patch over the eye not being tested. Once we finish with the right eye, I swap which eye is covered by the eye patch.

The tech titters and says, "You know, you're the first person who has ever moved that on their own. Normally, I have to do it for them."

"Not my first rodeo."

We test the next eye. I prefer testing the left eye because it's my better eye, so it makes me feel like I passed the test. This test is not pass or fail, but it certainly feels like it.

Then I pivot to another machine so they can take a picture of my eye. I hold still, eyes wide open as they snap the photo of each one. Then, my least favorite one. The tech cleans my forehead and under my eyes with an alcohol wipe, then sticks patches connected to wires to my forehead and cheeks. I stare ahead at a red cross, covering one eye at a time, as they flash a bright light to check my eyes' responses.

This test always makes me feel like a science experiment, the wires and all making it intense and somewhat sci-fi.

Lastly, we move into another room so I can wait for the doctor. I twiddle my thumbs while I wait, but before long, he enters with a knock on the door. We go through the standard greetings, then he pulls up the photos they took of my eye. He rubs his chin as he assesses them.

"Looks about the same as last time," he comments. "Have you noticed anything getting worse?"

"Not significantly."

"Good." He points out a few things on the scan, explaining what we're looking at. Tells me the pressure in my eyes isn't too bad, so I just need to keep using the eye drops I have been prescribed to keep the pressure down. I assure him that I use them as directed, twice a day.

Then he slides over on his chair and takes a look at my eyes himself. "The cataract forming on your right eye isn't terrible. I see a little clouding, but it's not bad enough to be removed any time soon."

"Cool," I say. People with RP have a higher likelihood of developing cataracts at a young age. My dad had to get his cataracts out when he was in his forties. I'm expecting the same.

Then we finish up. "I'll send in a refill of your eyedrops, and then we will see you again in six months."

"Sounds good," I say, hopping up from my seat. "Thanks." I head back to reception to schedule my next appointment, then exit the office.

I exchange my glasses for my sunglasses because the sun is extremely intense with my dilated eyes. Can I see well enough to walk around without my glasses? No. The world is a big old blur and fellow humans are oblong smudges. Am I going to anyway? Yes.

I walk back to the shop, slowly, but find myself bypassing it in favor of Somewhere Special. As I enter, I switch my sunglasses and glasses back out. Gemma is behind the counter and Isla is in the corner chatting with a customer. I catch her laugh before I catch sight of her.

"Hiya," Gemma says when the customer in front of me departs. "What'll you have?"

"An americano, please," I say, offering my regular order. "Let me pay for it this time."

"If you insist."

I tap my card quickly before Ben or Isla notice me.

Isla spots me then because I hear her shout, "Ben! Linny's here!" She pops up next to me and says, "I like the glasses."

"Thanks," I say.

She looks both ways before she whispers, "You're good for him, you know. He's been so *happy* since he met you. Or, *re*-met you, I suppose. It's obnoxious, but I've missed him being obnoxious."

Before I can respond to that, Ben sweeps out of the kitchen in his apron and throws his arms around me, surprising me and spinning me a bit. With a smug expression, Isla moves behind the counter.

I laugh out, "Someone's in a good mood."

"I am! Made these gorgeous orange and cranberry scones. They turned out incredible. I'll fetch you one when they cool," he says, then looks me over. "You're in your glasses. I love when you wear your glasses."

I blush involuntarily at the comment and accept the coffee Gemma reaches over the counter to hand me. "Eye doctor. Easier with the glasses."

"That explains why your pupils are gigantic." His voice lowers, ensuring this conversation is now one only for us. "Everything okay?"

"Yeah, yeah. Just a normal check-up." I mean, technically things are worse because that's how it works, but not aggressively, so good news in a way only not-terrible news can be. "Work going all right?" I ask, determined to shift the subject away from my eyes.

"Yeah, yeah," he mimics. He grabs my hand. "Come to the kitchen with me." I wave goodbye to Isla and Gemma as best I can with my coffee as Ben pulls me into the back.

"Don't tell me you need my help again. I feel like I ruined all your food that day."

"Are you kidding? My pride is still recovering from all the compliments we got on your muffins."

I settle in a spot that is hopefully out of the way as he taps a scone with his finger, determining the temperature. It's cool enough, so he picks it up and hands it to me, watching me with hopeful eyes as I take my first bite. The scone crumbles slightly as I bite into it, but it is delicious.

I cover my mouth as I chew before swallowing and saying, "Amazing, Ben."

He simpers. "Thank you." He refocuses on the scones, moving them one by one from the cooling rack to a sheet to take out to the case in front. "Do you want to chill here for a bit or do you need to head back to the shop?"

I finish another bite of my scone before answering. "I can stay for a bit. At least while I drink my coffee. Give my eyes time to un-dilate." I take a swallow. "Is everything alright?"

"Yeah, I'm all good," he says, opening the fridge and taking out butter. "It's been a while. I wanted to spend time with you."

Only the inside of my mug sees my grin. "Are you saying you miss me?" I joke.

He rotates to look at me seriously. "Yes. I am saying that." He swivels back to his work.

I find myself somewhat dumbstruck, as I always am with him.

We don't talk as he works and I finish my scone, but I like watching him. He seems so happy as he bakes. And it's fun to see him stop what he's working on to pivot and make a sandwich or avocado toast or anything someone comes in to order for lunch. Because he does so quickly and efficiently, then goes back to whatever he's baking.

Once my coffee is finished, I can't delay my return to my store any longer. He takes my mug to put in the sink and gives me a quick goodbye and see you soon. I bid Isla and Gemma farewell on my way out and go back into the store, a scone for Carolyn in my hand.

She accepts the pastry gleefully, then heads into the back, letting me resume control of the counter.

A few customers are milling around, but no one who needs

any assistance, so I continue the cataloging I had started that morning, even though my eyes are still a bit blurry. I'm happy for the mindless work and am not thinking about the handsome man next door who gives me coffee and scones and friendship. I'm definitely not thinking about how nice it would be if he were also able to give me love. And if I were able to give it to him in return.

CHAPTER FIFTEEN
Ben

I hang my pinny on a hook in the kitchen before slipping on my jacket. Today is one of those days where the end of my shift has come upon me rather quickly. Those are the best days, the ones where I get to spend the time chatting with customers, baking, and just reminding myself why we wanted to open this café in the first place.

Isla is behind the counter while Scott is cleaning up a few tables when I come up front.

To Isla, I say, "I'm gonna head out."

"Alright. See you tomorrow."

"Yeah, see you tomorrow."

I take one step, but she pauses me with an, "Oh." I twist back to her. "I keep forgetting. I have a gig tomorrow, if you want to come."

Isla used to be rather evasive about inviting people to watch her sing, but she's gotten a lot better about it since she started seeing Rachel. I think because Rachel constantly reminds her how much we all enjoy hearing her sing. However, it has been a while since I've agreed to go.

"Sure," I say.

Her eyebrows perk up. "Really?"

I shrug. "Yeah, of course."

She purses her lips. "David is probably going to be there."

I stiffen on instinct, my heart *pinging* when I hear his name, as it always does.

When I recover, I say, "Okay. That's fine."

"It's at McCarthy's."

Ah, that's why she's being weird. McCarthy's, aka the pub where I confessed.

I am so *sick* of this ache. Of being afraid to go places because of possible bad memories or feelings. I'm going. There's no stopping me. I am fed up with this, and I am so unbelievably furious that I let this stop me for so long.

I say, "I like McCarthy's." Because I do. "Fine if I invite Linny?"

"Yeah," she says, toying with the blue scrunchie around her wrist. "Are you only inviting her because of David?"

That question surprises me, though I can't say why. "No. I just haven't seen her in a few days."

Five, to be exact. Not that I'm counting. Except I am counting because I am tired of consistently going multiple days without seeing someone I would like to see every day.

"Cool. I like Linny." She drums her fingers on the counter. "When is the wedding again?"

"Two weeks." I sigh. "I know you want to tell Rachel, and I promise you can as soon as this whole thing is over. I just think it will be easier for her to not tell David if Linny and I are broken up in a way."

"Fine. I hate this, though."

"Me too," I agree.

I take my leave at that. Instead of heading home, I pivot and head into Better than New Antiques. I figure I'll go ahead and ask Linny about coming to McCarthy's tomorrow.

I don't see her or Carolyn when I walk in, which is odd. One of them is normally behind the front counter. Even if they're somewhere else in the shop, potentially hiding behind a tall piece of furniture or what have you, I'd expect them to shout out a greeting.

I poke around a bit, weaving through the aisles before I find Linny in the slightly elevated section at the back of the shop, arms crossed over her chest with her back to me. Even with the squeak of my approaching footsteps on the uneven hardwood floors, she doesn't seem to hear me.

I clear my throat, and with that, she pivots around. "Ben," she practically breathes. "What are you doing here?"

I cock my head to the side, confused by this response to my presence. "Just popping in to see you, cardamom."

"Oh."

I'm not saying she's always excessively enthusiastic about my presence, but this is different. She's indifferent about me being here. It's throwing me off. "Er, do you want to come with me to a gig of Isla's tomorrow? At McCarthy's pub."

"Why?"

I keep pushing through this extremely weird vibe of a conversation. "Because I thought you'd like to come?"

"Oh. Uh, maybe? I don't know. Do you need me there?"

I chuckle. "No, I don't *need* you there. I want you there. David is probably going to be there, but…"

She cuts me off with a sharp inhale and a slight roll of her eyes. My jaw tightens. "What?"

"I just…" she covers her face with a hand for a moment

before dragging it away and losing my eye. "I just don't have the energy for this right now."

"The gig is tomorrow—"

"No," she cuts me off. "I mean the whole David thing. The whole I'm in love with this guy but he doesn't love me back bullshit. People have bigger things going on, Ben. Move past it." Her eyes widen as she slaps a hand over her mouth, as though realizing what she said a moment too late.

My jaw manages to tighten even further. "Right."

She shakes her head rapidly, dragging her hand away from her mouth. "Oh my god. Benny, I didn't mean that. I'm sorry. I'm so sorry. That was horrible to say."

I blow out a huff of air, not meeting her eye. "Yeah, I didn't love that."

She approaches me carefully. "I'm sorry," she says again, gently grabbing my arm. "I'm being extremely self-centered right now. I wasn't expecting you."

"It's fine."

"It's not."

I use my hand to cover hers. "Really, Lin. It's fine." I swallow. "What's wrong?"

She sighs, glancing behind herself, and says quietly, "That couch is green."

I look at the couch in question. It's a small loveseat with a frame of brass and, yes, sage green upholstered fabric functioning as the seating.

"It is green," I agree, not sure what exactly the issue is.

"I thought it was gray."

"Oh. Like when you bought it?"

"No." Then she amends, "Well, yeah, but that's not what I meant. I thought it was gray until just now. The light hit it a certain way as it got brighter in here, and I could see that it was green."

"Oh," I say again, still not understanding the true issue.

She exhales a thick breath of air through her nose. "I couldn't see the color. I mean, I see it now, but I couldn't see it until a certain light hit it, then my brain changed the color for me, so I can see it now." She swallows. "RP can involve color blindness. I could have trouble with colors because of the cones, which help you see color, mutating. My aunt has a hard time with purple and brown. Red, pink, and orange. Gray and certain greens."

I think I finally understand where she's going with this. "Right. That really blows. I'm sorry."

She shakes her head. "It's not…I knew this was coming. And I'm not even surprised when things like this happen. I mean, I just noticed a pan that I've owned for years is dark blue on the outside. I've been thinking it was black. Whatever. I hate that, but whatever. But this color…" She trails off, pinching between her eyebrows.

"What, Lin?" I ask gently.

"I *like* that color." Her eyes meet mine, wet and open, but no tears fall. "I really love that color green and one day"—she points toward the couch, her hand shaking—"one day, I won't be able to see it. One day it'll stay gray, or whatever other fucking color it will turn into as my eyes continue to change and that just *sucks*. It sucks, Ben, because I like that color and I want to keep seeing it and it is so unfair that one day I won't be able to, but other people will be able to see that color for the entirety of their lives."

"Linny," I say quietly, unsure of what else to say.

She bulldozes on. "I am so tired of losing things. I'm losing my peripheral vision, I'm losing colors, I lost my…" Her hand forms a fist across her stomach before she presses it to her mouth.

"I am so tired. And I am so…so *angry*. I'm pissed. I am so furious *all the time*." She shakes her head, gazing up to keep the tears at bay. "Every day, I have to look at everything that I won't have one day. I have to stare at the world that I am losing. And I hate it. I hate it so much because I can't stop it." She looks back to me. "I know exactly what's coming for me. I watched my dad lose so much of his independence. I'm going to lose that too."

I reach out as gently as I can, hand on her arm, no idea what I can say, understanding my words are not what she needs right now.

"Do you know what it's like to know your future? To know exactly what's coming for you and to be completely defenseless against it? Until science decides to figure it out." She pulls out of my grasp, turning away from me. "Sorry. Some days, it hits me harder than others. Some days, I get so angry that I want to run and run until I am so far away that none of this matters. So infuriated that I could smash everything in this store. So upset that I could crawl in a hole and not move for the rest of my life and be totally content with that. Or so deranged that I could go knocking on the door of every doctor or scientist I can find and beg them to find a cure faster."

"I'm angry for you," I say. She turns back to me. "I wish you didn't have to go through this. I wish I could do this for you. I wish I could go bug those doctors myself."

"Thanks," she says, knowing what I know as well, that my words mean nothing because nothing can be changed.

However, something else she said prompted an idea. It won't fix anything, but it may help her feel better, if only for a little while.

"That box of broken teacups I saw one time I was here—what do you do with them?"

Her brow furrows adorably. "Sell them if they're still whole. I mean, people buy them to make candles or whatever. They don't care if they're chipped."

"How much do you sell them for?"

"Like fifty pence apiece. Why?"

I grin. "I have an idea." I pivot on my heel and head back to the office, where I find Carolyn polishing a silver pot.

She smiles up at me. "Bennett. Hello."

"Hiya, Carolyn. Can I steal Linny for the rest of the day?"

"Sure. She's here too often anyway."

"Hey!" Linny protests. "I *work* here."

I grab the box of teacups off the shelf. "Come on."

"Where are we going?"

"Just trust me on this."

She sighs, but proceeds to follow me out the door as I lead the way to my flat.

CHAPTER SIXTEEN
Linny

"You cannot be serious."

With the box of teacups in between us, Ben and I stand in his back garden—if it can be called that. It's a fenced-in slab of concrete with IKEA patio furniture in one corner.

"I'm deeply serious." He snatches one teacup out of the box, placing it in my reluctant hand. "Smash it."

I look at him doubtfully. After we arrived at his flat, he brought out two pairs of safety goggles from god knows where and made us each put a pair on.

"Come on," he urges. "This teacup is from TK Maxx. It's not an actual antique. It probably cost three pounds at most."

I now look at the teacup doubtfully. He's right. I saw this exact mug in the store the other day. Without letting myself give it any more thought, I let the cup tip from my grasp and explode into shards on the concrete.

Ben grins wildly and hands me another. "Good. Now throw this one at the ground. Don't just let it fall."

I carefully take the cup from him. I raise it in the air and heave it at the ground. It shatters powerfully. Oh god. *That* felt good. I grab another before he has a chance to hand one to me and throw that on the ground too, smashing it with a gusto I didn't know I had in me. A joyful laugh escapes. This feels *amazing*. I grab another teacup, smashing it with all the hatred I have for my eyes. Then another, smashing it with my frustration with every dark bar with random steps, every dim restaurant with speed-walking hosts, and every goddamn shop with *mood* lighting. And another, smashing it with the sharp hurt I experience every time I think about Atticus. With every broken cup, a twig of anger is released.

Maybe I should be frequenting rage rooms. I didn't know it would feel this *good*. Tears stream down my face, but I don't wipe them away. They are fuel to my power in this moment.

Ben finally takes his turn, grabbing one from the box and throwing it hard at the ground. The laugh he lets out is the most elated one I have ever heard from him. He too has a lot of things to work out. I feel horrible about what I said to him today. I know he cannot help what he feels for David. I know he is trying so hard to get over it. To move on.

I know because I'm trying to do the same thing. To let go of everything in the past that is determined to hold me back.

I smash another cup, letting go of the color sage. And another, letting go of my peripheral vision. And another, letting go of everything else I have lost or will lose. It will come back to me eventually, but to be free of it right now is the best feeling in the world. We keep going through the box until there are two left. My tears have dried by now, freeing me. We each take one teacup, looking at each other for a long moment before either of us lifts an arm to throw them.

"Thank you," I say, my voice thick and throat tight. "I needed this. So much."

His breath rattles out of his chest. "Me too."

With a nod, we each lift our arms. *One, two, three*—we smash the final two cups on the ground. With the final cup shattering, the last thread of my anger is released.

Ben and I lock eyes. *Shit.* That decides it.

"I'm gonna kiss you."

"Thank *fuck.*"

I chuck off my safety goggles, rip the ones off Ben's face, and capture his mouth. The instant *relief* that spreads over me is addictive. If I could live attached to him, I would.

Ben kisses me back with a similar gumption, dragging me away from the shattered ceramic lining his back garden. His mouth opens on mine as he backs me into the wall of his flat. Pressing me closer to the rough siding, his hands stroke down my body until they get to my flowing skirt. He bunches it up so his hands reach my bare thighs, then he lifts me, holding me up against the wall. My legs wrap around him tightly, and I loop my arms around his neck as well.

His tongue traces the inside of my mouth, pulling a moan from deep in my throat. The desperate *want* I have felt since, damn, since we met, bubbles to surface, threatening to consume me whole. I grind my body into his, feeling his hardness grow beneath me.

He pulls away, just enough to ask, "Linny, do you want to…?"

I understand the question without him having to finish it. "Ben, I do. I really do. I just…I don't…."

He nods, thinking he's comprehending what I'm saying. "We don't have to. It's okay."

I shake my head rapidly. "No. No. I want to. I do. I just…I don't do penetration." It's a firm rule I established after Atticus.

His eyebrows lift, surprised, but he says, "Okay. That's fine." He kisses me again, saying into my lips, "There are plenty of things I can do to you that do not involve penetration."

I inch back, regarding him curiously. "You don't want to know why?"

"Not unless you want to tell me." His hands tighten on my thighs.

I brush his disheveled hair back from his forehead, running my fingers gently through the short, soft strands of black and silver. "Can I tell you some other time?"

"Aye. Of course."

"Thank you." Our mouths reconnect, my body writhing against his. My skirt is bunched around my hips, pushed back by Ben's grip on me.

We keep moving in sync, so starved for each other that this alone may get me there. The belt of his pants brushes against my clit through the thin cotton of my underwear, and a scream gets caught in my throat. I press deeper into him, moving more intently, grinding hard. *Fuck*, I am so close.

"Lin," Ben says breathlessly, body pushing up into mine. "If we keep doing this, I'm going to…"

"Me too," I agree.

I grind against him more, needing him to move against me. His hips buck upward to meet my demand. Then, the lightest brush catapults me over the edge. I swear into his mouth as the pleasure races through me, my limbs tightening around him despite their desire to go limp. He groans deeply as he too finds release. Still held against the wall, I kiss him through swollen lips, consuming him like nectar.

When I can, I break the kiss, gathering air. "That was…" I start, not knowing how I want to finish. *Amazing, a bad idea, a great idea, just what I needed, potentially a mistake, something I want to do over and over again for the rest of my life?*

"We're not done."

"We're not, are we? Do you need a Gatorade or something?"

His eyes darken. "I just need to see how wet your pretty cunt is for me."

My mouth waters. "Okay. That answers that question."

"Hm?"

"I like when you say that word to me."

He grins devilishly, picking me up off the wall and carrying me back into his flat. My breath hitches as he takes me all the way to his bathroom, setting me down on the sink. His mouth claims mine again, teeth sinking into my lower lip, tugging gently.

Though I'd be happy to stay like this, curiosity gets the better of me, so I draw away to ask breathlessly, "Why are we making out in the bathroom?"

"Oh, right." He finally lets me go to pivot and turn on the shower.

Once the shower is on, he strips off his shirt.

"Your turn," he says.

I remove my top first, tossing it to the side, then go for my skirt.

"Let me," he requests.

He unzips the side, helping me lift my ass so he can remove it, letting the skirt slip to the ground. My hands find the top button of his ruined trousers, unbuttoning them and yanking them down as much as I can from where I sit. He helps get them off the rest of the way, along with his boxer briefs, so that he is standing completely naked before me. As I remove my bra, I scan him up and down, fully enjoying what I see—lean muscles, strong thighs, solid chest.

His hands stroke down my hips, fingering the top band of my panties. "These are fucking sexy," he mutters. "Do you always wear knickers like this?"

"They're just cotton underwear with a lace trim."

"It's the swoopy design of the lace, maybe."

Boldly, I say, "I think it's that *I'm* wearing them."

"Well, that was a given. You'd be fucking sexy in old days-of-the-week knickers with holes on the bum." He moves over the fabric and down to my center, feeling how positively soaked these fucking-sexy panties are. A satisfied groan escapes him. "How am I supposed to get through a single day now that I know what kind of knickers you wear? How wet they are because of me?"

I gulp, desire pooling low in my belly. He tugs the underwear off me. My legs spread involuntarily as I finger my breasts, watching how he stares down at me—predatory and thoroughly satisfied.

"Absolutely drenched," he comments.

"Absolutely."

With his hands on my waist, he helps me hop down from the sink, then pulls me into the shower with him. Under the stream of the water, he kisses me again, our slick bodies pressing against one another. He slides a hand down my stomach, moving toward my want. His fingers find my clit, stroking in succinct circles.

"Lin, when you say no penetration, do you mean any kind or just my cock?"

I swallow, finding it hard to form words with his fingers gliding over me. "Fingers are fine," I manage to get out. "Sorry, I-I can't…"

He caresses my face. "No, no, love. You don't need to explain right now. I just wanted to make sure." He kisses me hard on the mouth. "Tongue okay?"

"Tongue is great."

He rotates us so that my back is to the stream of water and

kneels before me. His mouth meets my sex with large, open-mouth kisses, thumb re-finding my clit as his tongue delves into me. My hand laces in his wet hair, grasping on and holding tight as the hand not focused on my clit locates my ass, taking a handful.

Into my skin, he murmurs, "You taste like sugar." The vibration of his voice makes my hand slam into the shower wall, clenching pointlessly against it.

"I highly—*fuck*." His tongue replaces his thumb, giving generous strokes before settling in. I draw in a breath and finish my sentence, "—doubt that."

He sucks on my clit, holding it between his lips before his tongue slides over it again. A finger gently strokes my entrance, waiting for approval. Once he has it, he dips that finger inside, shortly followed by another. As his mouth works my clit, his fingers curve in. They pump inside of me before hitting that perfect spot and—

Oh god.

I come hard, bending over at the waist as the ripples of pleasure ride through me. He would keep going, I can tell by the way his mouth continues to move intently, but I pull him back to his feet and bring his mouth to mine, tasting myself on his lips. Even though my legs are shaking and I'm not sure how much longer I can manage to stand, I guide his fingers back to my clit, still desperate for him.

I find his hard cock. "I need to touch you," I say. I stroke him, hot and thick, as I grind on his hand.

He puts two fingers back inside of me, but finds quickly that I want a third. His free hand twists in my hair, gathering it and tugging it enough for a delicious pinch of pain.

"Fecking hell," he murmurs. My inner walls grasp him tightly as the water runs over us in thick streams. As I focus on the head of his cock, thumb tracing over a pearl of pre-cum, he continues his attention on me.

"Come for me again, sugar. I want to feel your cunt pulsing around my fingers."

My body listens to his plea as bliss rockets through me, his name falling from my lips. Finally, that's enough. Legs threatening to give up, I gently push his hand away, letting him grasp my waist tightly as I continue to stroke his throbbing erection. I spit in my hand, water not offering enough lubrication for my efforts. His hips nudge forward, pushing into my touch.

"Linny," he growls warningly as he gets close.

"Come on my stomach," I instruct, positioning myself so he can do just that. I keep pumping him.

Soon enough, he comes, his pleasure pulsating onto my belly.

I use the wall of the shower to keep myself steady. His head drops to my shoulder as we catch our breath.

When it is well enough caught, Ben squeezes body wash onto a loofah and starts to clean my stomach. I laugh when I catch the scent.

"You bought my body wash!"

"I love how you smell."

He moves the loofah over my body, washing me carefully. He takes his time, ensuring every bit of me receives his apt attention. When he's done, I take it from him, enjoying the soapy trails I leave behind on his skin. When he turns around so I can clean his back, I spy something new.

"You have a tattoo," I observe. My eyes trail along the compass tattoo on his upper right shoulder blade.

"I do. I got it when I was eighteen because I thought I was going to lead a lot more adventurous life than I have. I had a year of adventure, but that's it."

I reach out to touch it, but halt before I make contact.

Ben must sense the heat of my fingers, because he says, "Sugar, I just cleaned cum off your stomach. I think it's okay if you touch my back."

"You don't have to be so crass," I grumble. My fingers trace the inked lines through droplets of water on his warm, wet skin. "I like it." I tap my fingers against the tattoo. "I think you still have time for more adventures." I trail over the tattoo and the rest of his back with the loofah.

"I do. But the problem is, I don't want to take those adventures alone anymore."

I place a light kiss on his back where the water just rinsed it clean, before I continue to wash him. "That's understandable."

The water runs cold by the time we're both washed up. Ben reluctantly cranks the shower off before we step out. He wraps me in a towel, letting me secure it across my chest, then grabs another towel for himself.

We have certainly crossed the boundary we agreed we would not cross, but in this moment, I cannot find it in myself to mind.

I fold my arms. "Thanks for today. I needed it."

He gives half a smile. "Me too." He mimics my crossed arms over his strong chest. "But we agree, a one-time thing, yeah?"

"Definitely, yeah." I lean against the counter, toeing the ground. "Pregnancy," I say without looking at him.

"Huh?"

"I don't do penis in vagina because of pregnancy. It's a simple reason, but it's the most effective way to keep from getting pregnant. I've been trying to get an IUD, but the NHS waiting list is atrocious, and I don't really want to pay for private care, so…it's easier to just not. I can't get pregnant."

"I understand. Thank you for telling me."

I gather my clothing from the floor, glad he did not inquire further. However, I suspect he knows my reasoning goes beyond simple preference. "I like being honest with you."

Whenever I'm with him, I'm in the safest place in the world.

He bends with me, fetching my underwear before I can grab it myself and holding it out to me, looped around one finger. I snatch it from his hand.

"If we're being honest, I recently learned that I rather like penetration."

I snort, surprised by what just came out of his mouth. "Oh yeah? I assume we're talking about you being the penetrate-e?"

"Indeed, we are." He wiggles his eyebrows at me, then swivels out of the bathroom, leaving me alone to get redressed.

I wasn't expecting this tonight, but really, I wasn't expecting Ben at all. When I sat down next to him all those months ago, I was not expecting him to become someone to me. But I am so incredibly glad he has. However, now that he has, I am terrified to lose him too. I refuse to add him to my list of losses.

When I exit the bathroom fully clothed and meet him in his living room, I direct my gaze to the back garden. "Should we clean up?"

"You don't have to help."

"I'd like to."

He agrees, grabbing a broom and two pairs of thick work gloves from the kitchen.

I take one pair of gloves and ask, "Why do you have these?"

As he pulls on the other pair, he answers, "I convinced myself I was going to garden. I bought all the things I needed to build one back here, but I never did. Maybe I'll get it going before next spring."

We go back outside. I crouch down to start grabbing at some of the bigger pieces of ceramic, throwing them into the box we brought from the store.

"Why a garden?"

Ben starts to sweep. "Rachel's brother has a garden, and he seems like a happy guy. I thought it would make me happy."

"Baking makes you happy," I comment.

"It does. Maybe chickens would be a better idea. Then I could use the eggs."

"Maybe," I agree while trying not to make a face.

He stops sweeping. "What?"

"Chickens freak me out. They're little, mean, cannibalistic dinosaurs."

He laughs loudly as he keeps sweeping. "If I got chickens, would you never come over here again?"

I seriously consider this. "I enjoy your company more than I hate the company of chickens, I suppose."

"I enjoy your company more than I enjoy the company of chickens," he says in return.

I smile to myself. "Thanks."

We finish cleaning up the broken teacups, filling the box with all the shattered bits and dust.

"I'll dispose of that in a proper way tomorrow," Ben says, pulling off his gloves. "Gloves," he says to me.

I hold out my hands, letting him pull them off for me one after the other. He uses his free hand to stroke a strand of my hair behind my ear, still wet from the shower. Leaving that hand on my cheek, he bends forward to press a kiss to my forehead. I lean into it, savoring the feeling of his lips on my skin.

Have we gone so far past the line that we won't ever be able to return?

CHAPTER SEVENTEEN
Ben

I'm sitting at a table in McCarthy's with David, Callum, and Rachel, and want to know something funny? I don't bother to think about how grateful I am that Rachel is here as a buffer. I mean, I do think it, and I am grateful she's here, but this feeling comes from me reminding myself to feel this way.

I'm sipping a pint as they talk about smart people things. The words "data processor," "cobra," and "microplastics" are thrown around, so I am very lost, but attempting to engage with an interested look here and a shocked gasp there.

I am alerted to Linny's approaching presence only by the, "Fuck, sorry," I hear after the sound of a scooting chair.

I glance behind me to watch her approach and notice that she apologized to an empty chair. I think she notices that as well because her face burns red. But instead of shrinking, she puts her chin up and keeps walking. However, her steps slow down, and her eyes scan and scan everything around her. I could get up and meet her halfway, but I know she likes doing this by herself.

When she makes it to the table, she drops into the chair beside me and says, "I made it before her set started?"

"Aye," I confirm, leaning in to kiss her on the temple, placing my hand on her lower back as I do so, before I bother to wonder if I should be doing either of those actions.

Callum offers, "She's still chatting with the bartender." He indicates his chin toward my sister, who is leaned against the bar with her guitar strapped to her back.

Rachel follows our eyeline and says, "She loves a good chat." She taps her phone to light it up and check the time. "Isles!"

Isla spins around to see Rachel tapping the invisible watch on her wrist. She grins, turns to say one last thing to the bartender, then weaves through the pub to first, come by our table and kiss Rachel on the mouth, then to the stool set up at the back of the bar with a spotlight shining on it.

"Hello, hello," she says lowly into the microphone. "Sorry I'm running a bit behind this evening. I can't even use the old 'I was flirting' excuse because the love of my life is sitting at a table in this pub"—she looks our way and Rachel squirms a bit under the attention, but smiles anyway, eyes only on Isla—"and I would never dream of flirting with anyone but her. So, in honor of her existence, I would like to start the set with her song."

Isla starts strumming a very familiar chord, following it with lyrics that are a bit less familiar. Rachel keeps her eyes on her, despite how her face burns red.

David leans across the table to say, "She's been starting every set with this song since she and Rach officially started dating."

Linny puts a hand over her heart. "That's cute. She wrote this? It's good."

I nod, agreeing. "She's always been good at the music bit but convinced herself that she was terrible at the word bit." I tickle Rachel gently on the arm. "Guess she just needed a muse."

Rachel swats me off and shushes us, but smiles even wider.

I find myself unable to be shushed, but I am agreeable to being quieter. I lean over to whisper in Linny's ear, "Are you feeling better today?"

"Yeah, yesterday really helped. Thank you."

I offer an over-emphasized wink. "Any time."

Her eyes narrow at me. She whispers, "You better mean the smashing shit thing because we agreed the other thing was a one-time occurrence."

There's a spasm in my chest at the knowledge that what happened yesterday will never happen again—likely because of just how *good* it was. Because it was. I mean, wet, naked Linny coming under my hand and my mouth. Obviously, that was a dream scenario.

But she's right. It was a one-time thing because we both have our reasons for not wanting to be together. And they are very good reasons. I know that. But…my reason is starting to feel forced—like I'm making it a bigger roadblock than it is.

David's laugh brings my attention to him. Callum has his hand on his back as he whispers something in David's ear with a smile. David lightly bites his lip, angling toward Callum to mutter something back.

My heart twitches at the sight. Dammit. *Still.*

"Of course I meant the smashing shit," I finally say. I swing my arm around her shoulders, letting her lean into me, thankful that even after yesterday, things are not weird. They are just as they always have been. Comfortable. Easy. The way a good fake relationship always is.

•••

"Walk you home?" I ask as we leave the bar, parting ways from the rest of our group.

"I don't need you to," she says.

"Sugar, you know the offer is purely a selfish excuse for me to see Oscar Wilde again."

She laughs. "Fine. Nice to know that you're using me for my cat."

I chide, "Better than using you for a body part of a similar name."

She lightly hits me on the arm. "You do not get to make jokes like that after seeing me naked."

I stop in my tracks. "I would never joke about seeing you naked. That was a magical experience. *Magical.* I mean, have you seen you? Fucking incredible."

She did not stop walking, so I have to jog to catch up to her. "You're not so bad yourself," she says once I retake my place at her side.

I put a hand to my ear. "I'm sorry, can you say that again? I believe you said, 'Ben, I think you're fit.'"

"I said you're not bad." She bumps me with her hip.

"Rude."

"Ben, you're absolutely beautiful and you know it. I kind of love looking at you."

I nudge her on the arm. "Well, then it sounds like the day you can't anymore will be devastating."

She doesn't say anything for a moment, so I think I've gone too far, but then she busts out laughing. "You self-centered dick!" she exclaims. "Yeah, yeah, you're right. In my old age, when my vision has completely deteriorated, the Highlands won't be at the top of my list, nor the ocean, it'll be *your face.*" She shakes her head and says with a smile, "You are such an ass."

I throw my arm around her shoulders as we continue to head in the direction of her flat. "You like it."

"I do," she admits with a sigh.

I don't remove my arm from her shoulders until we get to her door and I need to so she can dig around her bag to pull out her keys. She unlocks the door and leads me to her flat. As soon as I enter, I hear little legs running toward me. I bend down to greet Oscar Wilde, aka the love of my life.

As the cat plops before me, rolling on his back and showing off his soft stomach, which I am *not* allowed to touch, I lie down with him. Twisting to my side and propping my head up with my hand, I say, "Can I ask you a question?"

After kicking off her shoes, Linny joins me, sitting crossed-legged on the floor. "I already told you. He came with four legs, but decided I needed a little extra trauma, so now he only has three."

"He probably just wanted to ensure extra attention for the rest of his life." Oscar presses his head against my hand, begging for me to resume my stroking as if to prove this point. "That's not my question, though. Why don't you want to be in a relation-ship?" I add quickly, "I don't mean with me, I mean in general. You were engaged to Andy, but now you've sworn off rela-tionships altogether. Do you just want casual now? I mean, do you ever hook up with people, or no?"

She purses her lips, once again choosing to ignore my misnaming of her ex. "That was more than one question."

"Okay, can I ask you"—I count the questions I asked on one hand—"three, or wait, I have one more. Four questions?"

She just looks at me, but I take that as permission to proceed.

"What happened with you and Atti? I assume it was something big and awful."

She blows out a puff of air, then drops to her back on the rug. "I don't have the energy to get into that right now."

I'm a little disappointed, however, I don't want to push her.

"That's okay."

"The breakup with Atti is not technically the reason I don't want a long-term relationship anymore. I mean, it's connected, but not completely." She sighs. "And I do hook up, thank you very much. I'm not running around jumping every man I see, but if I have an itch, I know how to scratch it."

Well, she answered one of my questions, so I'll take it. And it turns out I have another one. "Is that what you were doing with me? Scratching an itch?"

She picks her head up to peer at me. "No. I was saying thank you." Her head drops to the ground. "Though, I think you ended up thanking me a bit more than I thanked you."

I chuckle. "Rather physical way to say thank you. Not that I minded doing some thanking myself." I really, really did not mind. As Oscar Wilde moves on to attack a toy mouse, I shift so that I am stretched beside her on the floor, leaving a sliver of space between us.

"Casual is easier," she discloses quietly.

I swallow before asking, "Are we casual?"

"We both know we could never work as casual." She turns her head toward me. "I was serious about last night being a one-time thing. If you can't agree to that, maybe we should stop what we're doing right now. Before either of us catches feelings."

Too damn late. I turn my head toward her as well, close enough to feel her breath. "I was just clarifying. We are strictly fake dating besties who have done some sexy stuff on the side, but will refrain from anything else sexy. I got it."

"Good." She swallows as she shifts her gaze back to the ceiling. "For me, no commitment is better. Then no one thinks I'm expecting anything from them."

My brow furrows as I keep my head facing her. "Are you

saying you don't want to commit to anyone, or you don't want anyone to commit to you?"

She chews her lip for a moment before whispering, "The latter."

"Why? Anybody would be lucky to commit to you."

She releases a sharp sound, shaking her head.

"What?"

"Ben, come on."

I pick myself up on an elbow to look at her full-on. "You come on. I'm serious."

With me still leaning over her, she whimpers lightly, eyes not meeting mine. "You don't get it."

"Explain. Please."

She huffs. "Committing to me is not just committing to be in a relationship with me, it's also committing to be there for me. Committing to take care of me when I need it. To drive me to doctor's appointments if I can't get there on my own. Committing to guide me through life as my vision gets worse. Committing to be the one who picks our kids up from school or playdates or…never mind. I've decided I'm not having kids. But you know what I mean."

"People who are in love take care of each other. That's how it works."

She groans. "That's not…it's different."

I shake my head. "I don't see how. Not sure I need to say this, but I guess I will because you seem to have convinced yourself otherwise. You deserve love. Like, duh."

She covers her face with her hands, letting out an annoyed moan. "That's not what I'm saying. I'm saying that I don't want someone whose love for me turns into a responsibility for them. I don't want to be someone's responsibility. I don't want to be someone's good deed. I don't want someone to think that I cannot take care of myself. That I cannot be on my own. It's infantilizing. And it's humiliating. And it's frustrating when people think that I cannot do things for myself. That I can't walk home alone in the dark. Or that I need them to drive me places buses don't easily access so they can feel good about themselves. That's what taxis are for! Maybe I need to pull out the flashlight on my phone. Or in the future, maybe I'll need to get a service dog or learn how to use a cane or whatever."

She takes a deep breath. "I'm getting off topic. I don't want someone to commit to me because they will fall out of love, but stay because they will feel bad leaving me on my own. Because they will think I will be unable to live on my own. Because no matter how they feel about me, I will not be a whole person to them. I will be their blind girlfriend or wife or whatever. They will be embarrassed by me when I make mistakes. They will treat me like I can't function as a human adult. There will be times when I *do* need help, but I don't want those moments to be used against me. For those moments to be used as evidence that I can't do life on my own. I would rather just cut all that out and be by myself. It's easier."

I look at her for a long moment, so many things I could say. So many things I *want* to say. However, I say what I think she needs to hear from me the most: "Do you need to break things again?"

Her mouth pinches as she attempts not to laugh. "That should be a limited activity because it might get addictive. And expensive."

I hope that impulse to laugh eased the hurt in her chest because the twitch of her mouth massaged the tension from mine. "You're wrong, by the way."

"I'm not," she argues, her eyes big as she gazes into mine.

"No, because I think if you let the right person love you, they will love you wholly and see you wholly. Not as the bits and pieces you are choosing to separate yourself into, but as the whole, perfect you. Because you are perfect, shite eyes or not, you're you and you is fucking amazing. You deserve to be loved wholly."

She swallows, still staring up at me with those big eyes. "The problem is, it's hard to find someone who will see me like that."

I lie back down beside her. I won't disagree. It is hard to find someone to love every part of you. Everyone has trouble with that. I almost offer to do it for her, but I can't yet.

Instead, I swerve the conversation a little and comment, "Atticus did a number on you." Her worry about embarrassing her partner comes strongly from him. I could tell by the way he acted the night of the stag and hen do.

"It's not just him. There have been other men…or just people in my life who have treated me like that. That feeling holds me back from making friends, too."

"Well, you have me."

"I'm glad I do."

I want to take her hand, but I hold back, wondering if that simple action would be a further element blurring the lines between us that she so desperately needs to remain drawn. We lie there in silence for a long while, me wondering what is going through her mind. What worries and pain has she not voiced?

In a need to fill the silence, I say, "Linny, there's something I need to tell you."

"Yeah?"

"I'm bi."

She lets out a surprised laugh. I feel so much joy from that simple sound. "I know! Did you think I didn't know? Was it a secret?" She sits up quickly, seeming panicked. "Wait, *was* it a secret? Are you not out? Am I not reacting correctly?"

I stay where I am. "I'm not not out. I wanted to verbally tell all of my people since it's a somewhat new development. I figured it out last May."

She lies back down. "Ah. Got it. Sorry, I assumed it was well-established. I mean, you never gave me a label, but you being desperately in love with your male best friend and the amount of time you spend staring at my boobs equaled bi in my head."

I scoff. "I don't spend that much time staring at your boobs."

"You do, but it's okay. I don't mind."

"I only stare because I know how nice they are." I know how a feather-light touch makes her nipples perk up. I know how she moans when I pinch them and how often I think about my tongue running over them.

She gently whacks me on the chest with the back of her hand, as if she can hear my lustful thoughts. "Shut up."

I force myself out of my libidinous haze. "Well, you figured right. I'm men-and-Linny-sexual." I swallow, staring up at the ceiling. "You're okay with it?"

She twists on her side to face me, hand landing on my cheek to turn my head toward her. "*Of course* I'm okay with it. Sorry, Benny, I really am not reacting correctly. Yes, I am okay with it. One hundred percent. One thousand percent. One *million* percent. It's who you are, and I like all of who you are. Okay?"

I swallow again, throat tight. Instead of saying thank you, I say, "I don't think that's how percentages work."

She groans silently before returning to her back. "Who else have you told?"

"Isla, Rachel, David, Callum, Josie. A few customers."

"Have you told your parents?"

"Och. No. Do you think I should do that?"

"Only if you want to. Do you think they'll react poorly?"

I shrug. "They were weird with Isla, but they've moved past the weirdness—or are at least making a conscious effort to. Let's see."

I pull out my phone to make a group chat with my mum and dad. I also throw Isla in to mix it up.

Me

Hey, just wanted to tell you I'm bisexual

Da

???

Is it a celebration day? I thought that was June

Me

No. I'm coming out

Mum

Coming out from where?

Da

Did we not already know you were bi?

Mum

Isla told us she was bi. Not Ben

Isla texts me separately.

We are not a group chat kind of family. Wtf are you doing?

I send back a shrug emoji and then go back to the group chat.

Da

> Ben is not also bi?

I scoff and say aloud, "Was it obvious to everyone that I was bi, except me?"

Linny makes a noncommittal hum.

Me

> Ben is bi. Isla is a lesbian who thought she was bi at first because of compulsory heterosexuality

> Then she tried and failed to date a boy and figured it out

> We know this

Isla

> I am firmly a lesbian

Da

> Right. Right. So Ben being bi is new information?

Mum

> Correct

Me

> Aye

Mum

> So you still like girls? Because there is a woman at my church with a daughter your age. She's very pretty

> But there is a woman at my hairdresser who has a gay son so there are options

Me

Thanks

Da

Congrats [picture of lesbian pride flag]

Isla

Wrong flag, da. That one is mine. This is the bi flag [picture of bisexual pride flag]

Mum

You're 30 years old, Ben. You really need to get married. Now you have more options

Isla

Mum, you can't say that

Mum

Why not? It's true

I show Linny the texts, who raises an eyebrow in a silent question.

"Better than I expected," I answer, knowing what she is wondering. "Just as confused as they were when Isla came out, but they've had time to do their own research over the years."

Isla texts me separately.

They're ridiculous. How ya feeling?

Okay

I feel a little lift in my heart, not realizing that I was waiting for this. All of the most important people in my life know. It's a little detail and an extremely grand one at the same time.

Linny and I continue to lie there in silence, happy to just exist in each other's presence. While we do, I resolve to keep doing everything I can to show her how deserving of love she is. Before we're done with this whole fake dating thing, I am determined to prove it to her.

CHAPTER EIGHTEEN
Linny

It's 7:30 a.m. and I am sitting at my kitchen table with my chin resting in my hand, a cooling cup of coffee beside me, and glasses slipping down my nose. This is how I start most mornings because it can take me forever to wake up. Oscar Wilde is weaving around my ankles, acting like I didn't just feed him.

"You can't fool me into second breakfast, my dude," I mumble. We do this every morning.

My eyes close as I take a sip of coffee, knowing the coffee from Ben's café will always be better than whatever I can brew myself. I set the mug on the table with a sigh.

A knock on my door makes my eyes shoot open and my arm swing out, sending coffee splashing from my mug.

I quietly approach the door so I can peek out through the peephole, which is slightly more difficult while wearing my frames. Ben is on the other side, wearing something bright and yellow. My shoulders un-tense as I unlock my door and pull it open, letting it drag across the doormat.

I scan him up and down. "What the hell are you wearing?"

It's not just bright and yellow. It's tight. My gaze trails down to a specific bulging area between his legs that I think about more often than I should—which is to say, at all.

He chuckles. "You like it, don't you?"

My focus shoots back up, my cheeks flaming. "You didn't answer my question. Also, second question, what the hell are you doing here?"

"You said the other day that there is no way anyone could look good in cycling clothes. I'm proving you wrong." He's wearing a long-sleeve yellow and black zip-up jacket that is windbreaker material and fitted black shorts with a neon yellow stripe down the side, reaching just above his knee.

I look him over again. "That color is horrendous."

"Yeah, but check out my arse." He spins around to give me a nice shot.

"Very…sculpted," I observe, eyes lingering. I shake myself out of it. "It is *so* early, Ben." I scan him again. "You said you don't wear that when you go mountain biking."

"Naw, I don't. Still fitted outfits, but lacking the spandex. I bought this when I thought I was gonna try out road cycling. Not as fun, and you're always in the way of cars."

"I guess that's why it's so goddamn bright." I sit back down at my table, gesturing him inside. He closes the door behind himself, but does not join me at the table. "Have you been mountain biking recently?"

"Too wet."

"Didn't think you'd mind the wet."

His eyes glimmer. "You want to see me wet again, sugar?"

"I feel like that's my line." I clear my throat, cheeks still warm. "It's *so* early," I say again. I have no defense against his joke flirting, and no defense against my honest enjoyment of it.

"Can I say hello to my nephew?"

"Your nephew?"

Ben's eyes light up as he spots Oscar behind me. "Hi, handsome boy!" He steps past my chair, scooping my cat up into his arms like a baby. Oscar Wilde nuzzles in. "Yes, you love your uncle Ben, don't you, you genius writer you."

"Don't call yourself 'Uncle Ben.' It makes it sound like you're going to try to stop a robbery and end up on the wrong side of a weapon."

"Are you Spider-Man in this scenario?"

"Obviously Oscar Wilde is Spider-Man in this scenario."

"He'd be a great superhero. What else am I supposed to call myself? My name is Ben. Uncle Bennett is too formal."

"You don't have to be his uncle anything."

"I can't just be 'Ben.'"

"He's a cat. He doesn't need to call you anything."

"Well, he has a mother. Does he need a daddy?"

"If you start calling yourself 'daddy,' you will get kicked out of my apartment."

He grins wickedly. "I knew you wouldn't like that. Uncle Ben it is." Oscar is rolling around in Ben's arms, rubbing his little head against Ben's jaw, then switching sides to rub against the other cheek.

My smile is uncontrollable. I gesture to him. "I assume you've been wearing that since you got into the café this morning?"

"Aye. When Isla asked and I said it was for you, she told me not to involve her in our sex games." He lets Oscar escape his arms, and then takes a seat at the table.

"Did you tell her we've had sex?"

"No, but I can't lie about blatant sexual tension." He gives an overexaggerated lift of his shoulders.

"You being a morning person is your worst personality trait."

He snickers as he reaches across the table to steal a sip of my coffee, afterward making an "eh" face.

I steal my coffee mug back and hold it with both hands. "Is this the only reason you're here? To show off your ass in those insanely tight shorts?"

"I also wanted to see if you're okay after last night."

My body stiffens. "I'm fine."

"You sure? I know you don't want to talk about what exactly went down with you and Atti, but I'm here for you if you'd like to talk."

"I don't."

His shoulders slump. "Lin, please. I want to know before I have to see him again. He's an arsehole to you, which is reason enough to hate him, I get it, but there's something else. I can tell there's something else."

"It doesn't matter."

"It *does* matter."

I don't say anything in response.

He taps his fingers on the table twice, seemingly trying so hard not to be irritated. I'm irritated with myself.

"I have told you *everything*," he says carefully. "I don't think there is an emotional trauma stone I have left unturned. I would love if you could do the same for me."

"Why do you care?"

"Because I care about *you*. That's why."

I scoff. "We're confusing things again."

"I'm not allowed to care about you?"

My eyes shoot back to his. "*No*, we're getting confused— pretending that this thing between us is anything more than an agreement. We keep crossing lines."

His jaw tightens. "Maybe there's a reason for that."

"What reason, Ben? Tell me what you think the reason is."

He doesn't respond, just looks at me, shaking his head.

My chin lifts. "This is over after the wedding—like we agreed. Wedding, then we never see one another again."

"Never see each other again? You can't be serious."

I'm thinking the same thing. *Am I serious?* Ben is my friend. I don't want to lose him. But I don't let on.

I end this discussion with, "Don't you have to open the café?"

He exhales sharply. "Aye. And change into something normal. See you later, Lin."

...

"Namaste," the instructor says once we sit back up after Savasana.

My yoga class is over, so the people around me start to shuffle, cleaning their mats, returning blocks and blankets, and packing up. The lights are still turned all the way down.

I was expecting this, so I just sit and wait in my spot near the back, where I had a direct eyeline of the teacher. I pretend I am still *so* into my meditation. I was unreasonably and unbelievably nervous before coming here. So much of my time used to be spent in this exact studio, but it has been ten months since I've been here. I let myself retreat into my solitude, give up things I used to enjoy. It's time to start taking them back.

The lights are brought back up, though still at a very dim level. Good enough. I stand, adjusting my ponytail as I evaluate the area, clocking people, mats, water bottles, and any other obstacles before I walk to the back corner to grab a cloth and cleaning spray. When I make it to my destination, my heart is beating like I just walked through high-speed traffic. I fetch the cloth and cleaning spray, and then narrowly miss a water bottle in the middle of the floor on my walk back.

As I'm cleaning my mat, the lights get brighter.

The instructor says in a pinched tone, "Oh, sorry, can you not touch the lights?"

Then I hear a familiar voice I haven't heard in a while say, "It was too dark. I couldn't see a damn thing."

I lift my head to find my old yoga buddy, Emma, who, by the way, could likely see just fine in the dim light. I shake my head at her as we lock eyes.

"Always making a scene on my behalf," I say as I roll up my mat.

She strolls over to me, making a weak attempt to fix the hair escaping from her bun, halting as she stands above me. "Would have said hi earlier, but I got here late."

"Ah, that was you. There is a way to keep the front door from slamming, you know."

"Eh, no harm in making my presence known."

"How have you been?" I ask as I stand, tucking my mat under my arm.

"I've been fine. How have *you* been? It's been so long, I thought you moved. Or, *did* you move? I remember your fiancé was from London."

I grimace and hold up my naked left hand. "Ex-fiancé," I correct.

"Oh," she says. "Well, then I have to say, I always thought he sounded like a real wanker."

A surprised laugh bursts from my chest. "He is. Very much so. You never met him, though, right? What made you think that?"

She sucks her teeth. "Little things you would say about him, that's all. You told me a story once about him getting upset when you knocked over a glass at a pub. That wasn't cool." She cocks her head. "Oh, and weren't you——?"

I cut her off with a quick shake of my head.

She nods, moving on. "So, are you going to start coming back here?"

"That's the plan. I've missed it. I just…I was in a funk that I'm starting to get out of. So, I'm back."

"Good," she says like she means it. "I've missed you. You were always so fun to talk to. Remember that time when the instructor kept glaring at us because we were talking in the back of class?"

"Yes, I do. Especially because that would happen in nearly every class we took together. It's not like we weren't participating."

"We were ruining the mood." She laughs and starts to walk toward the door. "Would you like to get lunch or a drink sometime soon?"

My heart lurches with nervous trepidation mixed with excitement. "Yeah. I would. Do you still have my number?"

Emma checks her phone as she says, "Can't imagine why I wouldn't. Ah, aye, there you are. Wow, under five unanswered direct questions I sent you."

I cringe. "Sorry, I was—"

"In a funk," she finishes for me. "It's fine."

I feel my phone buzz, Emma's name lighting up on my screen.

Hi ☺

"Got it," I say.

"Good. About time we took this friendship out of the yoga studio. I gotta check my schedule, but I'll text you?"

"Sounds good."

I follow her back to the reception area that is separated from the practice space by a thin, white curtain, and then out the front door. We go our separate ways.

I made a friend. A potential friend. No, an old friend. My own friend. Not one of Ben's friends. The urge to do a little wiggle of a dance in the street nearly gets me.

I'm halfway down the block when my phone buzzes in my pocket. I pull it out. It's Mel.

I stick in my headphones and answer, "Hello?"

"Hiya, so guess what? I hate the color pink."

"Pink is one of your wedding colors."

"I know!" Mel goes into a rant about how she still likes mint, but pink is a horrible choice and she should have gone with cream instead. I attempt to spit reassurances at her. It is far too late to change the colors now, but I avoid saying that.

However, I am distracted when I spot Ben across the street, shopping tote looped around his shoulder, changed from the cycling clothes I saw him in this morning. I offer a timid wave, hoping to mend what I tried to break earlier. I point to my ear to indicate that I am on the phone.

He smiles widely and waves back. Then he makes a circular motion with his finger.

"What?" I mouth back, crossing the street toward him.

He does it again.

Aloud, I say, "I have no idea what you're trying to say."

In my ear, Mel says, "That I think I *do* like pink."

I put my fingers on my headphone as I say, "No, sorry, Melly. I ran into Ben. But I will note, I love pink. It's a fun color to pair with mint. Very Spring-y."

Ben says, "Give us a twirl. I gave you one this morning."

In my ear, Mel asks, "What is he saying?"

"He's objectifying me because I'm wearing leggings," I answer flatly.

She says, "That's rude. Did you go to yoga?"

"I did. And it's okay. I objectified him earlier," I say, referring to his bike shorts.

Mel says, "Too much information," as I appease Ben and give him a little spin.

"Happy?" I ask.

"Exceedingly," he answers, falling into step beside me. I don't even argue as he begins to walk me home.

"Stop being cute with your boyfriend and focus on me," Mel says in my ear.

"Sorry," I say, the word *boyfriend* dragging its guilt across my chest.

"So, we think the pink is okay?"

"We think the pink is great."

Ben confirms beside me, "I am a sucker for a pink wedding."

"See, Ben agrees too."

"Okay. Okay, I'll keep it."

It's not quite dark outside, but getting there. Headlights from cars are shining in my eyes, making it more difficult to see. My eyes are moving quickly, scanning the ground, flitting side to side, looking forward, and repeat. If I were alone, I could manage, but Ben and his long legs are setting a pace that is quicker than I would be walking on my own. I grab Ben by the arm for extra ease of mind. He hardly reacts, just briefly pats the hand attached to his arm. As I talk to Mel, I am distracted, which is proven when Ben veers me away from the smallest dog I have ever seen in my entire life. Mel and I hang up soon after as Ben and I near my flat.

"Thank you for walking me back," I say, keeping a hold of his arm as we tread alongside each other. "Listen, I'm sorry about this morning. I shouldn't have snapped at you."

"I'm sorry I pushed."

I grimace, secretly hoping that he continues to push me even when I'm resistant. I need it.

I ask, "Did you have an okay day?"

"Yeah, it was fine. You?"

"Fine." I lift my mat in indication. "Yoga for the first time in a while. Needed some Zen."

"That's good. Erm…"

God, this is awkward. It's all my fault.

Ben nudges me with his elbow. "Am I allowed to say that your arse looks perfect in those leggings?"

I bite the corner of my lips to keep my smile at bay. "No."

"Really? I can't tell you that I am regretting not taking enough advantage of that arse the one and only time I was allowed to see you naked?"

My cheeks heat. "Nope."

He sighs. "Can I at least tell you, you look pretty?"

"No."

He sighs again. "Fine. So, I can't tell you that you look like a pure fantasy? All the damn time, Lin. You are sunlight in this dreary city. You are a breath of fresh air on an endless rubbish day. You are a perfectly browned crumpet just out of the oven. Is that crossing a line?"

I drop his arm and stop walking so I can stare at him, brow furrowed.

"Is that crossing a line?" he repeats, eyeing me down.

I rub my forehead as I recognize what he's doing. "Are you complimenting me because you're angry with me?"

He shrugs, looking defiant, so I take that as a yes.

"I said I was sorry."

"So did I."

"You express your anger in a very confusing way."

He shrugs again.

"It is crossing a line," I say firmly.

He scoffs. "Well, then the goddamn line needs to be pushed back because if that line says I can't *care* about you, I'm done."

"You're done?" I repeat, stunned.

"I'm done."

I purse my lips. This can't end here. I mutter, "You're allowed to care about me, Ben."

"Am I?"

"Yes." I meet his eye. "Because I care about you, too."

He seems satisfied. "Grand. So, the line has been officially pushed."

"Okay."

I relink myself to him as we start walking again, mentally crossing my fingers, hoping he does not bring up Atti.

He doesn't. Instead, he gets us back to normal and says, "So, I, er, I agreed to go to a football match with David on Saturday. Tomorrow."

My eyebrows raise. "Did you? Just you and him?"

"Aye."

"Are you nervous?"

"Very. But it's good that we're doing this."

I squeeze his upper arm. "I agree. I'm here if you need to talk about it with me afterward."

"Thank you, Linbolina."

"That's a new one."

"I think it's a new favorite."

I chuckle, shoving my key into my door. I'm personally a sucker for "sugar" or "Lin." But he doesn't need to know that.

CHAPTER NINETEEN
Ben

I arrive at the stadium, nervously fidgeting with my sunglasses as I walk the long stretch of pavement that leads to the gates. David texted to say he's waiting outside. This is a bit of an odd choice of activity for us. I mean, I love football. David likes it okay, but the American in him has always much preferred a baseball game to "soccer."

He suggested this because he knows *I* like it.

When I see him through the crowds, he throws up a hand in a wave. "Hi," I say as I reach him.

"Hey, man." He gestures to my kit. "I see the lucky jersey still fits."

I sigh dramatically. "I figured by the age of thirty, my bulging muscles would have made it tear in two from the bulk. But, alas."

"Those thighs are trying to do the work of that."

"I've ripped a trouser or two in my time."

"I know. I was witness to both of those occasions."

I click my tongue. "You liked it." I cringe, coughing as I reprimand myself for getting too comfortable. As much as I wish things were back to the way they used to be, we are not there yet.

But David smiles as though we are. "Should we head in?"

"Aye."

I follow him into the stadium. We stop for beer and snacks and then find our seats. Christ, I forgot how tight these little seats are. Our thighs are a sliver apart, and only because I am squeezing my legs together as best I can without crushing the goods.

I take a long sip of my beer, scouring my brain for a subject to discuss, praying the game starts early so we have something to focus on. It didn't used to be like this. I ruined this. I ruined us.

David breaks into my panic with, "Listen, at your birthday, I'm sorry I told Linny about the kiss. I...I figured she knew because you said she knew everything. I shouldn't have even brought it up, but I just started talking because I felt incredibly uncomfortable." He quickly corrects, "Not that I'm uncomfortable with you or her. But I don't want Linny to not like me because it's obvious how much you like her."

I chuckle lightly, patting him on the back. "Getting straight into it, aren't we? It's fine, mate. What you said to her was right. We should have talked about it then."

"Do you want to talk about it now?"

"At a footie match? Surrounded by all these foul-mouthed lads? Alright." I scratch awkwardly behind my ear. "Erm, I had been thinking about laying one on ye for a while. The alcohol gave me a little push. It was nice but..." I trail off, not sure I am ready to admit this fact.

He cocks his head. "But?"

"But there was no spark. I sensed it then, but we were pissed enough that I thought maybe if it happened again while we were sober, there would be a spark."

"What are you saying?"

"That, there's no denying my feelings for you, but I ignored evidence that you did not feel the same."

"I'm sorry," he says quietly, looking truly distressed.

"You don't have to apologize," I say quickly. "You don't have to love me like that. Just because we're best mates who are both queer—and both very handsome—and one of us fell, the other doesn't have to. Especially when he has a bloke already."

David smiles softly at the mention of Callum. "Are we still best friends?"

"Aren't we a little old to be using phrases like 'best friends?'"

"You said it first."

"Technically, I used the word 'mate.' But you never won't be my best friend, David."

"You never won't be mine."

I take a sip of beer, looking away, things getting too gooey for public. Thankfully, the match is starting. The ref drops the ball, and the Hearts take it almost immediately. The match is well fought, though, because the other team steals it, running down the pitch. The game keeps going.

After a particularly bad call, I stand in my seat to yell at the ref, then drop back down.

"So, what'd'ya like about him?" I ask.

David cocks his head at me. "Who?"

"Callum. Is it the hair? The hair is lovely. Or is it the fact that he is literally the nicest bloke I've ever met? I had a minging cold my first year of uni and he brought me soup. Like, what nineteen-year-old bloke brings another bloke soup? Him, that's who. And just when I thought I was special, it turns out he was doing soup runs all over campus, that soup slut."

David laughs loudly. "I'd appreciate it if you didn't call my boyfriend a 'soup slut.'"

"I mean it in the nicest way."

"Only you could." He shakes his head with a smile. "I do love him because he's kind. And because he's funny. And smart—I mean, he actually knows what I'm talking about when I tell him about my studies. But, you're right, he is so good at the little things. Remembering my mom's birthday. Remembering the town my dad grew up in. My favorite sweet. Kissing me like there is nothing else he would rather be doing, even if it's just a peck before we walk out the door. He's quiet, but he listens so well. And when he's not quiet, I love listening to him. He gets so heated about TV shows sometimes. Will rant for hours about inconsistencies or wrong choices. It's everything, Ben. I love everything."

"Sounds like he's treating you right, then." I knew Callum was a stand-up guy, but it's nice to hear it from David's lips.

"He is. And how about Linny? She's treating you well?"

I break out into an uncontrollable grin that I wish I could control. My *fake* girlfriend Linny. Who things are ending with after the wedding. My expression drops, but I may as well answer truthfully.

"She's a dream, mate. She's a little mean, which you know I love, very grumpy, which I also love, and so goddamn sweet. Her laugh is probably my favorite sound in the world."

Linny makes it so easy for me to find things I enjoy about her.

"That's amazing, man. And, sorry for prying, but does she have a little visual impairment thing going on? It's just, I've noticed her bump into things, and that you guide her in dark spaces, and I've overheard a conversation or two you've had. It reminds me of my uncle with Macular Degeneration."

"I'm sure she'd love to be compared to Uncle Earl. She's basically got the opposite. Macular Degeneration starts in the middle and moves out, RP starts from the sides and moves in. God, her eyes, though. Have you seen them? That blue? She has the prettiest eyes I have ever seen in my entire life. They'd be perfect if they didn't give her so much trouble." I shake my head. "I think they're perfect anyway, but she hates that this is happening to her, and it crushes me to see her sad about it. Or angry about it. She's both a lot of the time."

"She's lucky she found you."

"Naw, I'm the lucky one."

...

The rest of the game is great. There's this ease between David and me that hasn't been there the last few times we've seen each other. Though, admittedly, maybe it was missing because the last time we were truly alone together was when we were in the toilet the night we had supper. The match was a good idea.

After it ends and we exit the stadium, we get ready to go our separate ways. Before we do, I go in for a hug. Squeezing him tightly, I say, "Thanks for today, mate." I release him without doing anything peculiar like smelling him.

"It was a good day, Ben. I'll see you soon? Stop by Hoot sometime I'm working."

"Aye. Or you stop by the café before you head to campus or whatever."

"I'll do it."

I head back home, feeling the wild temptation to head for Linny's instead of mine. But I'm getting confused—just like she said. All that talk today about her and Callum got in my head, tricking me into thinking that we're actually in a relationship. We're not. I know we're not.

But I can't help but wonder if the only thing holding us back is ourselves and our stubbornness.

...

How was the football match?

The text from Oscar Wilde's Mother comes in after I get home. I'm lying in bed wishing there was a cat beside me. Or a pretty girl. Or both.

I type my response to Linny.

It was nice. Honestly. Normal, for the most part

That's great

Yeah, I think so too

I gnaw my lip, staring at the bright screen on my phone. I take a few beats, then send her another text.

We talked about you a bit

You did?

Yeah. I had asked about Callum. Real dramatic 'why do you love him and not me' type question. But in a nice way

So, David asked about you. I just told him everything I like about ya

Short list, yeah?

Incredibly long list, actually

Number one being: mother to the best cat in the whole world

Naturally

I mean, there's a reason your contact name is 'Oscar Wilde's Mother'

It is not

Oh, but it is

I send her a screenshot of her contact name. She sends back the rolling eyes emoji. Then:

Well, yours is just Ben. I need something better

Hottest man alive?

Eh

Silver fox?

Maybe in a few years

Benny

There's a slight delay before she texts me back. When she does, she says:

I'll consider it

I offer her an out.

Pheromone king?

Bingo. That's the one

I think that's probably where we're going to leave it, but then she sends another text.

The rehearsal dinner is Friday, just as a reminder. You don't have to come

> Do you not want me there?

> It might be boring for you is all I'm saying

> I always like when you're around

I bite the corner of my mouth. She's so good at that, letting me know that she wants me around, even when she thinks I might not want to be. Though that's where her assumption is wrong— I want to be anywhere and everywhere she is. Always.

> You'll be there, so I'll be there too

> Come by the café tomorrow? Or I'll come by the shop?

I miss you is the implied end of that text.

> I'll stop by the café

> See you tomorrow?

> See you tomorrow

CHAPTER TWENTY
Linny

"Hello?" Ben answers, tone confused because I have never called him before. "You okay, my crumpet?"

"Hey," I say, readjusting the headphone in my right ear. It always slips. "Yeah. Sorry. I can't text and walk, and I don't have time to pause. So, about the rehearsal dinner tonight…" I trail off, unable to both continue talking and open the door to the bakery I'm entering.

"What about it? Aye, I know. You *do* want me to break out the tartan. I warned you, the kilt may be a little short. Though, since this will be the welcome dinner and not the wedding, that may be warranted."

The image of him in a kilt flashes across my mind. Me kneeling before him, dipping my head under to—

"Huh? No, no kilt. Uh, I just wanted to say that you don't have to come. I just need you at the wedding, really."

He sighs into the phone. I know why. We've had this conversation before. And every time he tells me no, he's happy to come as long as I want him there. Of course, I want him there. It's just, his end of the deal carries so much more weight than mine. All he needs me for is a meal with his friends every now and then. To show up at a pub or get a coffee from his café. I'm requiring him to attend all these huge wedding events that scream commitment.

"I'd like to go. Oh, may I please, please go to your cousin's rehearsal dinner?"

"That makes it sound like you don't want to go," I grumble into the phone. I greet the woman behind the counter. "Hi, I have a pickup for Jenkins?"

The woman pivots around to retrieve my order.

"What are you picking up?" Ben asks in my ear.

"Some dessert for tonight. Mel is obsessed with this bakery right off of Princes Street. They don't do wedding cakes, so her compromise was to have them make something for the rehearsal dinner. The restaurant let the dessert be outsourced, and they agreed to keep it in their kitchen for tonight, so I'm getting it now, taking it over to the restaurant, then heading to the church for the rehearsal part of the rehearsal."

"Do you want me to meet you at the church or at the restaurant?" Ben asks, but I don't respond because the bakery worker comes back out, carrying two large boxes of mini carrot cakes.

I carefully take the boxes from her and say, "The bill has been settled already?"

"Huh?" Ben asks.

I ignore him as the woman says, "Yes. You're all sorted."

"Thanks!" I call as I push my way out the door using my back, tripping only a little on the slight drop down.

"You're welcome," Ben says. "Church or restaurant?"

"What?" I adjust the boxes so I am better balancing them.

He chuckles in my ear. "My god, woman, you are unable to multitask. Shall I meet you at the church after the rehearsal so we can head to the restaurant together, or just at the restaurant?"

"Oh." If I'm being honest, the church, but if I'm being realistic: "The restaurant is fine."

"Okay. What color are you wearing?"

I pause at a crosswalk, glancing both ways multiple times before I cross, my dad in my head telling me, *Always look twice.*

"Purple."

"Dark or light?"

"Dark. Plum." I turn the corner, arms already tired. Jeez, I need to work out more, don't I?

"Ah, yes. I have the perfect tie. See you tonight?"

"Yeah. Later, Benny."

Ben hangs up, so the music I had playing before resumes in my ears. It's too loud, distracting me, but I don't have a hand to grab my phone to turn the volume down. At the next crosswalk, I stop, balancing the desserts in a precarious way that Mel would murder me for, to remove one of the headphones and slip it into my purse. Now, with only one playing music, I feel like I can see again.

I get to the restaurant and ring the bell because the door is locked in anticipation of the private event tonight. A man in a black and white uniform opens the door and says, "You must be the lass with the pudding."

"I am indeed," I say, stepping into the restaurant through the door he holds open for me.

I take small, cautious steps, blinking a few times as my eyes take their time adjusting to the change in light level.

"I'll take these," the man says, lifting the desserts from my arms. "We're to keep them in the fridge?"

"Yes, please," I say, arms relieved by the sudden lack of weight. "Thanks so much."

I bid him goodbye, then walk to my bus stop, adjusting my dress as I do. I'm wearing a thin-strapped, midi-length dress with embroidered tulle over the solid plum underlayer. My exposed legs are cold and my coat is too warm. As I wait for my bus, I unbutton the coat, then stand with my arms loose in an attempt to prevent sweating. My feet are already threatening mutiny because I'm wearing heels.

The bus comes and I take it five stops. I walk a small ways before I turn the corner and arrive at the church. I see Mel standing outside when I do. She waves with both hands before nearly tackling me in a hug as I get closer.

"Wedding rehearsal!" she yells in my ear.

"Yay!" I pull away. "Desserts have been secured and taken to the restaurant, by the way."

Her shoulders sag in relief. "Ugh, thank you, Linny. You're the best."

"It's what I'm here for."

She takes me by the hand and leads me into the church. It's old, which means lights are not the church's friend, and the bright sun outside is making it appear darker in here for now, but I'll be alright. My eyes will adjust. I spot Atti standing at the end of the aisle with his arms crossed, talking to Julien. Mel keeps hold of my hand as she calls everyone to gather in a group. The entire wedding party is here, all the groomsmen and bridesmaids, Mel's parents, Julien's parents, Gregory and Claire's daughter Emery, who will be the flower girl, and Mel's and my little cousin Michael, who will be the ring bearer.

Mel finally releases my hand as she begins to explain the order we'll be walking down the aisle in, and starts to pair us up. For a brief moment, I fear she's going to stick me with Atticus despite her assurances that that would not happen. However, that was only my panic speaking, because she pairs me with Darren. Obviously. Mel would not put me with Atti. Atti will be walking with Amber. Poor Amber.

We easily proceed through the rehearsal, then Mel tells us we are free to head to the restaurant.

As we're walking out the door, Paul asks, "Need a ride?" His car keys jingle in his hand.

"Sure, thanks," I say, following him to his car. I was going to ask my aunt and uncle or Kensie for a ride, but I'm happy to go with Paul. "Is this your car?"

"No, I rented it. I'm heading up to the Highlands to do some hiking after the wedding. Ben gave me some recs."

I can't hide my surprise. I wasn't aware that Ben and Paul were in communication. Not that it matters. Ben can talk to whomever he wants. Paul unlocks the car, and we both get in.

"That'll be nice," I say, recovering slightly as I buckle my seatbelt. "I'm sure Ben gave you some great recs. He really likes hiking. Or just the outdoors in general. He's really into mountain biking and things as well. He took a gap year before uni and went to the States and visited all these national parks. He's shown me pictures and they're amazing. He has a list that he wants to check off, but I don't think he's gone back since then."

Paul turns the car on and backs out of the lot. "Maybe you two can go together. Unless you're not outdoorsy?"

I weigh my head. "I'm not, not outdoorsy. Hiking is fun. Though I think he's a bit more intense than I am."

"I like intense."

I almost say something then. Something to push him to pursue Ben because they seem to have a lot in common—a much better match than he and I. A more realistic one, as well. But I stop myself because Paul thinks Ben and I are dating, and he cannot know that we're not. No one here can. At this point, if anyone finds out that we're not really seeing one another, it will be extremely embarrassing.

I also stop myself because I don't *want* Ben to date Paul. Okay? I can admit it. I do think they would be good together, but I want to keep Ben for myself, even if just for a little longer. I don't care how selfish that is. I have agreed to let him go after tomorrow. He's mine until then.

Paul pulls up to the restaurant, pausing on the street to let me out. "I'll go around the corner to find somewhere to park," he says.

"I can come with, if you want."

He waves me off. "No biggie. I'll see you in there."

I close the car door behind me, already hearing music and chatter from inside the restaurant. The temperature has dropped since this afternoon, making me glad for the coat I chose. I push my way in. It's darker than it was when I was here earlier, but it's fine. I pause in the doorway to give myself a little extra time to adjust. A man comes from nowhere and asks to take my coat. I give it to him to take to the cloakroom, accepting the tab with my number on it and sticking it in my pocket, because yes, this dress does have pockets.

I don't see Ben (not that that's saying much), so I focus on finding someone I know. I locate Kensie standing near the bar with her girlfriend, Jen, so I head toward them. I give Jen a quick hug hello, then ask the bartender for a glass of water.

The three of us move away from the bar once beverages are in all of our hands. There are more people here than were at the church as partners and additional family members were invited. I search around for Ben, still not seeing him.

My mom and my sister Chelsea were supposed to be here, but

their flight got delayed. They're in the air now, so they'll make it for the wedding. My dad and my other sister, Sarah (who came a week early to stay with him), are heading here on a train tonight.

I feel a hand on my shoulder and jump so hard I spill a bit of my water. I know that hand and it is not one I ever planned on touching me again. I crane my head to see Atti standing behind me. "Hey, Linny. We didn't really say hello at the church."

"By design, Atticus."

"Where's that guy you were seeing? Are you not seeing him anymore?"

"No, I can still see him," I respond flatly.

He rolls his eyes obnoxiously. "Funny."

I mutter, "You used to think so." I sip my water, glancing back at Kensie and Jen, who look equally as annoyed by Atti's presence. "He's not here yet. Where's Bridget?"

He shifts uncomfortably. "We broke up."

If I had a few drinks in me, all the horrible things I want to say in this moment would slip out. But I am completely sober, so all I say is, "Ah."

An arm slides around my waist, but this touch does not surprise me. I melt into it, so familiar and comfortable. Ben.

"Hi," he says in my ear.

"Hi," I say back through a grin.

I glance back at Atti, who has taken a step away and looks down at us uncomfortably. Without another word, he gives a stiff jerk of his head and wanders off to prey on someone else for the evening.

"You're late," I scold Ben.

He frowns. "I know. I'm sorry—time got away from me. I was searching for this tie. An embarrassing amount of my things are still in boxes. But look." He holds it to my dress. "It matches perfectly."

I bump him lightly with my hip. "This isn't prom."

"You guys are so cute," Kensie interjects. "Jen and I love to match. We're matching tonight."

Indeed, they are. The light pink flowers on Kensie's dress match the color of Jen's jumpsuit. They're also wearing the same shoes in different colors. That is cute.

I nudge Ben to the side so I can talk to him privately for a second. "I got you something."

He lights up. "You did?"

From my pocket, I pull out a pin I spotted in a shop the other day, about the size of my thumbnail. It's a tri-colored cat. Pink, purple, and blue. He takes it from my hand and holds it up to his eye.

"A bisexual cat?"

My face heats. "Yeah. Sorry. It's silly. I saw it and thought of you. Not that you being bi is like the only part of you I can see. You don't have to keep—"

He cuts me off by pulling me into his arms. I let out a surprised, "*Oof*," but wrap my arms around him as well, my head pressed to his chest. "You're hugging me," I observe.

"I am hugging you," he confirms, dipping his head down to nuzzle closer to my neck. "Thank you. I love it."

"It was five pounds."

"I love it," he repeats. He releases me and immediately pins the cat to the collar of his shirt.

We make our way over to an assigned table with Kensie and Jen. Paul and Amber are sitting there as well. Ben and Paul say an excited hello to one another, causing guilt to rattle through me for being the reason they can't give it a try. I remind myself that Ben is perfectly able to pursue him after the wedding. And what a great story that would be of how they met.

Dinner is soon served. Once we finish eating, the speeches start. One from the father of the groom, and one from Mel, which is unconventional, but she loves a bit of that.

"Thank you all for being here to help us celebrate our special day, which starts in *four* hours!"

After the speeches are done, we are left to mingle. Ben and I get up from the table, making the rounds together. He leaves me to go grab us a drink, returning rather swiftly with a cocktail in each hand.

I take a sip and cough. "Whoa. How much vodka did they add to this?" I hold the glass in front of my face to get a better look. It's pink. Vodka cranberry should be red, typically. I laugh. "I'm going to see if the bartender will add more cranberry juice to this."

"I can do it if you want," Ben offers.

"Nah, I got it." I squeeze him on the arm before navigating my way to the bar. I ask the bartender for a bit more cranberry juice, and we joke together about his heavy pour.

I turn around, glass in hand, and start to make my way back to Ben. Someone is walking my way, so I swerve a little too much as an overcorrection and bump into a chair. It scoots on the ground, and I let out a little groan, but nothing was spilled. No one was hurt. I really hate chairs, though. Why are they always in my way?

I round that one, but then I hit another one that someone pushed out too far.

I'm about to let that be as well, more than ready to get back to Ben, but a deep voice says, "God, Linny. You should walk slower."

Atti is watching me with pure distaste. I freeze up, wishing I wouldn't. His embarrassment of me burns through me, churning in my core like molten lava.

"Or go easy on the drinks," he says, eyeing the glass in my hand.

"It's my first one," I say tightly, not knowing why I am bothering to defend myself from him.

He holds his hands up as though I'm yelling at him. Like I'm the one being overdramatic. "All I'm saying is that you should be more careful. That guy isn't going to want to date someone always making a scene." My jaw tightens at the mention of Ben. "It's easier for everyone if you just stand still."

Before I get my mouth to work, Ben slides in out of nowhere and says, "Apologize." Atti chortles like Ben is joking, but Ben doubles down. "I said, *apologize*."

Atti's lip curls. "Sorry."

Ben steps closer, encompassed by fury. "Say it like you mean it." Even though Atticus has a few inches on him, with the expression on Ben's face, Ben seems much taller.

I grab Ben's arm, saying his name quietly. I don't want to cause a scene. No one seems to be looking at us, thankfully. Ben's hand covers where mine grasps his arm.

Atti tsks and peers down at me. "Sorry, Linny. I just think you should be more careful. I'm looking out for you."

Ben laughs at that. Loudly. "Looking out for her?" he asks. "You think she needs you to look out for her? You think you *deserve* to look out for her? That is hilarious. Truly." Ben turns away, taking my hand in his.

But Atti isn't going to let this go. "She's not worth it, mate. You say one wrong thing in the heat of the moment, and she'll drop you. Dump you like you never meant anything to her."

My entire body is so rigid that I am in pain.

Ben turns back slowly. "She's not worth it? *She's* not worth it?" He laughs like that is the most ridiculous thing he has ever heard.

"*She* is worth the world, and *you* are hardly a blade of grass."

My heart catches in my throat. He takes my hand to pull me away from Atti and back to the center of the room. He stops, but I tug on his hand to keep walking, eyes trained ahead as I am now on a mission.

I set my drink on a table before I push our way through the curtains and down the hallway that holds the restrooms and the cloakroom. The bathrooms are both occupied, so I shove open the door to the empty cloakroom. I lock it behind me.

Ben followed me willingly, but is incredibly confused as he asks, "Linny, what—?"

"Shut up," I say, pulling his mouth to mine.

CHAPTER TWENTY-ONE
Ben

Linny's mouth is scorching as her hands pull at my tie, undoing it and dropping it to the floor. She pushes me back into a wall of coats, the hangers clanging together when our bodies rattle them.

My hands stroke over her hips, taking fistfuls of fabric to pull her closer. I'm…confused is not the correct word. *Elated* is better. But something is tapping at the back of my mind, making me break the kiss so I can ask, "Is this you saying thank you again?"

She shakes her head, fingers tangling in my hair. "I don't want to see it like that." Her mouth meets mine again, hot and heavy. She moves to my jaw, murmuring, "You're just so…*ugh*," as her lips make trails of searing kisses. Her fingers work at the buttons of my shirt, undoing them one by one before she pulls it open, hands stroking down my chest and over my shoulders. "You would wear a V-neck undershirt," she mutters, mouth on my neck.

"That feels like an insult," I say, eyes blinking closed at the sensation of her lips.

"Not at all." Her hands stroke down over me again. "*Ugh*, your chest. Your fucking chest." My fucking chest is heaving, heart pounding from all the attention she's giving me. Her mouth meets the skin above the collar of my undershirt, sucking lightly, sending a thrill through me, before she moves downward.

She kneels before me, undoing the belt of my trousers.

"Linny, you don't have to—"

Hand gripping my thigh, she says, "Please, shut up. I want to. I really, really want to. I mean, it's almost absurd to me how much I want to. I can't stop thinking about it." She looks up at me, long lashes fluttering. "Ben, I need your cock in my mouth."

I gulp, giving a small nod. "Then I need your mouth on my cock."

She next undoes the top button and zipper, yanking the trousers downward. As her fingers trace the waistband of my pants, her head tips back with a strangled laugh, which isn't typically what you want from the person kneeling before you. But I know why she's laughing.

She puffs out a lip and whimpers out, "They match my dress."

I glance down at the plum boxer briefs I'm sporting. "To be fair, you weren't supposed to be seeing them."

Her head shakes as she pulls my pants down, revealing my stiffening erection. I must be dreaming, this gorgeous woman with her mouth so goddamn close to me.

"Linny," I say again.

"Ben, do you not want me to—"

I cut her off, "No, no. I do." I spy my coat on the rack next to us, grabbing it to hand to her. "For your knees."

One side of her mouth quirks up as she takes the coat from my grasp, folding it so it acts as a cushion from the hard floor, and kneels on it.

Then her wet tongue strokes up my cock, hardening it completely. She meets the tip in a kiss as her hand wraps around the base. Her tongue swirls over the crown before she takes me in her mouth, covering the head and—

"*Fuck*ing hell," I swear as she sucks. My hand flies out to grip the top bar of the cloak rack. She blinks up at me innocently, mouth stretched widely around my shaft.

My other hand moves to lace tightly in her hair as her head bobs back and forth on me, her hand following her lips to stroke the parts her mouth cannot reach. My hips itch to thrust forward and move with her, but I hold back.

The hand gripping my cock moves to grasp my thigh as she takes me fully and deeply to her throat. *Bloody hell*, this woman will be the death of me.

I stroke her hair, grounding out, "Sugar, you look so pretty with my cock in your mouth."

Her eyes are watering as she blinks, peering up at me through wet lashes. She bobs backward, moving off my cock with a pop.

"Fuck my mouth," she instructs.

I don't need to be told twice. "Pinch me if it's too much."

As her mouth re-closes around me, I rock my hips into her, moving with her, faster and faster as she chokes on my erection. Her fingers bury into my thighs, digging in tightly enough that I'll have bruises in the shape of her fingertips tomorrow. I'd allow those bruises to stay forever if they could.

"Lin, " I warn as I feel ready to detonate, in case she wants me to come somewhere other than her mouth.

Lips wrapped fully around me, she blinks up at me again, communicating all I need to know. I find my release, spilling into her mouth as my hips jerk. My hand falls from the coat rack, impressions from the tops of hangers buried in my palm. She pulls away from my cock and swallows, eyes locked on mine the entire time. I stroke a hand down her face, thumb catching on a bit of cum at the corner of her lips. I dip that thumb into her mouth, her tongue working over it, lapping the last bit of me up, then sucking.

"Sugar," I ground out, "you have no idea what I can do to you."

And I'm about to start doing it, but then something slams into the door.

"It's locked!" someone angrily proclaims from the other side.

The knob rattles as they continue to try and open the door.

"Shite," I say, pulling up my pants and then yanking my trousers up as well, the zipper giving me grief.

I hear someone else say, "No bother. I have the key."

The key shoves into the lock. Linny snatches my tie as I grab her and yank her into the back corner of the room behind a rack of coats. I press her front flat into the wall, my body covering hers like a shield as we hide and pray that whoever is coming in does not have their coat stored back here.

The door opens, and footsteps enter.

"Och, a coat fell," the second voice says, causing Linny to let out a sharp laugh. My hand covers her mouth, both of us breathing heavily. I bury my face in her neck to quiet my pants. I hear them pick up my coat from the ground and rehang it on the rack.

Thankfully, they stay on that rack as they find the coat they were searching for and hand it to the other person, a muttered, "Cheers," offered from them.

They leave the room, closing the door behind them. We let out collective sighs of relief as my hand falls from her mouth. I drop my head on her shoulder, letting out the winded breaths I wasn't able to release before.

Linny laughs lightly, resting her forehead on the wall. "We should get back out there."

"Naw, not yet." I'm still covering her body with mine, pressing her against the wall. "I haven't had my way with you."

She angles her head to look at me. "Not necessary."

I guide a hand down to her waist, gazing at her pleadingly before drawing her hair to the side so I can kiss her neck. Into her skin, I say, "Please, sugar, let me see how wet that sweet cunt of yours is for me. I know you liked it when I came in your mouth. I saw you clenching those pretty thighs together."

She visibly swallows. I knew that word would get her. She gives me a nod, so I let my hand stroke up her leg, slowly drawing up the skirt of her dress. I find the devious lace of her panties and stroke over the drenched fabric.

"Soaked," I confirm in a rasp. Her hands brace on the wall in front of us, and my free hand finds its way across her stomach, holding her to me.

My hand dips under the waist of her panties to find her hot pussy very ready for me. I use one finger to dip inside her pulsing center, before I drag it out and focus on the clit.

"Ben," she whispers, hands clenching into fists against the wall. "Ben," she says again, strangled.

"You just saying my name, sugar, or is there something you need?"

"*Ben*," she moans, which confirms that she just fancies saying my name.

I rub hard and fast, knowing that she does want this to be quick, even though all I want to do is take my time with her. Some other time, when we're not hiding in a cloakroom at her cousin's wedding welcome dinner. She comes forcefully on my hand, a stifled cry pressing into her fist as the other hand hits the wall once, pointlessly clutching against it.

As she rides through this, I keep moving my fingers, but she says noncommittally, "We should get back." She angles her head to kiss me, opened-mouthed and full as I drag my nail across her clit.

Her loud moan seems to surprise her as her lips leave mine to press into her shoulder, fists again forming tightly in her hands. "Ben," she pleads. "I can't…"

My fingers pause.

"Don't *stop*," she demands.

I chuckle silently. Another drag of my fingertips and she finds her second release, practically sobbing in her muffled cries.

Reluctantly, I remove my hand, taking my fingers and dipping them into my mouth, witnessing her pupils dilate as she watches me. I finally release her from the wall, letting her turn into me to press a long kiss to my lips before pulling away, adjusting her dress as she does.

Her heaving chest and still watery eyes become the only evidence of anything untoward between us. I finish rebuttoning my shirt and loop my tie back around my neck. She pulls me out to a better-lit area of the small room and runs quick fingers through my hair, fixing it.

I wipe the corner of her eye, clearing a smudge of makeup away.

"I don't know about you," Linny says, "but I am ready to go home."

I agree, so we find our coats before we exit the cloakroom. Since we've been gone a while, I go first, looking both ways to ensure the hallway is clear before I pull her out after me. She clings to my arm as we walk back toward the main room to say our goodnights.

However, we're met by Melanie before we make it there. "Here you are!" she says. Her face softens toward Linny. "Oh, babe, you've been crying. Are you okay?"

Linny's eyes widen, and I nearly laugh, knowing that I am purely the reason for her tears tonight. "I'm fine," she says.

Mel tuts. "Atti left in a huff already, so I was wondering if you guys got into it and left too."

My face hardens at the sound of his name.

Mel catches that expression, spinning on me. "Ben, I know we don't know each other well and I know Atti is an utter arsehole, but if you cause a violent scene at my wedding tomorrow, I will actually kill you."

I promise, "Never have been one for violence. Though, I have never met someone as deserving of a punch in the face as our dear Atticus."

Linny snorts as Mel shakes her head at me. "You better not make me commit a crime on my wedding day, but I will if I have to."

Mel hugs Linny, muttering something in her ear. Linny smiles. "Of course, Mel." Then says in a loud whisper, "You're getting married tomorrow!"

Mel claps her hands together excitedly. "I'm getting married tomorrow!" She spins around and goes back into the party.

We follow Mel so we can say our goodbyes to the rest of the wedding party, then start our journey back to Linny's place. I don't ask to walk her home—I just do, and she doesn't complain. She holds my hand the entire walk.

When we get to her door, she asks, "You want to come in?" Then, almost as an afterthought, she adds, "To see Oscar Wilde?"

"Sure," I say, following her inside, wondering if she is just inviting me in for a hello to her cat or if she will let me spend the rest of our night with my head buried in her thighs.

As per usual, Oscar Wilde comes hopping up to us as soon as

we walk through the door. I bend down to greet him as Linny heads to her bathroom. She crosses the hallway to her bedroom a bit later with her face washed, glasses on, and hair pulled into a haphazard bun. Oscar Wilde seems finished with me, so he slumps away. I stand up, not sure what I'm supposed to be doing.

When Linny comes back out, she's in sweats and an oversized T-shirt, which I think answers my question of whether or not this night will continue as it did in the cloakroom. It's perfectly fine that it won't. I'm her friend first. I figure she has invited me into hers tonight to be her friend and nothing more.

She stops before me. "Why are you just standing there?"

"I don't know," I admit.

Amusement crosses her face. "Well, take your coat off. Stay a while."

She helps me pull my coat off, then hangs it on a hook by the front door. Then she comes back and removes my tie, tossing it on her coffee table, then unbuttons my top two buttons. Lastly, her fingers trace through my hair, messing up the style she helped me get it back to in the cloakroom.

"Och, not the hair," I say, even though my head is pushing into her fingers like a cat wanting to be pet.

"I love your hair," she says absently before pulling away.

My tongue clicks. "I knew you only liked me for the hair."

"Caught me."

As I roll up the sleeves of my shirt, she switches off the overhead light in favor of a lamp on the side table. Then she sits down on the couch, angling herself against the arm and pulling her legs up to wrap her arms around.

"I'm ready to talk about Atti," she says quietly.

A rush of anticipation hits my chest. This was the one thing. The one thing she was using to keep a distance between us, and now, she's ready to offer it away.

"Okay," I say just as quietly, taking a seat across from her on the couch, one leg propped up on it so I can face her.

She loses my eye, picking at her fingernails as she says, "I had a miscarriage."

I jerk up straight in my seat. "Oh, fuck, Lin."

She adds unnecessarily, "When I was with Atti."

"I'm so sorry," I say. I hold my arms out to her. "Come here, sugar. Please."

She nods barely, scooting over on the couch until her back is pressed to my chest. I swing an arm around her shoulders and place a kiss on the top of her head as she snuggles into me.

"Talk to me about it," I softly plead.

She burrows deeper into me, scooching lower so she can press her head to my chest. "It happened while we were engaged. We got engaged, and then about two months later, I found out I was pregnant. We weren't ready for it at all, but we were happy about it. *I* was happy about it. I was excited because I thought I was having a baby with the man I loved, and I thought because of that, everything would work out."

She swallows. "But, four months in, I woke up in so much pain I couldn't see straight, bleeding all over the bed." She clears her throat. "We went to the hospital and they told me I lost the baby. I don't think I have ever cried that hard. So hard I could have thrown up."

I don't say anything, just continue to stroke her hair as I let her tell me this story at her own pace.

"We went home, and I stayed in bed for a solid week. During that week, Atti was great. He took care of me. He held me when I needed to be held and gave me space when I needed space. I mean, we were both going through this loss. When I finally got out of bed, I guess he figured I was over it. I still wasn't okay, but I was showered and eating breakfast in the kitchen. While he was making coffee, he said…and he said this so casually, he said, 'It was for the best.' I didn't know what he was talking about at first because in my mind, there was no way he could be talking about the baby. But then he kept talking. 'We weren't ready for a kid.' I remember nodding, thinking he was trying to make me feel better, even though it was a bad method. I said, 'Probably not. We can try again after we're married.' But then he shook his head and said, 'I don't know, Linny. I mean, do *you* even want a baby?' And it was the way he said 'you' that I knew I did not like where this conversation was heading." She swallows again and is quiet for a long while.

I keep my mouth shut, pressing another kiss to her head.

She starts speaking again. "He said, 'With your eyes, it would be easier on us to just not have kids.' And of course, I argued and said, 'My dad did just fine. My aunts did just fine. My grandmother did just fine.' But he said, 'You know what I mean. Hell, you said yourself you were worried about it. What if you pass it on to our kid? I don't know if I can take care of more than one of you.'"

A blind fury washes over me for her. I could kill him, the right bastard. Mel warned me against causing a violent scene at the wedding, so maybe I can do it before? Linny's hand strokes over my thigh, bringing me out of the livid haze and back to reality.

She keeps speaking. "With that, he implied that if our kid had my eyes, he would love them less. Like my eyes made him love me less. I kicked him out. I screamed and yelled, but I did not shed one tear because I had used all those up over the week. We broke up, and he still to this day acts like he does not understand why."

Finally, I feel like it's okay for me to speak. "He was wrong for that, Lin. He's a daft idiot. The biggest idiot I've met, in fact. You and any child you have are one hundred percent worthy of all the love anyone has to give."

She stays in my arms, but I feel as she turns away from me. "The thing is, I agree with him. It would be best if I didn't have kids. If I didn't risk passing on my eyes. My eyes suck. Why would I want the person or people I love most in the world to go through this like I am?"

I swallow over a thick lump in my throat. "It's your choice, sugar. But you want kids. You said how excited you were when you were pregnant."

"I changed my mind. That's why I don't do penetrative sex—it makes me feel safer. That way, I will never get pregnant again."

"Okay, but is the risk that your kids might have RP the only thing holding you back?"

"I mean, I think it will be too hard to take care of them with my eyes."

"I don't agree. I think sometimes you may have to take care of them differently, but it won't be impossible. How likely is it to get passed on?"

"I don't have a percentage. My dad and two of his three siblings all have it."

"How many of your siblings have it?"

She purses her lips. "Just me."

"Mel doesn't have it."

"No. Only one of my cousins does." Her jaw tightens. "But still, Ben. I'm not going to change my mind about this."

"I'm not trying to make you. I just don't want that man in your head, making you think you can't have the things you want."

She says quietly, "It's not that I can't. It's that the responsible thing for me is that I shouldn't."

I hold her tighter. "Fuck society's fucked up view of responsibility."

She hums slightly, but I can't tell if it's in agreement or not.

I gnaw my lip. "Can I ask the timeline for all of this?"

"July 9th," she answers instantly. "We broke up about a week later, so uh, July 16th or 17th?"

"This past July?" I confirm.

"Yeah."

It's been less than a year—no wonder she was so *pissed* at Atti when she saw him happy and laughing at that pub in early September. My face presses into her hair.

We sit there together for a while longer before she finally pushes herself up and away from me. "I'm tired."

That'll be my cue. "I'll get out of your hair."

"Can you stay the night?" She looks at me hopefully.

My heart pinches in a good way. "Can I sleep in your bed with you?"

"Where else would you sleep?"

Linny lets me borrow her facewash and an extra toothbrush so I can brush my teeth. I take off my trousers and my shirt so I can climb into the bed in my pants and undershirt. Before I do, I grab pillows from off the floor and start to build that barrier between us.

Linny laughs and throws the pillows back at me. "Just get in the bed."

I smirk and climb in beside her. She flips off the lamp on her bedside table, then slides across the bed to snuggle in my arms, her back to my front.

"Shut up," she grumbles into the pillow. My arms tighten around her with the intent to stay that way for the rest of the night.

"I didn't say anything," I mutter, my grinning mouth pressing a kiss to the back of her head.

"You were going to."

"I was only going to say that you *do* like to cuddle. We're cuddle buddies."

"*Ew*," she emphasizes.

With my arms secure around her, I shake her a little bit and taunt, "You like to cuddle."

She lightly kicks me, but doesn't try to move. "Only with you, you jerk."

I sigh against her, the dark room offering courage. "Lin, you make me feel whole."

Almost automatically, and without much gumption, she says, "You can't say that."

I squeeze her body to mine. "Why not? It's true. You have somehow managed to tape together the shards of me into something resembling a real person."

"I am too tired for you to be this poetic." Her body shifts against mine, burrowing in. "I think you did that for yourself, though."

"I think you helped. As did my therapist."

"You're helping me too," she murmurs before drifting off to sleep.

CHAPTER TWENTY-TWO
Linny

I wake up on my back, one arm resting above my head and the other resting across my chest, holding on to the hand attached to the arm Ben has draped across me. His face is nuzzled in my neck and he is breathing deeply, still sound asleep. I allow myself to lie there for a bit in this morning bliss, unwilling to check the time because I know whatever time it is will be a signal for me to get up. I could stay here forever with Ben this close to me.

Ugh, I really should get up. Ben and I aren't supposed to be doing this. This is not "fake" dating, this is just dating. We spend time together whenever possible. We have deep conversations. We have sex. We sleep an entire night in each other's arms. Then we lie to ourselves and say that this is nothing. That we're not dating. That we're nothing more.

We *can't* be more. I've let myself get in too deep. I really, really care about this man, but I cannot let myself fall for him. My head will remain below my heels. I *can't* do it. I refuse.

But the problem is, he makes me feel whole, too. He's not supposed to do that—because it will hurt so much more when he realizes that he does not want what my future holds.

However, I'm content to enjoy the rest of this morning—the rest of today, rather. The last day I will allow us to have.

Carefully, I stretch an arm out to grab my phone and glasses from the nightstand. I slip the glasses on first, angling them awkwardly on the tip of my nose so I don't have to lift my head to look at my phone. When I do, I see three missed calls from Mel and two from Kensie, along with over a dozen panicked texts.

"Shit." I slide out from Ben's arms and run to the bathroom, putting my contacts in as I try to call Mel. She doesn't answer, so I try Kensie.

She answers on the first ring. "Linny, thank god. Mel is flipping out. She got so worked up that she didn't sleep a wink last night. She showed up at our hotel room early this morning in tears because there was a black mark on her dress. We got it out, it's fine, but now she has locked herself in the loo and won't come out."

"Shit," I say again. "Okay. Okay. I'll be right there." I pause. "Not to be insensitive about this, but do I have time to shower? I mean, I'll get there and I'll get her out of the bathroom and the wedding will go on, so I'm going to need to be clean, right? Or no, I should just come."

Kensie lets out a light laugh. "Shower. Please. But do so quickly."

I hang up and turn on the shower, hopping in before the water fully grows warm to start scrubbing myself down. I opt out of washing my hair because I washed it yesterday, but I do take the time to shave my legs. It's a chop job, and I surely left some patches of hair on my knees, but my dress is floor length, so I don't care. I wrap my robe around myself before I grab a large cosmetics bag from off the shelf in my bathroom and throw all of my makeup into it, my curling iron, dry shampoo, and hair-spray.

I run back into my room to find Ben awake and sitting up in bed. God, he's cute as he smiles at me, sleepy and happy with his hair sticking up all over the place. But his smile drops when he sees the panic on my face.

"Mel locked herself in the bathroom," I explain, stripping myself of my robe, not caring that Ben is watching me, and pulling on leggings and a T-shirt. "I have to go talk her off the ledge." I sit down on the edge of the bed to tie my sneakers. "Can you feed Oscar Wilde for me? You can let yourself out. I'll leave my keys, and you can give them back to me at the wedding." I get up and grab my dress from off the door and shoes from my closet. "Is that fine?"

He stands from the bed and places both his hands on my shoulders. "It's fine. Go on. I'll take care of everything here."

My body sags gratefully—and even though I want to kiss him, I don't. I turn on my heel and rush out of my building. The hotel that Mel and everyone coming in from out of town are staying at is closer to the church than the city center, so I have to catch a bus there. I take the bus, then run the entire ten minutes it takes to get to the hotel on a road with very little shoulder with my arms very full. I get to the hotel and rush past reception to head toward the elevator, wondering too late if I need a key to get up to the rooms. Thankfully, I don't, so I press the button for the fourth floor with my foot.

I find the room quickly once I get to the correct floor. The door flies open before I even have the chance to knock.

"I heard you coming," Kensie says, gesturing me inside. She's in a pink robe with her dark hair done up and about half her face etched with makeup. I'm sure with nothing else to do with Mel locked in the bathroom, she started to get ready. Which I get. A wedding *will* be happening today. Jen waves at me from the bed, still in sweats, but her hair also done.

I drop my things over the desk and chair, and then go to the bathroom door. I knock hard. "Mel? It's Linny. Can you let me in?"

No response or indication that she even heard me. If we weren't on the fourth floor, I'd be afraid she climbed out a window.

"Melly?" I try again to no response. I sigh. Fine, I'll do this the invasive way. I go back to my bag and dig out my wallet. From it, I pull an old gift card. Kensie watches me curiously, likely wondering what I plan to do with it.

I stick the card in the door and wiggle it until I hear the lock click open. I smirk back at the other women. "My mom taught me that."

I push into the bathroom, saying, "Mel?" She hardly glances up at me from the bathtub where she has stationed herself. She's in her white, silk robe, hair poorly pulled into a claw clip and eyes red from lack of sleep. I close the door behind me, the wedding dress hanging on the back of it slapping against the wood.

I slip off my shoes and climb into the tub across from her. She still doesn't say anything, but holds the open Champagne bottle, likely meant for mimosas, across the tub for me to take. I play along, accepting the bottle and having a swig of it before setting it down outside of the tub.

I take her hands in mine, sliding my feet across the porcelain to interlock with hers. "What's wrong, Melly?"

Her shoulders lift, then she lets out a little Champagne burp.

"Classic case of cold feet?"

She says softly, "Julien doesn't look at me like that anymore."

I cock my head. "Like how?"

"Like how Ben looks at you." She pulls from my grasp and throws her arm out in a gesture toward the bedroom. "Like how Kensie looks at Jen." She drops her forehead on her knees.

I can't say anything for how Ben looks at me because I've never noticed any significance in it, but I do know what she is talking about with how Kensie looks at Jen. It's the same as how Jen looks at Kensie. How Isla and Rachel look at each other. How David and Callum look at each other. And, the same as how Julien looks at Mel. I've seen it. I've seen it and been so deeply jealous of it.

"Yes, he does," I say firmly. "Maybe you stopped noticing it because you're used to how he sees you, but he looks at you like that. He loves you so much, Mel."

She glances up at me with big eyes. "You think?"

"*Yes,*" I say vehemently. "My eyes are not always to be trusted, but I have seen the way he looks at you. He is crazy about you. And I've seen the way you look at him, too."

"I love him," she says, a tear slipping from her eye.

"I know you do." I grab her hand again. "You want to marry him. And he wants to marry you. You're a little scared. It's perfectly natural."

She nods slowly, then stares at her dress. "There was a black mark on my dress this morning. It felt like a bad omen."

"Kensie got it out. It's not a bad omen. I bet it was just grease on the door hinges that you hung it on. But it's in plastic now, so it's safe."

"But..." She shakes her head.

"But what?"

"But is that it? One thing goes wrong and we fix it, but it completely breaks me. What if something worse happens?"

"Nothing worse will happen. Something always has to go wrong, but this was it. And it's been fixed. Everything else will be fine." I knock lightly on her head. "Knock on wood."

She swats my hand away, but smiles. "Yeah."

"Mel, do you want to marry Julien? Like, if you didn't marry him today, would you be sad?"

She stares at me like I'm crazy. "I'd be devastated."

I lean back in the tub. "Then, that's that. We get through the ceremony, which we rehearsed quite well yesterday, then we have a party. And you'll be married. And you'll have so much good sex tonight."

She laughs wetly.

"And you'll continue to be outlandishly, obnoxiously happy. Okay?"

"Okay." She leans across the tub to pull me into a tight hug. "Thank you, Linny."

"Of course." I sigh, thinking about what she said about how Ben looks at me. When I pull back, I say, "Not to make this about me, but can I tell you something?"

She waves me off. "I welcome the distraction."

"Ben and I aren't dating."

She cocks her head to the side, confused. "You broke up?"

"No. We were never actually dating. I lied. He's been pretending to be my boyfriend."

She continues to look extremely confused. "Why?"

I lose her eye. "You told me Atti would be at the hen do, and I freaked out. I needed someone by my side." Quietly, I add, "I also wanted to show him that someone else could love me."

"Oh, Linny. Of course someone else could love you. Things didn't work out with Atti because he's a wanker." She purses her lips. "But Ben is not. Why aren't you actually dating him?"

"I don't want to date anyone. You know this. And he's in love with someone else. It's complicated."

"Huh," she says. "I did find it odd that you suddenly had a boyfriend after going on for months about never wanting to be in a relationship again. But I figured I wouldn't say anything because you seemed happy with him, and I didn't want to accidentally talk you out of the relationship."

"I *am* happy with him," I moan into my hands. "I absolutely adore him. I told him about the miscarriage last night. And what Atti said afterward. I haven't told anyone but you, my parents, and my sisters about that."

Her eyes squint. "What did Atti say afterward?"

I drop my hands, aghast that she could have forgotten the worst thing anyone has ever spoken to me. "What do you mean 'what did Atti say afterward?' How can you not remember?"

"You never told me what he said! You just said he said something horrible, but you were too upset to elaborate."

My mouth drops open. "I never told you? I know I told my mom and dad. I swear to god I told you."

"You most certainly did not."

"I did too! I tell you everything!"

"You *did not*. I would remember. I remember every detail about his I'm-rich-so-let's-go-to-Paris proposal, so I *know* I remember every detail you told me about the breakup. I swear you did not tell me, Melinda."

"Oh. You're sure?"

She nods, so I tell her, and her mouth falls open.

"Shit. Maybe I'll be the one committing a violent act at my wedding. How could you not tell me that! I would have kicked him out of the bridal party, Julien's cousin or not, if you told me he said that." She groans and says, "I honestly don't think Julien will allow Atti in the wedding party anymore once he learns what he said. Which will mess up our numbers." She grimaces and asks quietly, "Can I tell him tomorrow? No, that's horrible. He should know today."

"You can tell him tomorrow. I've moved past it. I don't want to mess with your numbers."

"We could ask Ben to fill in."

"Ben and I are not dating," I remind her. "Even if we were, we have not known each other that long. Do you want to look back at your wedding photos many years from now and see a rando?"

"I don't want to see Atti. I like Ben better than I like Atti."

"Well, yeah, but Atti is going to be your family, whether you like it or not. We can always ask him to go grab something and quickly take a bunch of pictures without him."

She laughs, then sighs long and hard. "Atti always said he said something in the heat of the moment and you overreacted."

"He would frame it that way."

She grabs both my hands and says earnestly, "I'm so sorry, Linny. He's wrong, you know. He's a terrible, bitter, tiny man, and he is *wrong*." She pulls me into her arms again. "You will be a wonderful mother, if that is what you want. And I *know* it is. Your future child will be perfect, just like you. My mum is the best mum in the world, and her eyes did not keep her from being that wonderful, perfect mother. They kept her from driving me places. That's *it*. And there are so many workarounds for that. *Do not* let him keep you from trying again. I suspect your family told you the same thing."

I swallow roughly. "So did Ben."

"So, logically, *we* are all right and that little man-child otherwise known as Atticus the arsehole is *wrong*." We sit there, in the bathtub, holding each other until there's a knock on the door.

"Mel? Linny? The makeup artist is in the lobby."

Mel pulls away, wiping her eyes. "Shit. I have to go." She yells, "I'm getting married today!"

"You're getting married today!"

We get Mel back to her hotel room with the makeup artist. After we're all ready, we climb into cars to the church. We head straight to a room in the back where Mel can finish getting dressed.

When it's almost time, I run out to make sure everything is in order and run into Paul in the hallway, dressed in a gray suit with his tie the same color pink as my dress.

"Hey!" I say. "Julien ready?"

"Yep," Paul says, messing with one of his cuff links. "I was just coming to find you. We're all set."

"How is he?"

"Grossly excited," he confirms with a smile.

"Mel too."

Paul asks, "You have the rings?"

Fucking fuck.

"Oh my god," I say. Then again, "Oh. My. *God.*"

Paul cringes. "No chance that's a good 'oh my god?'"

I let out a frustrated groan. "I forgot the fucking rings. Shit!" My hands flutter around me as I try to figure out what to do. "Can we stall, do you think? I know where they are. We can go get them. Or, wait. Ben. Ben might not be here yet. It'll be quicker if he gets them."

Paul nods, trying to remain calm. "Okay. Good plan. I'm sure we can stall for a bit."

My hands shake as I find Ben's contact. I can't believe I did this. I told Mel nothing else would go wrong. Fucking fuck.

Ben answers, "Why hello, sugar. May I help you with something?"

I let out another frustrated whimper. "Benny, I forgot the rings. Do you still have my keys? Are you on your way here? Can you go back and get them? I cannot believe I forgot the rings. Mel is going to kill me. They're on the table by my front door. Just, if you could go get them, it would be quicker, I think. And it would really help—"

He cuts me off. "Lin, I have the rings."

My heart skips a beat. "What?"

"I saw them sitting on the mail table as I was leaving yours this morning. Figured you would need them. I texted you."

I look at Paul and say, "He has the rings."

Paul's body sags, relief spreading over his features. "Thank goodness."

My voice is small as I say, "I didn't see the text."

"That's okay. You were busy. I'm pulling into the car park now. Where are you?"

My hand covers my heart as I force myself to take in a few deep breaths. "We're in the back of the church. Cut through the church and go through the door on the back left."

"Got it. I'll see you in a sec."

I pace while we wait for Ben. Moments later, he comes through the door. He bows before me, extending his arm to hold out the ring box. "Your rings, my lady."

I take them and immediately hand them over to Paul, who pivots to make sure the ring bearer has them. When Ben stands up straight, I wrap my arms around his neck to pull him into a tight hug. "Thank you," I say, squeezing with all my might. "Thank you. Thank you."

He squeezes me back. "Of course, love."

I finally release him and smooth down my dress.

"You look beautiful," he says.

"You too," I say, because he does. He's wearing the pin I gave him yesterday on the lapel of his suit jacket. I can't help but ask, "No kilt?"

He grins. "Naw, didn't want to outshine Mel. Though I saw a fair few on my strut up the aisle, so I'm a tad jealous."

"Next wedding," I say, toying with the amethyst ring on my right hand, mind once again straying to him in a kilt. Damn, it only took me five years of living in Scotland to realize I had a thing for kilts. Maybe I just have a thing for the idea of Ben in a kilt. I have a thing for Ben, period. I shake myself back to reality. "I've got to get back to Mel."

"Right. I'll go find my seat."

We head in our separate directions, but I can't help but look back at him before I turn the corner. I catch him looking back at me as well. He smiles, then disappears through the door.

I go tell Mel that we're ready to start. She's getting married today.

CHAPTER TWENTY-THREE
Ben

I head into the church and choose a seat on the bride's side.

I couldn't sleep last night. For a while, at least. I held Linny until she fell asleep, then, when I realized my brain was not turning off, I slipped out of the bed quietly, going to her kitchen for water. Oscar Wilde met me at the sink, weaving around my legs. I had picked him up with a grunt and admitted, "I'm falling in love with your mother, Oscar."

He stared back at me with big, black eyes that said, "Duh."

I stare at my phone while I wait, not having anyone to talk to since I don't know anyone here. Except that doesn't last for long. A hand grabs me on the shoulder, so I turn quickly to see Linny's father. I shoot to my feet.

"Sir," I say, but don't attempt a handshake this time.

He sticks out his hand, which I gratefully meet. "Ben, I thought that was you. I told you, you could call me Harry."

"Right," I say, the thought of it making me a tad uncomfortable. "Harry."

He gestures to the two women behind him, whom I am just now seeing, one with ginger hair the same color as Linny's and the other with deep brunette hair. "These are my other daughters, Chelsea and Sarah. Girls, this is Linny's boyfriend, Ben."

The way he says *boyfriend*, I wonder if her sisters don't know about the whole fake dating thing—it came out naturally. Maybe he's just a good liar. I say hellos to them as well, and both take their time scanning me up and down, studying me with full suspicion.

I squirm under their prying eyes and say, "Well, I'll let you guys find your seats."

Harry shakes his head. "No, no. Come sit up front with us. You're honorary family."

I shake my head back at him. "Harry, you know…" I trail off, hoping he will understand the end of that sentence.

He winks at me and says, "Today, I don't know a thing."

Harry puts a hand on my shoulder and guides me out of my row. He keeps that hand on my shoulder and has me lead the way to the front, where I find a woman who can only be Linny's mother. They have the same face, albeit thirty years apart, only her eyes are brown. I turn around in an attempt to let Linny's sisters in first so they can sit next to their mum, but Harry ushers me in so I end up sitting between him and Linny's mum. Right. I would end up here.

I introduce myself to her. "Hi, I'm Ben."

Her face brightens. "Ah, Linny's 'boyfriend.'" She puts air quotes around the word.

Harry says, "Emily, put those fingers away."

She rolls her eyes, but just says, "Sorry. Hello, Harold."

He grins. "Hiya, Em."

I know they're divorced, but there is an odd sexual tension between them that I have uncomfortably been put in the middle of. I glance around Harry, hoping for some reason that one of

Linny's sisters will step in to save me, but from the looks on their faces, I think they find my current position rather funny. I've seen a very similar expression of amusement in Linny's eyes before. They want to watch me sweat.

Emily focuses back on me. "So, Ben, what do you do for a living?"

I resist the urge to gulp. "I run a café. Right next door to Better than New, actually."

"Really?" She looks around me at Harry. "Harold, did you know they worked next door to one another?"

"I did."

She huffs. "Linny never mentioned that to me. She said you met on a bench."

"We did meet on a bench, to be fair."

"But you work next door to one another?"

"Yeah. Lucky coincidence."

Harry nudges me. "Some would call that fate, son."

I gulp now. "Yeah, some would." I look at him seriously. "I am very lucky to have met your daughter."

"Damn right," he confirms.

We quiet down when Julien and Paul enter the church, knowing the ceremony is about to begin. The minister is not far behind them. The music commences, and the bridal party starts to walk in. Linny enters the church linked to Darren. I want to catch her eye, but she is looking straight ahead. She squeezes Darren's arm before she lets go of him and takes her place at the front of the church.

As the rest of the bridal party enters behind her, she glances over our way. I think she sees her mum first, then her dad, her gaze glancing over me. Then she notices me and where I am sitting, stuck between her parents. Brow furrowed, she looks back and forth between them, then catches my eye. I give a small shrug, making her giggle into her bouquet.

Then the bridal march starts, so we stand, all eyes turned to Melanie walking in with her father. I glance back at Julien, who has a smile so wide on his face as he watches the love of his life walk down the aisle. I've been to plenty of weddings before, but I think this is the first one I have ever felt jealous at.

My attention shifts to Linny, who is watching Mel with tears in her eyes. I should keep watching Mel, but Linny has stolen my focus. As she always does.

We take our seats as soon as Mel's father gives her away and Julien takes her hand. The ceremony continues, and my eyes stay on one specific woman in pink rather than the one in white.

...

I meet Linny outside the church after they proceed out, only for a moment, as they need to go back inside to take photos.

"Hi, again," I say as soon as I see her.

"Hi." She adjusts my tie, then smooths it down. "How did you end up between my parents?"

"Blame your dad and your sisters. I was sitting happily on my own near the back of the church before he came to get me." I lower my voice. "So, your parents…?"

"Are still completely into each other? Yes. It's disturbing. Divorce was grossly good for their relationship." Linny's hands are still on my tie. "It was nice to see you sitting with my family."

Linny turns when someone calls her name. "I've got to go. Are you fine getting to the reception venue? I think Kensie or Paul is going to drive me."

"Aye, I'll see you there."

"I know it's not super fun being the date of someone in the wedding," she says.

"I don't mind. I get to dress up, I get to see you dressed up. Free dinner and drinks. Pretty good day for me. Go on then." I lean down to kiss her on the cheek, but her head moves fractionally, so I catch the corner of her mouth.

Her lips twitch, then she grabs my face with one hand and presses a kiss to my mouth. Her lips linger on mine before she pulls away, just a breath, then she fully retreats and jogs off back into the church. I shove my hands in my pockets, watching after her even when I can't see her anymore.

I don't want this to end. This day. This fake relationship. I don't want it to end.

A hand clasps my shoulder, and I see Harry. "Come on, son. Cocktail hour."

I go with Harry and Linny's mum and sisters to the reception hall. Harry gets Sarah to put a cocktail in my hand pretty quickly and starts introducing me around to the rest of her family. I get to meet every one of her cousins, aunts, and uncles on this side, minus Mel's parents, who are still back at the church. I get called Linny's boyfriend about a thousand times, and while I have been called that before, this is the first day where it has truly bothered me. It bothers me because it's not true.

I wish it was.

…

Linny finds me at the cocktail hour, drink in her hand and shoulders sagging in relief.

"I think I'm done with pictures for the night," she says.

I loop an arm around her waist. "That's good. More time for me, then?"

She gives me a funny look, perhaps at the overt flirting, though it's not like I haven't done it before. Maybe she can tell it's real this time—*more* real, rather. I was never jokingly flirting with her.

However, all she says is, "Yeah, more time for you." She glares at her family members who surround us, but focuses on her dad. "Please stop torturing him."

Harry holds up his hands in surrender. "Torturing? I've just been introducing him 'round to everyone."

She gives him a hard look, but resigns to settle into my side, pulling me back from the circle by a few steps. To only me, she says, "Apparently, I never told Mel exactly what Atti said to me after…you know. So, she feels really bad about letting him stay in the wedding party. She's waiting to tell Julien about it until after, so he doesn't freak." She says the words seriously, but I can see the undercurrent of joy in her.

"You're happy with that response, aren't you?"

"Yeah. It's not that I didn't think Mel and them were on my side, I just always had it in the back of my mind that they thought I was making a big deal out of nothing. A storm in a teacup, as Auntie Carolyn would say."

I kiss her on the side of the head. "You're definitely not. Where is she, by the way? I haven't seen her."

Linny searches, then finally points to the bar. "Over there talking to the corner. I think she saw a ghost."

That tracks.

Soon, they let everyone into the reception hall and we find our seats. Mel sits at a table with Julien, her parents, and his parents. She didn't organize the room so the bridal party all had to sit together, so Linny and I are sat at a table with her family.

I laugh along with Linny's family, enjoying being a part of the nonsensical conversation they're having. Eventually, Carolyn and her date join, completing our table of eight. There's a lot of focus on me, but I don't mind. Linny, however, squirms at all of the attention toward me. At one point, she looks my way to say something, but Chelsea taunts, "They're whispering sweet nothings, how precious."

Linny's mum adds in a tone that sounds like an attempted whisper, "Is this what fake relationships look like? I think I'd like one if that's the case."

Linny gives a glare and says, "Oh, please." She picks up one of the place cards set on the table, unfolding it and holding it up between us. She leans forward, using the open place card as a tiny shield that I meet her behind. "I'm sorry you're having to deal with my family so much," she whispers, seeming genuinely distressed.

I smile. "I don't mind. I like your family."

"They're ridiculous," she argues.

"I like ridiculous." I grab my glass of water from the table, bringing it behind our shield so I can take a sip and say into it, "I also like you."

Her eyes squint suspiciously. "Fine."

She drops the place card back on the table, and soon enough, our suppers are brought out. We eat, continuing to chat with her family. Carolyn launches into a very dramatic tale about a haunted armoire that the shop acquired a few years ago, and I swear Linny keeps inching closer to me. I'm not sure I can prove *that*, but I can prove that her hand soon comes to rest on my thigh. I at first think it's an accident or a momentary gesture of her trying to communicate something, but she leaves it there throughout the meal. I like that her hand is there, as though she is laying claim to me.

Since no one at the table can see it, it feels like something private. Something just between us. But I glance behind us and notice someone whose eyeline would hit our backs. Someone who may be able to see her hand on my thigh. Atti. And when I look behind us, his eyes dart away.

Well, that is what I'm here for, so I can't say that I'm surprised, but my focus droops toward her hand in disappointment.

It doesn't matter. I place my hand on top of hers, entwining our fingers. Linny doesn't falter for a moment as she speaks to her sister, like this was the most natural thing I could have done.

She turns to me to ask, "It was Yosemite, right?"

"Huh?"

Her hand squeezes mine. "Where you almost fell into the waterfall."

She and Sarah were talking about me. I had zoned out, concentrating too much on someone who she perhaps didn't realize was watching us after all. "Right. Yosemite. Got a little too close and slipped on a wet rock. Nearly busted my head along with my arse."

"I'm glad it was just your ass."

I bring her hand to my mouth, kissing it gently, making her lips quirk up. She turns back to her sister, but her hand stays in mine.

The speeches start before dinner is taken away. First, Paul, the best man, then Kensie, the maid of honor, get up there to give their speeches. Then Mel's father. We clap and hoot and holler for them. Finally, Mel takes the microphone and says, "Please, everyone, for the love of god, start drinking and dancing!"

Most people don't have to be told twice. I get Linny and I each another drink, and then I drag her somewhat reluctantly to the dance floor.

"I am not wearing the right shoes for this," she argues.

"Take them off," I say.

"No!" she laughs out. She takes a sip of her drink, soon finding the rhythm of the music and moving with it. We dance together until our drinks are gone. I get rid of the glasses and rejoin her on the dance floor for another song. After that one finishes, she complains, "My feet hurt!"

"Take off your shoes," I suggest again. "Kensie's not wearing shoes anymore. You won't be the only one."

She looks around suspiciously but does not move to take them off. I drop to my knees before her, grabbing her ankle and lifting her foot in the air to remove the shoe. I repeat the action with the other foot, then stand back up, using the back straps to loop the heels around my wrist.

With her feet now flat on the floor, I ask, "Better?"

"Better," she grumbles, annoyed that I was right.

However, she soon gets past it, and we're dancing again. At one point, I go fetch her another drink and me a water since I'm driving us home. Then another drink for her, by her request. I'm glad she's taking advantage of the opportunity to have a good time. She's been so stressed. By the time we make it off the floor, she is more than a little tipsy, the lightweight.

We both sit down heavily in chairs at our empty table, though Chelsea soon joins us. She's on her phone talking to her two-year-old and her husband, who are still back in New York, leaving us in our own little bubble.

Linny props her foot up on my legs and whines, "My feet still hurt."

I chuckle to myself and proceed to massage her foot as she makes adorable, happy little whimpers.

Out of nowhere, Atti walks up to us and says, "I heard a rumor."

Linny groans and says to me, "If we're really still, he may not be able to see us."

Atti does not take that hard and instead says, "I heard your mother say to your father that you two are not really dating. Who would do that? Pretend to date? Seems a little sad."

I stiffen, ready to say something in retort of that, but Chelsea beats me to it, holding her phone away from her ear. "Atticus, he is literally massaging her feet. People don't do that for people they're not in a relationship with."

I figure that may settle it, but Linny laughs. "Ben would. Ben's the nicest person ever." Okay, maybe she's a little more drunk than I thought. I figure she'll end it there, but she keeps talking after she takes another sip of her drink. "We're not dating!" she pronounces. "We *lied* because we're liars. But I don't care because Ben is my friend and I like Ben."

Atti tsks like he's going to scold her. The absolute wanker. "Why would you lie, Linny? Like I said, it's sad."

She snorts. "We're not sad. You're sad. You're pathetic. You let little bullshitty things embarrass you. Like blind people. Who's embarrassed by blind people? You, that's who. Ableist garbage face." She leans back in her chair and says, "I don't know. I wanted a friend, and I wanted to show you I was lovable. Not because I wanted you to love me again, 'cause no way, but because I wanted to prove it to myself, and Ben did that. Ben made me know I'm lovable. And I am. I am so goddamn loveable."

I smile, pressing a kiss to her toes because that's all I can reach. "Damn right you are, sugar." To Atti, I say, "It might be time to walk away."

He stands there, stunned. But he does not walk away. And because he does not walk away, Linny keeps talking. "And even though we're not dating, his dick was in my mouth last night."

Chelsea snorts loudly from across the table, coughing up her wine. "I have to go," she wheezes into her phone.

And then I hear Harry say, "I clearly walked up at the wrong moment." He looks at Atticus and says, "Arsehole," then takes his seat with Sarah by his side.

I'd think Linny would be done speaking, but she keeps going. "And not only was his dick in my mouth, I really *wanted* it in my mouth." She cups a hand around her lips like she's going to whisper something to me, but says at full volume, "I want it other places too."

My shoulders shake as I attempt to contain myself.

She drops the hand. "Atti, I don't think I ever wanted your dick in my mouth. Like it was fine. I was happy to assist, but I didn't fantasize about it. I fantasized about Ben's dick in my mouth and once it was, I was thrilled." She looks at me. "Right, Benny? I was thrilled."

I clear my throat, caught between wanting to show off to Atti and being fully aware that Linny's father is also looking at me expectantly. "Sugar, this might be a private conversation that we can have later."

She sighs and leans back again. "He could tell I was thrilled after he stuck his hand between my legs. But, Atti, do you know how rare it is to fantasize about having a dick in your mouth? For me, at least." She looks at me again. "Ben, are there any dicks you've fantasized about having in your mouth?"

I reply, "A few."

"But not Atti's dick?"

I glance up at him and say, "Definitely not."

"See, Atti just doesn't have a fantasizable dick. I think it's his personality." She looks up at him and rears back in faux surprise. "Oh my god. You're still standing there. I didn't see you." Then she cackles to herself.

I give her foot a squeeze before I stand up. "That's enough for now." I place a hand firmly on Atti's shoulder. "Let me walk you back to your table." He shakes me off and storms away.

"Fucking prick," Harry and I say together. Then I direct my attention back to Linny. "Likely time to head home."

She groans. "Finally. I am so tired." She hops up, shoes forgotten on the ground beside her chair. She gives her family hugs one by one, promising to see them all tomorrow. She spots her mum across the room and jogs over to her to say goodbye as I bend to grab her shoes and go fetch our coats.

I help her put her coat on, but she refuses to put her shoes back on. When we get to the exit, I sweep her up into my arms and carry her to my car, placing her in the front seat. I loop around the car and get in as well, turning on the ignition and driving us home.

"Can I spend the night?" she asks me. "Your bed looks comfy."

I chuckle. "I'd love for you to spend the night, but we have to go to yours and feed Oscar Wilde."

"Shit," she says. "You're right. Bad cat mom."

I park outside her building, lifting her and her bare feet out of the car and inside. I have to let her walk up the stairs on her own, though, my strength only going so far.

When we get inside her flat and Linny sees Oscar curled up on his cat tree, she shouts, "My baby!" She rushes up to him, placing kisses on his head and stroking down his back. His purring intensifies with each little head kiss he receives, practically vibrating the entire flat.

With a snicker, I usher her away from the cat and into her bathroom so she can get ready for bed while I take care of feeding him.

Once her face is washed and teeth are brushed and contacts are out, she wanders back out into the living room to plop down next to me on the couch. I hand her a glass of water, which she chugs down before thrusting the empty cup back at me.

"You should go to sleep, Lin."

"I don't wanna," she whines. She reaches behind herself in an attempt to yank at the zipper on the back of her dress, but gives up after one try. She moans loudly. "I can't get it."

"Och, you're a whiny drunkard, aren't you?" I pull down her zipper. I help her back up to her feet and only take one glance at her bare back as she walks into her bedroom.

She changes into pjs and crawls into her bed, then calls me into her room like I'm not standing in the doorway. I tug the blanket up so it fully covers her, leaning down to press a kiss to her forehead.

"Get some sleep," I say.

"*You* get some sleep," she argues back. Oscar finds us, hopping up onto the bed and nestling himself by her feet. Linny flips on her side and sighs. "This has been fun, Benny. I think I *will* miss you the most." And with that nonsense, her eyes close. Before she falls asleep, she says, "Too bad this is over."

Right, I… Right. The wedding is done, meaning our arrangement is done. I planned to stay the night, but it's best that I don't. I should go. I really should go and cut myself off while I still can.

I leave her flat, closing the door and ensuring it is locked behind me, saying a goodbye I am not ready for.

CHAPTER TWENTY-FOUR
Linny

I lean forward in my bed with a groan. It's been a while since I've been hungover and, my god, is my head pounding. I snatch my full water bottle from my nightstand and take a sip, letting out a, "Blech," after the first taste, my mouth disgusting. I force myself to drink the rest of the bottle before I get up to pee. When I do stand, I immediately sit back down, bile rushing to my throat. I lean forward again with another groan.

My bed was empty when I awoke, which was surprising. I'm pretty sure I asked Ben to spend the night last night. Or, no, I think I asked to spend the night at his place? Did he stay here or go home? I don't know. I feel like I would know if I got to spend another night in his arms.

"Oh god," I say as a memory rushes back to me. I talked a lot about dicks last night. My hands cover my face. While nothing I said was particularly mortifying, or untruthful, I don't love that I said it in front of my dad. He will never let me live that down.

Once I finally manage to get up, I wander into the bathroom. Oscar Wilde is not too far behind me, weaving between my feet as I sit down on the toilet. I sit there for longer than I need to, my stomach swimming. When I finally get up, I schlump into the kitchen to give Oscar Wilde his breakfast. The scrape of the spoon in the wet food can is too loud, making my head pound even more. I drop his bowl on the ground, then go back to my room, lying face-first on my bed.

A little while later, there is a cat loafing on my back.

When I can manage to move again, I fish my phone out from the sheets, doing my best not to disturb Oscar Wilde. I see a few texts from my sisters, my dad, Emma, and one from Ben. I open the one from Benny first.

Drink water, please

But that's it. I hate that I'm disappointed. I mean, it's still a nice text. I heart the message, then change my mind and throw a thumbs up on there instead, hoping he did not see the heart.

I meant the heart, though. I release an audible sigh. This wasn't supposed to happen.

There were moments last night, as there have been so many times since I've met him, where it was *just him*. We were on the crowded dance floor, yet all I could see was him. We were sitting at the dining table with my whole family, but he was practically under a spotlight in my vision. Mel was actively getting married, but one glance at him sitting in the pew with my parents, and I was done for. He was the only other person in the room.

I go through the rest of the texts. First, from Emma, confirming lunch plans for next week and making sure I'm going to yoga on Wednesday. I say yes to both. Then I move on to the messages from my family. I'm supposed to meet them for brunch at the hotel where the rest of the bridal party and my family are staying. In thirty minutes.

I groan for the millionth time this morning, then carefully

nudge the cat off my back. I drag myself into the shower, another day gone without washing my hair. When I get out, I braid it in two French braids down my back. Then I wander to the window to check the weather. It's sunny, so I think I should put in my contacts, even though my eyes are screaming at me not to. I want to wear sunglasses, though. I should invest in prescription sunglasses, but switching from glasses to sunglasses sounds annoying. I already have trouble keeping my sunglasses on in the shade, feeling my vision impaired by the change in light created by shadows.

I go back to the bathroom and put in my contacts, but I don't bother with a stitch of makeup, not even concealer to cover the massive dark circles under my eyes. I wasn't planning on putting on jewelry, but I spot a bracelet I haven't worn in a while. I slip on the bracelet made of black tourmaline beads. Before I leave, I fill up my water bottle so I can take it with me, then I'm off.

As I lock the door to my building, I glance at the café. Ben's probably in there, back in the kitchen. He didn't say anything about taking the day off today. I could go in and say good morning. Pop in just to see him. But I don't. I instead head the other direction toward the bus stop.

It's very sunny, so the shade is very shady. My sunglasses stay on my nose in the sun, then get pushed to my head in the shade. I wait for the bus, my stomach still swimming. Oh god. I better not vomit on the bus.

When it comes, I choose a seat by the window, leaning my head against it and focusing on my breath. If I breathe slowly, I will not vomit. I repeat that to myself over and over in my mind so my body believes it.

After the bus finally comes to a stop, I find the hotel, following my nose to the dining area. My family is at a group of tables with a few of the other guests who stayed in this hotel.

I slide into the seat next to my dad. Before I even have a chance to say hello, I feel arms around my neck from the back. I recognize the perfume, so I don't even need to look to know it's Mel.

"Hello, Mrs. Parker."

She giggles in my ear. "Hiya. Where's Ben?"

"I was wondering the same thing," my dad says.

"The café, probably. How should I know? Do I need to remind you two that Ben and I aren't actually dating?" I clear my throat and say loud enough for everyone to hear, "Ben Pyeon and I are not dating." No one reacts, because everyone already knows. "It's over, anyway."

Chelsea chuckles into her coffee.

"What?" I ask, glaring.

She toys with a strand of her red hair, giving me a classic big sister look that says she knows more than me. "You should be dating, though. I mean, he was massaging your feet last night."

Mel slides into the open seat beside me. "From what I hear, you have a great love of his penis."

I wrinkle my nose. "Ew, don't say 'penis' to me this early in the morning."

My dad grimaces. "The word she used excessively last night was 'dick.'"

"I prefer 'dick,'" I say, then hear what I said and groan as everyone around me laughs. "And I really don't want to talk about this with my father."

Everyone can most likely tell I am too hungover to discuss this now, so they leave me be and let me get my food. Most of the bridal party is here, but one person is missing: Atti. I slide up next to Paul at the egg station. "Where's the tall one?"

Paul flashes his eyes. "Left early this morning, apparently."

"Good," I say.

"Yeah." Paul turns to me. "So, you and Ben *aren't* dating?"

"Nope," I say. I take a scoop of eggs and glance at him. "If you're interested, I can put in a good word."

Paul chuckles. "Ben's great, but I generally don't go after men who are desperately in love with other people."

I take a bagel next, before moving onto the coffee that my stomach is not prepared to drink. My head needs it badly, though. "Ah, he told you about David, then?"

Paul cocks his head. "Who's David?"

I stare at him, confused. He doesn't say anymore, just gives me a wink, then heads back to sit at a table with Kensie, Jen, and a couple others from the bridal party. I rejoin my family, my mother now at the table as well.

She looks me up and down and says, "Someone's hungover. I heard you were comparing dicks last night."

I bite into my food. With a partially full mouth, I say, "Comparing implies that there is a question of which is better"— I swallow—"when in fact the answer of which is better is obvious. Mostly because I like the human better that the better dick is attached to."

My dad sighs into his tea. "Perhaps we could stop saying the word 'dick' at the breakfast table?"

"You said it first," I remind him. I force down a sip of coffee with a grimace. "Though, I agree."

With that request, talk of dicks stops. We finish up our breakfast, and then my family insists I show them around Edinburgh (even though they have all been here many times before).

"We want to see *your* Edinburgh." Which is exactly what they said last time.

Mom and Dad together for the first time in probably three years, since Chelsea's wedding, is weird, but they act as they always do. As old friends who are in a petty argument that could be solved simply by sleeping together. It's weird having divorced parents who still love each other, but are not *in* love anymore. Though, as situations like this go, I know how lucky I am.

I take them all over the city. And, while I go back and forth on it for a while, I end up taking them to Ben's cafe. They asked to see it, so what was I supposed to say? No? I have complicated feelings for the owner that I'm not willing to face at the moment?

Isla is behind the counter when we walk in. "Hey," I say. "It's a Sunday. What are you doing here? Did Ben take the day off?"

"Ben's in the kitchen," she says carefully. Okay, my voice may have been a bit panicky. She continues, "Gemma needed the day off and I never mind working." She glances at my family looming behind me.

"Right. Then let me start with an apology because I have brought my entire family with me."

Half her mouth quirks up. "The more the merrier. The entire Jenkins clan!" She looks to my dad first, "What'll you have?"

As Isla takes their orders, I slip around and head into the kitchen to see Ben. He doesn't acknowledge me when I enter, but jumps when I place a hand on his arm. He removes a headphone from one ear and smiles when he sees me. I might be imagining it, but I swear he looks…relieved?

"Hey, sugar. Sorry—playing my music too loud. Isla has been playing moody, hipster music all day. It's driving me mad."

"What are you listening to?"

"Don't make fun." He hands me one headphone, and I slip it in my ear. The music resumes, playing *Spice Up Your Life* by the Spice Girls.

I bite my lip. "Why would I tease you? This is a great song."

"I've been listening to their entire discography."

"Okay, that may be a little excessive."

"Hard disagree." He removes the headphone from my ear and slips them both into the pocket of his jeans. "How's your head?"

"Pounding."

"Did you drink water?"

"Yes. Thank you for filling up my water bottle. And for taking care of me."

"It's my favorite thing to do." There's a heavy pause before he says, "So, what's up? Just wanted to see me?"

My dad's loud laugh echoes from the front in answer.

"Ah, they nagging you about coming here?"

"Nonstop. You do not have to come out and greet them. They wanted to see the place, and we were stopping by mine to say hello to Oscar anyway. I can tell them you're busy." I poke him on the arm in an attempt at nonchalance. "This is over between us anyway."

His eyes darken. "Yeah. I suppose it is."

I squint back at him. "Everyone on my side knows we were lying. The wedding is over. Unless you need me for something with David?"

"I don't need you for David anymore."

"Are you…I mean, are you still…?"

"Erm, well." He looks at me seriously. "Lin, I really like you. I want to—" He sighs, rubbing his forehead. "I shouldn't say that. It's not fair."

I purse my lips, desperate to ask for the end of that sentence, but knowing it's best if I don't hear more.

"Our hearts aren't ready," I offer softly. His is stuck on someone else, and mine? Mine has too many holes to hold anyone inside.

Ben shakes his head, but I can't tell whether or not he's agreeing with me. "Can we still be friends?" he asks quietly.

I chew my lip to keep it from wobbling. "I don't know if that's a good idea. Maybe…maybe this should be our goodbye."

His throat bobbles, and he gives one stiff nod. "I can never say goodbye to you, Linny."

"Ben…"

"No, I mean, you work and live right next door. We'll see each other all the time."

I heave out a laugh. "God, okay. Way to take the dramatics out of it."

He wrinkles his nose. "Yeah, sorry. I usually live for the dramatics."

He holds out a hand for me to shake, and I nearly cry at the sight. The hand that has held mine now a countless number of times, the hand that has brushed my hair behind my ears, wiped away my tears, been inside of me. After all that, I only get a handshake.

I take that hand in mine anyway. "See you soon, then."

"See you on the streets, Melinda." He winks.

"On the *streets*?"

"Yeah, like outside the café and your shop."

I frown. "Please, never stop being you." I finally drop his hand, feeling a bit of my soul drop with it. Before I can say anything else, I rejoin my family, spitting out some lie about how he literally cannot walk away from whatever he is baking right now.

I may attempt to keep it so our streets don't cross again. It will be easier that way.

CHAPTER TWENTY-FIVE
Ben

When Linny's family takes off, Isla comes into the kitchen and throws a muffin at me. I catch it before dropping it on the counter.

"Why were you hiding back here?" she asks.

"I was busy," I lie.

Her eyes meet the ceiling. "Sure." She leans against the door-frame, hands in the pockets of her loose trousers. "What happened?"

"Nothing happened. We just…" I can't say *broke up*, because that's not what we did. We just stopped. We are no more. The terms of our agreement have expired. It all went kaput. "We're finished with the whole fake relationship thing," I finally land on. "There was no need for me to come say hello to her family."

Isla jerks her head. "So, I can tell Rachel now? I mean, I'll ask that she keep it from David."

"I don't care," I say honestly. "At this point, I couldn't care less who finds out. David can find out, and it doesn't matter."

"Well, good, because Rachel already knows." I'm not even surprised. Isla purses her lips. "Are you okay? I know you fancy her."

"I more than fancy her." I drag a hand down my face. "But yeah. I'm fine."

"You sure you don't want to try for real with her?"

"There's no point. It's not what she wants."

Isla looks doubtful. "If you say so. My only request is that you stop breaking up with people I like. Your next person should be unlikable so I don't get attached."

"I'll make sure I hate them so you can too." We shake on it, then she pivots out of the room, heading back up front to wait on a customer who just walked in.

I cannot believe I shook Linny's hand. I shook her hand like I didn't even know her. It's just, I thought about hugging her and smelling that citrus scent I love so much. The idea of it alone was enough to break me. I couldn't let her see me broken. I've only just begun to repair.

...

Nearly a week goes by, and I don't see Linny once. Trust me, I'm looking for her, but I think she is doing everything in her power to avoid me. Likely for the best, though. Seeing her would hurt in ways I can't even begin to describe.

I've gone back to using my old soap so I don't smell like her anymore, but that hasn't stopped me from popping the cap and taking a deep whiff of her body wash every time I enter my bathroom. I can't bring myself to throw it away.

After I leave the café on Friday, I'm back home lounging on my couch and scrolling endlessly on my phone. I come across a cute cat video and am tempted to send it to Linny, but hold myself back.

Now that I'm thinking about her (like I even stopped), I read the last text I sent: **Drink water please**. She hearted it at first, but changed it to a thumbs up, probably hoping that I didn't notice. I noticed.

I toss my phone to the side only to immediately pick it back up, in need of a distraction. I text David.

You working tonight?

Till close. You want to stop by?

Aye. I'll see you in 30

I force myself up to put real trousers back on and change out of the stained T-shirt I'm wearing with the café's logo on the chest. I mess with my hair a bit, fussing over a new silver strand that will not settle down, *this* close to plucking it out. Ergh. The bar is dark. No one will notice.

I leave my flat, finally deciding to walk to Hoot. When I get there, I head down the familiar staircase, push my way through the door, and slide into a seat in front of David, who is cosplaying as a classic bartender, wiping out glasses with a little rag.

"Hey, man," he says. "Want anything?"

"Death," I say, naming one of their signature cocktails. I lean my chin on my hand as I watch him make my drink. He slides it over to me, and I take a slow sip. "Thanks."

"You doing alright? How's Linny?"

The person I came here to stop thinking about. That lasted, what? Two minutes?

"Fine, I assume."

His eyebrows shoot up. "Shit. Did you guys break up?"

I hang my head and confess, "We were never dating in the first place." And there we have it. Everyone who thought we were together now knows we were not. A surprising weight leaves my shoulders.

"What does that mean?"

"It means you assumed I was dating her at the café, I let you believe it, she needed me to pretend to be her boyfriend for a joint hen and stag do because her ex is the devil, and I asked her to come to dinner with us as my girlfriend, then we just kept pretending."

He sets a glass down with a heavy *clink*. "Why would you do that?"

"To prove to you that I wasn't in love with you anymore."

"Were you still?"

"Yes."

He stiffens, asking carefully, "Are you still?"

I assess him thoroughly. The perfect line of his jaw with a light, sharply cut stubble, his strong hands splayed on the bar, the bright orange shirt he wears that practically glows in the dark.

"No," I say honestly, surprising myself. "I'm not." I laugh, giddy. "I'm not in love with you anymore. I mean, hey, I still love you, but I'm not *in* love with you anymore."

Another patron hears that as he approaches the bar and pivots away, saying, "Tough break, mate."

"Aye, tough break! Christ almighty, David, I'm over you!" I keep laughing. I'm sure I look like I've gone doolally, spinning around on my bar stool, but I don't care. I feel so free. I still love him, but in the way I used to. As a friend. As my brother. My love for him has shifted back to where it should have stayed.

David grins. "Your excitement over this is somewhat insulting."

"Good. Be insulted. Your go for that." I laugh still. "Bloody hell. I mean, look at you, gorgeous, perfect, wonderful man, but everything I felt, it's gone. I don't know where it went. I don't know *when* it went, but it's gone."

David's hands clench on the bar. "Does this mean we can go back to normal?"

"We can," I say. "We really, really can."

"You're going to make jokes about the fact that you were in love with me for the rest of our lives, aren't you?"

"Yes, yes, I am."

"If you make those jokes in mixed company, you might make people uncomfortable."

"Why? Because of the explicit homoeroticism I'll work into every conversation?"

"No, I think they'll be down with the homoeroticism."

Someone slides into the seat next to me. Rachel.

She grimaces slightly. "I've been standing back there for a bit. I wanted to give you guys your space, but then I felt like I was in the way. And your conversation was starting to get weird."

"You heard all that?" I ask.

"Yeah." She lowers her voice. "Isla told me about you and Linny."

"Oh," I say, at a normal volume. "Yeah, the fake relationship. Wild thing to do, right? I told David."

Rachel squints. "I meant the breakup."

"'Breakup,'" I correct with air quotes, though my chest aches as though there were no air quotes.

"Where is Isla, by the way?" David asks.

"Her place working on a song. I got kicked out so she could concentrate, but she's been texting me since I left, so I assume she'll be here as well soon enough."

"Good deal. Callum is heading over as well." David directs his attention back to me. "So, when did the thing with Linny go from fake to real?"

I furrow my brow. "What do you mean?"

He and Rachel exchange a look. "You're completely obsessed with her," he says.

"I'm not *obsessed*."

"No," Rachel agrees. "You're in love with her." She says that like it's an established fact.

I look between them. "I-I care about her a lot. I felt myself falling, but I never…landed."

David scoffs. "Okay, and that long-winded rant you gave me about how amazing she is at the football match was, what? You trying to match my energy with how I talk about Callum?"

I scoff back, leaning my forearms on the bar to address him. "No, but how can I not rant about how amazing she is? Have you met her? Have you *seen* her?" I shake my head. "Sorry, I directed that last bit at the wrong person." To Rachel, I repeat, "Have you *seen* her?"

"Yes, I've seen her," Rachel says flatly. "I've also seen you interact with her."

"Same," David agrees. "You're in love with her." He picks up a rogue lime and tosses it in the bin behind the bar.

I huff. "How would you know?"

"I have eyes, man."

Rachel sighs and says, "Let's work this out the long way. How do you feel when you see her? Think about her? Anything."

"Happy," I say without thought. "But love is about more than happiness. I mean"—I hook a thumb toward David—"when I was head over heels for this guy, it was devastating."

Her hands wring together as she glances at David, whose stance has gone stark straight. I hate to admit it, but I find a bit of joy in making him uncomfortable like this. Quietly, Rachel says, "Because it was unrequited, Ben. When love is mutual, it doesn't hurt. Not the love itself, at least. The simple act of loving and being loved is joyful."

I shake my head, even though she may be right. Okay. Fine. So, I fell all the way. I'm in love with Linny, but…

"That doesn't matter. She doesn't love me back." I grasp my drink with both hands, the condensation chilling them through. "I can't…I can't do that again. Confess my feelings only to get rejected. It took me forever to get over that buff genius. If I move on from Linny now, I don't have to deal with that again." I stare down into the glass.

David cuts in, "I do enjoy how you keep referencing me like I'm not standing right here, but I have to say, I think you're already dealing with it, Ben. You decided it was over before you gave it a chance to start."

With a tentative hand, Rachel touches my arm. "Listen, I think you've come to associate love with hurt. *That* is why you thought you were in love with David for as long as you did. Because every time you saw him or thought about him, you felt pain. Not because you still loved him, but because of how him not loving you made you feel. Love shouldn't hurt like that, Ben. Especially when the person you love loves you in the same way."

"Oof," David whispers.

My mouth twitches, but it stills as I stress, "Linny doesn't love me, so the hurt is still there."

Rachel clicks her tongue. "Are you sure?"

"She doesn't want to be in a relationship."

"That doesn't mean she's not in love with you."

"Well, shite."

"Shite, indeed."

"When I tell my therapist about this, he's going to accuse me of cheating on him." I stand up, backing away from my stool and my friends. "Fecking hell. Don't make me do the grand confession thing again."

Rachel exchanges another look with David.

I drop my head back. "I have to, don't I?"

"Yes," they both confirm, seeming satisfied that I finally managed to get there.

They're right, though. I need to go talk to her. I need to talk to her immediately.

When I right my head, David is looking at me seriously. "She loves you, man. I have no doubt."

"Seconded," Rachel agrees.

"If you two are wrong, you owe me something big. I don't know what yet, but I mean *big*."

"Just *go*," Rachel says.

I laugh stupidly, slapping David's bicep forcefully over the bar, squeezing, then hold my hands as close to Rachel's face as I can get without touching her. "You little love goddess. Do I have permission to kiss you aggressively on the top of your head?"

"Go for it."

I do so, practically slapping my mouth against her hair. I wave a big goodbye to both of them and then sprint up the stairs. I sprint all the way to the antique shop.

The door up to Linny's flat is unlocked, her having not closed it correctly, the wind doing its job to open it. I run up the stairs, and once I get to the top, I am breathing so heavily I have to lean against the wall while I catch my breath. Okay, this is my sign to start focusing more heavily on cardio.

My phone vibrates in my pocket. It's Linny.

"Hello?" I answer in a whisper.

"Benny?" she whispers back. "Sorry, I'm not sure why I called you. I just…I think there's someone outside my door. I hear very heavy breathing. It's too loud to be the ghost. I shouldn't have called you. I need to call the police."

I chuckle. "Linny, wait. It's me." I say louder and knock on her door, "It's me, Lin. Let me in." The call ends.

A moment later, the door unlatches and she opens it up. She's in her glasses, sweats, and a fitted tank.

"You look beautiful."

I mean it genuinely, but she squints at me like I'm joking. "Why do you look like you're dying?"

"I ran here. Can I come in?"

She steps to the side to let me enter the flat. Out of habit, I search around for Oscar Wilde and finally spot him curled up on the top of his cat tree, sound asleep.

"Here to see the cat?"

I twist back to her. "Always, but I wanted to see you more."

"He'll be disappointed to hear that."

I step forward and grab her lightly by the shoulders. "Linny."

She glances at my hand on her shoulder, then angles her chin up toward me. "Yes?"

"I love you."

Her mouth opens, then closes. She shakes her head like she didn't hear me. "What?"

"I love you," I say again. Then expand. "I'm in love with you." She shakes her head again, so I keep going. "I want to spend every day with you. Laughing with you, crying with you, holding you, living the rest of my life by your side and with you by mine. I love you, Linny."

"Ben. I…" She sighs, looking away.

Not again, my heart pleads. *Not again. This cannot happen to me again.* I was so sure, this time. I was so sure.

No, not was. *Am.* I am so sure she loves me back, that I hold on. I don't crumple yet. I let her take her time.

Her eyes move back to mine. "Ben, I love you too. I am in love with you too." My heart explodes in my chest. She loves me too. I *knew* it. "But—"

"Don't say but," I beg.

"*But* we talked about this. Neither of us…" she trails off, contemplating which point to bring up first because I know she has many. "What about David?" she lands on.

"What about David? Who cares about David?"

"You're still in love with him."

My shoulders droop. "I'm not," I say. "I haven't been for a while. I'm not sure when my heart fell out of love with him and in love with you, but it's been a long time now. I'm so sorry it took me so long to figure it out, to admit. I was too hurt by everything with him to see what I had before me. What I had inside of me. You said our hearts aren't ready, but mine is. It got a head start on me and ran straight to you."

As if feeling it in her chest, she covers her heart with both hands. "I don't know if *mine* is ready. You deserve a whole heart, but mine has been shredded to pieces more times than I can count. I don't know if it can take that again. If *I* can take that again."

"I won't shred your heart."

"You don't know that."

"I *do*. I'll be so, so careful with it, Linny. I'll cradle it in my hands and give it all the love and care it deserves. I'll feed it, I'll burp it, I'll wrap it in warm blankets and…" I shake my head with a heartbroken laugh. "I don't know. I don't know what I'm saying. I just know that I love you. I want you. I need you. Please, you love me too. You said it. You do. Can we please, please just take care of each other? It's not going to be perfect, because life never is, people never are, but we can make our own version of perfect."

"Ben," she argues.

"Come on, sugar. I'm spitting out poetry here. Give me something."

"I *can't*." She says it so firmly I have to take a step back. "I meant it when I said I did not want to be in another relationship. I can do life alone. I am capable of it. I don't need someone. I don't need anyone. I'm my own person. I am capable," she says again. "I...I..." she trails off, tears now falling.

I thumb away a tear. "Just because you can, and sugar, I know you can, doesn't mean you have to."

She backs away from me gently, so I reluctantly drop my arm.

"I can't do this, Ben. I'm sorry. I'm not ready."

I give one stiff bob of my head. "Then I'll wait."

"Ben..."

"No, I will wait until you are ready because there is no one else for me, Linny Jenkins. No one else."

She argues, "There are so many other people out there. People who can love you so much better than I can. People who aren't going to be a burden on you in the future."

"You will *never* be a burden on me. Never." I regard her seriously. "Don't you dare presume that. Don't you dare think that I would *ever* feel that way. You will never be a burden on me."

She throws up her hands. "Fine. *Fine.* But you could be dating someone else. Anyone else. What about Paul? I mean, he likes you, you like him."

"What about Paul? Who cares about Paul?"

"Paul is great."

"Then *you* date Paul."

"Paul is gay," she shoots back.

"Then neither of us will date Paul! Why are we talking about Paul? Stop bringing up other people." I exhale, rubbing my forehead. "I feel like we're getting off-topic, so let's go over this again. I love you. You love me, but are not ready to date me. Fine. I am willing to wait, so that's what I'll do."

"Ben…" she starts again, but I cut her off.

"Lin, every argument you have, I have a counterargument prepared. That's it. We're in love with each other. I am waiting for you. Done."

With that, I pivot on my heel and am out of her flat in a flash, closing the door behind me. I get to the bottom of the stairs and pause, anticipating the click of a lock that does not come. I sit at the bottom of the stairs, waiting, just as I promised I would. I will leave when she locks her door. She always deadbolts her door because the one at the bottom does not lock very well, so she will lock it.

While this isn't exactly how I hoped this would turn out, I can't get over the one fact that is making me giddy. *Linny loves me.* She loves me. So, I am perfectly happy to wait. I'll wait for days, months, years until she is ready. And once she is, I'll be here, arms wide and heart open.

I think I sit on the stairs for an hour before her door opens.

"Ben." My name comes out like a breath on her lips.

I look up at her whilst keeping my seat on the bottom step. She's still in her sweatpants, but has slipped on a pair of white trainers.

"Fancy seeing you here," I say.

She huffs out a laugh. "I thought you went home. Uh, do you…do you want to get dinner?"

I stand up, parking myself at the bottom of the stairs. My eyes narrow. "It's nearly midnight, but I'm sure there's a kabob place open somewhere."

"No, I mean, sometime. Do you want to get dinner with me

sometime? Or go to a movie?"

"A film? I like films. What film?"

"Ben, I'm trying to—" She cuts herself off with a groan. "This was cuter in my head. I'm asking you out. I am asking you on a date because I would like to date you. Oscar and I had a long talk, and we decided I'm being stubborn, so I'm trying to rectify that. I don't want you to wait for me because I think the two of us have done enough waiting. I'm ready now."

I smile uncontrollably and walk back up the stairs. "Sugar, we're already dating. We've been dating for a while."

She groans again. "I know. God, we're thick."

"We really are." I reach the top of the stairs, gently grabbing her face with both my hands. "Are you sure about this?"

She clutches my wrists as she nods in confirmation. "Are you? You're choosing a hard route."

"No, I'm not," I say firmly. "Linny, falling in love with you is the easiest thing I've ever done. Staying in love with you will be even easier."

"It'll be easy for me, too."

With that, I gently pull her mouth to mine, wanting to slam into her lips, but refraining because of her glasses. She soon removes them, pinching the earpiece with her fingers as her arms loop around my neck.

"I'm sorry," she says through kisses. "I'm sorry I was being stubborn."

"No, sugar," I say. "Don't apologize. You were being careful. I can't fault you for that." I kiss her again. "You came around quicker than I thought you would."

"I can't believe you sat there for an hour."

"I told you I would wait."

CHAPTER TWENTY-SIX
Linny

I cannot believe I tried to say no to this man. I love this man.

Don't get me wrong, I'm terrified—so worried that we have both been swept up in the excitement of it all. Swept up in the rush of feelings a new love can bring. However, at the same time, I am so confident in my feelings for him and his feelings for me that all that worry and terror is washed away. My heart can hold him. I know this because it has been holding him for a while.

So right now, I put all my focus on him.

Ben backs me into my flat and kicks the front door closed with his foot. Without taking his lips off mine, he reaches behind us to lock it shut. He keeps walking me backward until we hit a wall. Once I hit that wall, I drop my glasses on the mail table to be retrieved much, much later.

"I missed you so much," I get out between kisses.

The noise he makes is nothing short of elated. "It hasn't even been a week." His leg slips between my thighs, pinning me in place.

"It's like I was going through Ben-withdrawal. I want to see you every day. I need to talk to you every day. I can never get enough of you, Benny."

He finds the strip of skin between the bottom of my shirt and the top of my pants, pushing my shirt higher so he can grasp at my bare waist. "I can never get enough of you, either. I missed you like hell, Lin. Let's never pretend we're not in love with each other again. Deal?"

"Deal."

Once his lips cover mine again, his hand trails down, dipping beneath the waistband of my sweats and over my underwear. He groans into my mouth, feeling how wet I already am through the cotton. He strokes me over the fabric, causing my toes to curl on the ground.

His mouth separates from mine, giving me room to say, "I've been thinking."

"Fuck, that's sexy," he says, lips frantically moving over my jaw.

"I want you to fuck me."

He pauses, drawing back to look at me, fingers now moving in slow circles over my clit and pure lust in his eyes. "Like, with my fingers, or have you a toy for me to use?"

"No," I say, hand trailing down his stomach until I meet the stiffening cock pushing through his trousers. I stroke him over the fabric, a deep whimper emanating from his throat. "You. I just want you."

I do. I've been thinking about it a lot. It's another thing I've refrained from due to fear as opposed to true opposition.

His throat bobbles. "Lin, you know I don't need that."

"I know, but I want to. Really."

"Are you sure?" His hand pauses, forcing me to shift against it for more friction. He restarts, much to my relief.

"Never ever has a man wanted to talk me out of this. Yes! I

want to. I would still very much like to use protection, but I'm willing to risk it. If you are."

"Aye, sugar. I am." He takes his hand away to scoop me up with a small grunt. I wrap my legs around him as he carries me to my bedroom, dropping me down on the bed. He then shuts my bedroom door. "Oscar Wilde does not need to see me defiling his mother."

I prop myself up on my elbows. "Defiling, huh?" I scan him up and down, blurry but all him. "We are both wearing entirely too much clothing for that."

"I can fix that." He throws off his shirt, then bends over the bed to tug at mine. I help him remove it, my bare chest exposed, nipples tight and pinching in the sudden cool air. His hands find the waist of my sweats and pull them off, leaving me in only my underwear. "You're wearing these sexy knickers again. It's like you knew I was coming over."

"They are literally just cotton panties." I loop my fingers through his belt loops, tugging him down to meet my lips.

"Fucking sexy cotton panties," he mutters.

A terrible realization occurs to me. "Wait, I don't have any condoms. Should we go to your place?"

He smirks above me. "I actually have one on me, but we'll get to that."

He backs down my body until his mouth is at my ankles. He presses a kiss there, then moves up to my calf, murmuring, "All these goddamn bruises." His lips meet one of said bruises.

"I told you," I say, "I have a tendency to run into things. I barrel forward with more confidence than I should have."

"Keep the confidence. You have me at home to kiss the bruises and make them better." He kisses at one by my knee to prove his point. When his mouth reaches my thighs, I wriggle in desperate anticipation, nearly over this teasing. Instead of kissing my inner thigh, he bites it, only to soothe the sting with his tongue.

My teeth sink into my lower lip. "Okay. *Yes*, to that," I praise.

He fixes me with a cheeky grin. "You liked that? Tell me where you want my mouth next."

Using one finger, I point to a spot on my other thigh. He bites, then soothes again with his tongue, sending a thrill through me. I move upward, touching my upper thigh close to my hip. He follows with those wicked teeth and gentle tongue, causing me to whimper. Next, I move my finger to my clit, stroking myself over the cotton for a moment before I let Ben follow. He does, eyes locking with mine before he gently guides his teeth over that spot, making me gasp, only to follow with a swipe of his tongue against the fabric.

He yanks off my panties, tossing them to the side, saying, "I'm buying you a pair of those in every color."

His mouth lands on my clit again, repeating the action he did before, scraping his teeth then soothing with his tongue. He stays on that bud of nerves, my moans growing louder and louder. His arm travels up my body, searching for my hand, which he finds resting on my stomach. His fingers clutch my palm as he settles in, my legs spreading wider to give him better access. As he keeps licking, I squeeze his fingers tight enough to break a bone. He swipes that tongue just right and—

"*Fuck*," I moan, my back bowing. I see sparkles as a flood of ecstasy rushes through me.

His mouth is still down there, but I need him to keep moving. With my free hand, I tug on his hair to get his attention, then tap my stomach so he takes his mouth upward. Mouth now shining with traces of my arousal, he moves to my stomach, biting then coaxing. I draw my finger upward in between my breasts. He lightly bites both, then proceeds to kiss both. Finally, I drag my finger up to my mouth, tracing over my bottom lip. He prowls up to my face, mouth meeting mine before his teeth sink into my lower lip, tugging before releasing and letting his tongue delve into my waiting mouth. I can feel his hardness pushing through his jeans against my leg.

"Where is that condom?" I ask, voice muffled by his lips.

"You are highly impatient." He pushes himself off me to shove a hand into the back pocket of his jeans, pulling out a wallet and handing it over. "In there, love."

My heart attempts to find a steady beat as I ask breathlessly, "When did you put this in here? High hopes for tonight?" I dig through the wallet until my fingers trace the foil wrapper I'm after.

"I put it in there before London. I wasn't planning anything, but wanted to be prepared for the best-case scenario."

"Glad you're an optimist. Take off your pants."

He chuckles lightly as he strips down, revealing a thick erection, then kneels between my splayed legs. I open the condom wrapper and slip it on him, my eyes pleading desperately.

His hand strokes down my stomach before finding his cock. He stares at me as he pumps it once, twice, and says, "Look at that pretty cunt. Dripping and ready for me."

"So ready for you," I confirm heavily.

I spread my legs wider, welcoming him as he slides inside inch by inch, his arms caging me. His thrusts are slow, testing the waters, almost as if he is waiting for me to take back what I said. I won't. This is so, so good.

"Harder, Ben," I plead.

His head shakes above me. "I need you on your hands and

knees, sugar. If I go any harder while looking you in the eye, I will come here and now. I want this to last as long as possible."

"Okay," I agree.

He pulls out, and I feel inexplicably empty without him inside. I shift so I'm on my knees facing away from him. Bent forward, I grab my headboard. His hands stroke over my backside, muttering, "I promise to appreciate you."

The man is talking to my ass. It's a good thing I love him.

His hands move down to my thighs, spreading them wider before he slips back inside fully. His thrusts get more intense, harder, faster as his body lays over mine, one arm wrapping around my waist and the other hand meeting mine on the headboard. Gripping me tight, he pulls me upward, my ass out and back arched as he pounds into me, holding me to him with an arm across my chest. The movement to this position alone nearly leads me straight into oblivion.

"*Fuck*, sugar. I love the feeling of you on my cock. You're going to come for me, okay?"

"Okay," I choke out.

He continues to move inside me. I angle my head so his lips meet mine in a heavy kiss. He thrusts upward, and that is enough to send me spasming, crying out as I find that release.

"*Fucking* hell," he mutters. "I want to hear the noises you make when you come every day for the rest of my life."

I make a sound of agreement, knowing I want him to be the cause of those noises each time.

He removes himself from me, flipping me onto my back before pulling me up so that I am straddling his bent legs. My thighs are trembling, but my body is still begging desperately for more.

"I need to see you," he says through heavy breaths.

I nod, agreeing, still blinded by stars as I attempt to re-enter reality. Together, we guide him back inside. My hips roll against him, feeling every inch. I touch his face, hands gliding over it, learning each little bit, knowing I need to see him too, with every sense I have.

"Come for me one more time, sugar? I need to feel that pretty cunt pulsing on my cock."

"Yes," I agree readily. "Yes." I move up and down with his thrusts, wet and slippery between us. I glide on his cock, the position we're in perfect for my clit. "Ben," I say, only wanting to say his name. "Benny," I plead as he gets me so close. "Oh, *fuck*." I come a third time, and this time, he comes with me, releasing himself as his head drops to my shoulder, brow moist with sweat.

We stay in that position, connected, as we catch our breath, just exchanging our own air for each other's. I cling to him, feeling boneless and happy. I'm not sure I'll ever be able to move again, but that's fine by me. When I have enough air, I kiss him lightly. "We should do this again."

"And again," he agrees.

...

My fingers trail down Ben's face as we lie side by side in bed. Once we tired out, we opened the door to let in a very disgruntled Oscar Wilde, who is now resting at the edge of the bed between our feet. It's 2 a.m., but I'm not tired.

"It will be your face," I say quietly, trailing my finger down his cheek, the askew glasses on my nose and the dim light of the lamp offering a visual.

"Hmm?" he asks through heavy lids.

I swallow. "What I'll miss most when I can't see *anything* anymore. When I'm like seventy or whatever. It'll be your face."

He smiles giddily. "Well, then you better spend so much time looking at it that you won't forget."

"Okay." I stare at him, taking in his dark eyes, his graying hair, and the smile lines I know will eventually form. He leans forward and kisses me, mouth opening on mine. I sink into him, but I pull away as soon as I can. "I can't see you if you're kissing me."

He inches away, resigned, as we just stare at each other, both trying to memorize every little detail. The natural quirk in his eyebrow, the slight stubble growing on his face, the singular small pockmarked scar on his cheek. I love his face.

I scoot my feet around the cat so that they are touching Ben's. "I think I finally have to admit that I'm a cuddler."

He laughs. "Like I didn't already know that." His foot nudges mine. "You've said that to me before," he says quietly. "About my face. But I didn't know what you meant."

"When?"

"After the wedding. You said you'd miss me the most. I figured you were talking about our arrangement ending, but that's not what you were talking about, was it?"

I shake my head. "By that night, I knew I never wanted this to end, even if I wasn't ready to admit it."

"Now it won't."

...

In the morning, I drag myself out of my flat and down to the shop, forgoing coffee in favor of forgoing a scolding from Carolyn for being late. However, I end up getting scolded for another reason. "Och, you're letting out Fergus! Close the door, child."

I swing the front door closed tightly. "Did we lose him?"

"No, no. He's still here. A lot grumpier, mind you." She looks me up and down as I approach the front counter, commenting, "Someone didn't sleep well. You alright, Melinda?"

I yawn as if to prove her point. "I slept well once I finally got to sleep," I say. And I did, solidly and in Ben's arms until my phone started buzzing in an effort to wake me up.

There's a mischievous glint in her eye. "Up doing other things?"

My cheeks redden involuntarily. "Other things that do not concern you," I admonish. "Ben is still upstairs. He's off on Saturdays, so I figured I'd let him sleep. He always has to get up so early." I add, "We're officially dating."

"Good, good. Wondering when the two of you would figure it out was wearying."

About half an hour later, I hear footsteps descending the stairs on the other side of the wall. I expect him to walk into the shop after I hear the door close, but he does not. I can't help the visible disappointment on my face.

Carolyn tuts. "That'll be the ghost who lives in the hallway, lass. Ben'll pop in later, surely."

"That ghost doesn't normally walk down the entire staircase. He stays at the top," I argue weakly. "I'm sure he wanted to go home and shower or something."

Even though the body wash he loves is in my shower. I shake my head. I'm being ridiculous. Just because we're dating does not mean we're not allowed to live our own lives. I was just expecting him to come say good morning to me, that's all.

I usher Carolyn out from behind the counter so I can take my place and start going through new inventory while she gets to work on the orders that came in overnight.

The bell over our door jingles. I peer up to find Ben walking in, three cups of coffee in his hands. I laugh to myself because of how insecure I was being. He went, from the looks of the cups, into his café to get coffee. He sets down all three cups before he leans across the counter to kiss me. I have to stand on my tiptoes to meet him.

"Morning, my love. I come bearing the source of all power: caffeine."

I giggle, so overcome by this goddamn man to act like a normal person. "My hero," I swoon like Olive Oyl. I choose my cup and then take a grateful sip. "Ugh, *this* is why you sleep with a man who owns a café."

His head is thrown back in a laugh. "Where's Carolyn? In the office? I'll bring this to her."

He takes the cup meant for Carolyn into the back. I hold my cup to my chest, a near-permanent smile etched on my face. I am so happy. Unbelievably. I mean, this came out of nowhere. I was not expecting him, but that's what they always say, right? That love will find you when you least expect it. I think I just didn't expect to find love and new friends.

Emma being back in my life is great—and I'm going to put in the work to keep it that way. And Rachel asked me to come with her to help look for a car. Super random, but I love doing random errands with friends. Two months ago, I felt like I had nothing and no one except for Mel and Carolyn, but I now have friends.

That's what should be found in a partner, right? Someone who helps grow your community, not deplete it.

Ben comes back out, and I lean my head up for another kiss. I'll never grow tired of casual kisses with him. I love him. "I love you," I say aloud, like I think I need a reminder.

He simpers, hands meeting my hips. "I love you, too, sugar lips."

"Big no to 'sugar lips.'"

He pouts. "Fine." He removes one hand to take a sip of his coffee. "Isla had a real go at me just now."

"How come?"

"She's miffed about missing my whole I-need-to-go-confess-my-love-for-Linny revelation at Hoot last night."

I laugh lightly. "I rather enjoyed that love confession. You can repeat it if you want. For her benefit, of course."

"Of course." He has another drink of his coffee, then asks, "Will it drive you mad if I loiter around here all day? I've nothing else to do."

"I'd like it if you loitered."

Ben does hang out at the shop for the rest of the day. Carolyn is tickled pink by his presence—she makes him start dusting, still dissatisfied with my continual effort. At one point during the day, while I'm talking to a customer about a chest of drawers with a mixture of original brass handles and new ones I attached myself and made look original, I feel his eyes on me. As soon as the customer retreats to the counter to purchase said chest of drawers from Carolyn, I say to him, "You're staring at me."

He gives me a goofy smile. "You're pretty."

My eyes water a bit—not at that specific compliment, just because of *him*. "You're so nice to me," I say quietly.

His mouth twitches downward as he makes it to me in two big steps. "Of course, I am, sugar." He grabs me by the cheeks, making me look up at him. "I will always be nice to you. If I am ever not, I will apologize and grovel as much as I need to grovel."

I nod, tears still brimming. "I promise that, too." I swallow and ask thickly, "Want to get dinner tonight?"

"Linny Jenkins, are you asking me out on a *date*?"

I press my lips together in an attempt to keep my smile at bay. "Well, you never actually said yes when I asked you last night. So, Ben Pyeon, would you like to go on a date with me?"

He kisses me and says into my lips. "Yes, please."

CHAPTER TWENTY-SEVEN
Ben

Linny and I are asleep in her bed—I'm asleep at least. That is, until I hear her aggressively whisper, *"Ben."*

I've no idea of the time, but it's the middle of the night. I feel it in my bones. Without opening my eyes, I reach out to her—finding her face, then her shoulder, then back to her face.

She swats me off. "Ben."

"Hmm?" I mumble, my hand still searching for her arm. I find something.

"That's my boob," she says.

"Hmm?" I mumble again. I become somewhat more alert to the bare lump beneath my palm. Into the pillow, I say, "Nice boob. Do you want my hand off it?"

She doesn't respond.

I'm attempting to open my eyes. I am. It's not working. "Lin?"

"I'm trying to decide if it's comforting or not."

I nod into the pillow. "Mmhmm. Emotional support boob."

"Okay, hand off my tit. Ben."

"What's wrong, sugar?" I mumble.

"Do we know how to be a normal couple?" she asks.

"I think we did some very normal couple things tonight," I reply.

"Not sex. I mean, our whole relationship so far has been defined by the excitement of our so-called fake dating. And we started off by going to all these big events. A weekend trip to London, a rehearsal dinner, a wedding. Do we know how to do normal things? Will we not mesh in daily life?"

I roll onto my back, eyes finally opening to her dark bedroom. I reach across her to turn on her lamp. Oscar Wilde picks up his head from the end of the bed, one eye open, giving me a very disgruntled glare before settling back down and closing his eye.

"Might I remind you," I start, "that we have already done a million normal couple things. We celebrated my birthday with my friends and family. We've hung out at pubs, eaten supper, and drank coffee together. I'm sure there's more that I'll think of when the sun comes out."

She shoots back, "But we've never sat down and watched TV or a movie together. I'm not sure we've really talked about TV or movies. What if we don't like the same kinds of things?"

I rub my eyes with the heels of my palms. "My interests are not narrow enough to not have a single media preference in common with you." I throw the sheets off my legs and get out of bed, finding my pants and pulling them on. I then retrieve my glasses from the nightstand. "Come on. Out to the living room. Let's watch telly."

She huffs a sigh. "I didn't mean I wanted to watch TV right now."

I leave the bedroom anyway, finding my way to her living room and her plush couch. I pick up the remote to flip on the telly. She joins me a few moments later, partially dressed, glasses on, and carrying a blanket. She sits down on the couch with me, settling into my side as my arm automatically wraps around her.

"What about *Taskmaster*?" I suggest.

"I like *Taskmaster*," she grumbles.

"See, we like the same things." As I click play on an episode, I squeeze my arm around her and kiss her on the temple. "We know how to be a normal couple, Lin. We have the most important things going for us: One, we love each other. Two, we get along incredibly. Three, we have great sex. Four, we have similar interests, and even where we don't, we are willing to learn. Five, I'm pretty sure we have similar life goals. Right?"

"Yeah," she confirms quietly. "Okay, you win."

"I'm not trying to win, sugar. But I am proving a point."

She snuggles into me. "Point proven."

...

After a week of living in our own little bubble, Linny and I are walking hand in hand from a park where we were taking a stroll when we run into Isla coming from the opposite direction.

"Hey!" she yells with a big wave, like I didn't see her only four hours ago, then turns on me with an aggression. "I've been texting you. Game night tonight at Rachel's. Come on."

My nose wrinkles. I was rather looking forward to getting Linny back to my flat and bent over my counter, but Linny squeezes my hand. "Game night sounds fun."

I sigh dramatically but smile. "Fine. Who's bringing snacks? I can bring dessert."

Isla points a hostile finger at me. "You've an hour, so don't go all out. And don't you be stealing supplies from the café."

I hold my hand up in defense. "I would *never*."

"He would," Linny counters. "But he won't."

I squeeze her hand and say, "You're supposed to be on my side, you know."

There's a glimmer in her eyes. "Future reference, I guess."

We part ways, finding our way to my flat so I can make something easy—simple biscuits.

As they're baking, I do manage to bend my girlfriend over the counter. We don't have an abundance of time, so I enter and thrust quickly while my hand works her clit. She comes with a sexy, sharp intake of breath, and I release myself with her. The timer still has not gone off, so I drop to my knees, mouth finding her wet cunt.

"*Ben*," she moans, heels lifting from the ground.

She comes again as the timer on the oven dings. I stand up, satisfied, kissing her deliciously on the mouth before turning off the buzzer.

While the biscuits are cooling, we freshen up. As I'm messing with an annoying new strand of gray hair that will not settle, she comes into the bathroom and wraps her arms around me from behind. She's wearing heeled boots so her chin can rest on my shoulder, though she still needs to stretch a bit.

"Your hair looks good," she says.

"It's being frustrating," I say back, fingers running over the silver stripe on the side of my head.

"Do you ever think about dyeing it?" she asks.

That question surprises me. "Do you want me to?"

"Absolutely not, but that wasn't my question. Do *you* think about dyeing it?"

I hum. "Sometimes. But then I figure that would be a hassle, and I am trying to grow into it naturally. Some days it bugs me more than others, especially as all my roots are starting to gray. But I know it's just hair and I should be happy that at least I have it." I twist my body so I'm facing her, back now pressed to the counter. She's pulled back, but her arms are still around me.

"I love your hair," she says earnestly. "The gray looks great on you."

I lean down and kiss her. "I think you're a bit sweet on me, Melinda Eugena Jenkins."

"I am. Also, so not my middle name. It's Charlotte."

"Mine's William."

"Ah, like your dad." She pulls her arms away. "We should get going."

We arrive at Isla's place a little bit later. As she ushers us in, I hear other voices besides Rachel's speaking. I don't see anyone else, then notice that she is on a video call on her laptop with a man and a woman.

"I should let you go," Rachel is saying. "Ben and his girlfriend are here."

"Wait!" I shout. "Is that Nick and Piper?"

She twists around in her chair. "Of course. Who else do I talk to?"

I nudge Rachel out of her seat at the kitchen table, stealing it and immediately getting excited chatter from her best friend and brother.

"Wolftrax!" Piper shouts, offering me the nickname she gave me after we first met last June. They were having trouble with an electric car outside my café early in the morning. Piper ended up leaving behind a necklace that I was fortunate enough to find and return to her when I came to Edinburgh to see David.

"How are you?" I ask.

As they answer, I overhear Linny ask Rachel, "Does he actually know them?"

Nick glances behind himself and says, "I've got a new batch of jam going that's almost ready to come out of the pot."

"Och, your jam. Please send the blackberry next time you

send it. Rach let me borrow some and I used it in these mini cheesecake cups and they were…" I kiss my fingers, then explode them. Chef's kiss.

Nick chuckles and says, "Sure. I'd be happy to. Rach isn't giving all of the jam to you, is she?"

Rachel cuts in, "Not all! But you send me an excessive amount. I am one person who just kind of likes jam. I spread the love. Ben uses it more than I do, anyway."

"Speaking of love." I gesture Linny over with exaggerated arm motions. "Let me introduce you to my girlfriend." I scoot over so we can share the seat. I can tell Lin feels mildly uncomfortable by this situation, so I rest my hand on her back. Piper, however, looks thrilled at her appearance. "This is Linny," I say.

"Hi," she says with a little wave.

"Hi!" Piper shouts back. "Linny! That is such a cute name. Is it short for anything?"

"Melinda," Linny and I say together.

"Ugh, Linny. That is so cute. I love it!" She nudges Nick beside her. "Isn't that such a cute name?"

"Very," Nick agrees, appearing lovingly amused by Piper's excitement over Linny's name. "So, how'd you guys meet?"

Linny and I look at each other, considering whether we'll tell the real version. Or, the whole version, rather.

"We met on a bench," Linny finally says. "We were both having a bad day, and he made me feel better."

"Me as well," I agree. "But then we ended up opening the café next to Linny's antique shop and re-met."

Piper covers her heart with her hands. "Ugh, that is so cute. Like destiny. Did you start dating right away?"

Linny laughs. "No. Not at all. Well, actually, in a way, I guess? My cousin Melanie was getting married in Edinburgh and I needed Ben to be my date for things so I wouldn't be alone. Everything got better from there."

"That's *so* cute," Piper says again.

Nick adds, "Yeah, that's really nice." His brow furrows. "Linny, you said your cousin's name is Melanie and she just got married in Edinburgh?"

"Yeah?"

"That wouldn't be Melanie Riedel, would it?"

"Well, Melanie Parker now, but yeah? Do you know her?"

Nick grins. "Yeah, we work together. I'm in the St. Louis office and she's in London, as you know, but we collaborate constantly. I actually met up with her last June when she was in Edinburgh visiting…" He laughs as a realization hits him. "When she was visiting her cousin. I assume that's you?"

"Yeah, the one and the same. This is insane. What a small world." She cocks her head to the side. "You know what, I think she mentioned you to me a few weeks ago. She was feeling guilty about not inviting her American co-workers to the wedding and said that one of them even had a sister who lives in Edinburgh."

"That sister would be our dear Rachel," I say.

Nick smiles. "Yeah, that would be me. I hope she doesn't feel too guilty since I would have declined. Pip and I are already planning a trip back to Scotland in June. To visit Rachel and…" His eyes widen before he coughs and adds, "that's it. To visit Rachel."

Piper narrows her eyes at him, but doesn't address the odd end to that sentence. "And hopefully to actually get on the Jacobite this time."

Rachel laughs from behind us. "I will be driving, so we will make it this time." She says to Linny, "Don't let them give you a long speech about the troubles of electric vehicles in Scotland.

They have a list of grievances."

"Ugh," Piper argues. "A list of accurate issues with the number and quality of charging stations. We have nothing against electric cars as a concept. If you get traumatized by something, I think it's valid to warn others."

Linny laughs, looking lost. "Well, my eye doctor advised me against driving, so I don't think that will be an issue. But I will make sure Ben heeds the warning."

I kiss her temple, then turn back to Nick and Piper. "I think we've stolen enough of your time. We'll let you be. Talk to you guys soon."

We stand up from the chair together, and Linny adds, "It was nice to meet you!"

"You too!" they both say, Piper a tad more enthusiastically than Nick.

Rachel slides back into our seat to finish her goodbyes with them.

I ask Isla, "Who else is coming?"

"Corrine and Madison. Aileen and her boyfriend. David and Callum. David is bringing wine."

I click my tongue. "You should have mentioned that. I would have told him which kinds to buy."

"He knows what you like."

"But he doesn't know what Linny likes."

Linny cuts in, "Linny is not picky."

My arm snakes around her waist. "A little picky, though, right?"

Her eyes lift to the ceiling. "When it comes to the people I spend my time with, yes. Not with wine."

Isla says, "My kind of girl." There's a knock on the door. "I'll get that."

She opens the door to David and Callum. David does come bearing multiple bottles of wine. I give David a hug—and it's the most natural thing I can do. Finally.

"I never got a thank you," he says.

"Thank you for rejecting me," I respond.

"Not what I meant."

"Thank you for being so bloody fit?"

"Still no."

"Oh. Thank you for shoving me when I needed it."

"There we go."

I move on to Callum and say, "Sorry about the whole confessing my undying love to your boyfriend thing. I should have apologized before."

Callum snorts and says, "Not to sound like a complete prat, but you never had a chance, so it's fine."

I laugh loudly as I rear back, hand over my heart. "Och—straight for the nuts."

David gets to work at pouring wine for everyone, jokingly complaining about how he does this at work, so he shouldn't have to do it at parties. After we get our glasses, I guide Linny to the couch, leaning into her as we sit down.

"Lin, I feel so light. I feel so much lighter than I have in months."

"You look it," she says. "In your eyes, in your face as a whole. You seem so happy."

"Of course I'm happy. The café is doing well, I got over the thing with you know who, and I found my soulmate."

"Soulmate?" she questions.

"Oscar Wilde."

Her face falls flat with a glare, which I deserve.

I bite back my grin. "I'm only teasing. I mean you, sugar."

"You believe in soulmates?" she asks.

"Yeah. Don't you?"

She considers this question, and I give her time because the term "soulmate" is powerful. It encompasses a tie so strong to one another that will never break.

"Yeah," she says. "I think I finally do."

Linny

I hold a coffee in each hand, severely regretting not grabbing a drink tray to carry them, but I have an unwarranted prejudice against drink trays because of this one time I went to fetch coffee for Carolyn and me at a café about a ten-minute walk away (this was obviously before Ben's café moved in next door). I put the two drinks in the drink tray and carried them all the way back to the store, to the back, and as I was about to set the drinks on the desk, one of them tipped out and spilled all over the floor. I never forget a betrayal like that.

After walking down the hill of a very populous and colorful street, I take a right and find Ben exactly where I expect him to be: on our bench.

I sit down next to him, handing over his coffee. "Maybe we should make a significant memory on a bench with a better view," I say before taking a sip of my hot beverage.

"I think the view here is pretty nice."

I turn toward him to find just what I was expecting: his eyes on me. "Smooth," I comment.

"Always." He grins into his coffee cup as he takes a swallow. "Where'd you get this? It's good."

"I don't remember the name of it. Somewhere Significant, maybe?"

"Huh," Ben muses. "Sounds familiar. Was it perhaps Somewhere Special?"

"Ah, right. That's it."

"I hear the owner is hot."

"The woman? Hell yeah." His nose wrinkles. I laugh lightly. "Oh. The guy. Yeah, I'd say he's pretty good-looking as well. Good kisser. Great pheromones."

Ben snickers. "I have heard his pheromones are better than the rest."

"They are to me, at least."

Ben throws an arm around my shoulders, pulling me into him and kissing me on the temple. "So, I have news," he says.

"Do you? Me as well. Two bits of it, actually."

"Well, you go first."

"Mel is pregnant."

Ben lights up. "You're going to be an aunt!"

"I'm already an aunt. And technically, I will be this child's…what is it? Second cousin? Your parents' cousins are your second cousins. Then your cousins' children are your first cousins, once removed."

"Why do you know this?"

"I honestly don't know."

"Well, still exciting. She's excited, I assume?"

"Oh, thrilled."

"What's your second bit?"

I grimace. "Atti is engaged."

His eyebrows lift. "Poor lass."

I chuckle. "Mel says he's been"—I curve my fingers in the air—"'working on himself.'"

Ben's lip curls. "To each their own, I guess. How you feeling about it?"

"Neutral. He took her to Spain to propose. He took me to France."

"Where do you want me to take you?"

I sip my coffee to hide my smile. "If you take me anywhere but this bench, I will say no."

"Noted."

"Do you have plans I should know about, Bennett?"

He shrugs noncommittally. "I don't know, Melinda. Have you plans *I* should know about?"

I throw a similar shrug back at him, then bump against him. "So, what was your news?"

"Ah, well, lots of engagements."

"Rachel and Isla?"

"Och, no. They're so annoying. They're waiting until they're better set up in their individual lives. Healthy, sure, but frustrating. I want to be best man at a sapphic wedding. Or would I be the man of honor? Butler of honor?"

I shake my head with a snort. "It's definitely not 'butler of honor,' Benny. But I know your day will come. So, is it Callum and David?"

"Aye."

"That's exciting. You told me they both came to you separately about proposing, but with no specific plan. Who asked who?"

"They asked each other." Ben beams manically. "They went down to the Lake District this past weekend and apparently, both pulled out a ring while they were on a rowboat together. So, my and Rachel's hinting at them both that this was the weekend for it worked."

My hand covers my heart. "That's so precious. How are you feeling about it?"

"Absolutely thrilled," he says without pause. "At least I'll get to be butler of honor at that wedding." He squeezes me tighter, kissing me on the mouth.

"You taste like coffee," I say fondly.

"You taste like sugar, sugar."

"What an egregious lie."

He shifts next to me, arm still resting comfortably around my shoulders. "I was thinking…what if I got a cat?"

"Oscar Wilde will be wildly offended, but I think ultimately he'd like to have a sibling."

"He won't feel insulted by our choice of a four-legged feline?"

"No, if anything, he'll make this new cat feel inferior." I mimic Oscar's voice, "'What do you mean you need *four* legs? I'm doing better than average with three.'"

Ben chuckles. "Yeah, you're probably right." He angles his head toward me. "Hey, Lin?"

"Yeah?"

"I love you."

"I love you too. Wholly." I kiss him.

Into my mouth, he mimics, "Wholly."

ACKNOWLEDGMENTS

It is honestly so hard to believe that I am writing the acknowledgments section for my third book. Third! That's wild. Three whole books.

I went a tad off the rails in the acknowledgments for *Down to a Science*, so I think I'll keep this one rather simple.

As always, thank you to my mother for your constant support and your willingness to let me go on and on about the process of self-publishing. It's so stressful and so much work and so damn expensive! But in the end, so worth it because, hey, here's a book!

Second, I would like to thank my friends for also listening to me talk about this practically nonstop. I feel like the author-thing takes over my brain sometimes, and I can't focus on or talk about anything else, so I appreciate you putting up with that.

Next, a thank you to Andrea, my wonderful beta reader. Your comments were insightful and helpful, and assisted in getting this book to where it is today.

The next thank you goes to my cover designer, Katie Pridige. The cover looks beautiful, and I appreciate all your hard work.

As always, thank you to my ARC readers. You all are the best. It's so exciting that with every book, I have found new readers.

My last thank you goes to the real Hoot the Redeemer. This

was a real bar in Edinburgh that I featured in all three books in the *Love in Edinburgh* series, to varying degrees of significance. They unfortunately permanently closed their doors back in January 2025, but I hope the memory of this really cool place can live on in these books.

Readers, thank you for being here and thank you for reading. Whether this was a one-star or five-star, or anywhere in between read for you, I appreciate you taking a chance and I hope to see you soon.

This will be the last book in the *Love in Edinburgh* series, but I will not rule out ever revisiting this universe—I already have a few ideas.

Also, side note, I included an Easter egg in this book for a book that I don't even know if I'll publish. Can you guess what it was? I'll give you a hint: it's in chapter two.

Farewell and on to the next. It's time to get spooky, y'all.

BRITISH TO AMERICAN TRANSLATION GUIDE

U.K.	U.S.
Football/Footie	Soccer
Boots	Cleats
Pitch	Field
Kit	Jersey
Wellies	Rainboots
Trousers	Pants
Pants	Underwear
Knickers	Underwear
Pinny	Apron
Plait	Braid
Fringe	Bangs
Baws	Balls (testicles)
Tadger	Penis
Fanny	Vagina
Wanker	Jerk-off
Numpty	Silly/Ridiculous person
Bloke/Lad	Man/Guy
Lass	Woman/Gal
Minging	Bad
Doolally	Nutty
Bonnie	Beautiful
Wee	Pee or Small/Little
Lead	Leash
Plaster	Bandage

Pavement	Sidewalk
Loo/WC/Toilet	Bathroom/Restroom
Tube	Metro/Subway
Telly	TV
Takeaway	To go/Takeout
Hen/Stag do	Bachelorette/Bachelor party
Pudding	Dessert
Ground floor, first floor, second floor, etc.	First floor, second floor, third floor, etc.

ABOUT THE AUTHOR

Kat Paige is a writer of romance books with humor, heart, and a touch of spice. She lives in New York City with a roommate who is more like family and an abundance of personified succulents. When she's not writing, she's probably reading, baking, going to Broadway musicals, or watching TV shows she will inevitably get too emotionally invested in.

LINNY & BEN'S PLAYLIST

My Kind of Lover - *BILLY SQUIER*

I'm Fine (No Really) - *DRURRY*

eyes don't lie - *KINGFISHR*

Good Hands - *TOPHOUSE*

all-american bitch - *OLIVIA RODRIGO*

It's Okay - *ZACH SEABAUGH*

Drama - *SPENCER SUTHERLAND*

i can't get my shit together - *BABY QUEEN*

The Man Who Can't Be Moved - *THE SCRIPT*

Little Chaos - *ORLA GARLAND*

Untether - *SOPHIE TRAUX*

I Don't Want To Live Like This - *JAMES MARRIOTT*

I Believe in a Thing Called Love - *THE DARKNESS*

The Weather - *DAVID WIMBLIN & THE COLLECTION*

Yes I'm A Mess - *AJR*

Where The Light Gets In - *BEN BARNES*

Glitter In The Air - *P!NK*

crooked the read - *MON ROVIA*

hey, honey - *THE 502S, HEY, NOTHING*

Sugar, Sugar - *THE ARCHIES*

Slutty - *THE SCARLET OPERA*

Clothes Off - *ALEKSIAH*

Spice Up Your Life - *THE SPICE GIRLS*

Sight of You - *SIGIRD*

Bloom - *THE PAPER KITES*

GET OVER YOU - *VERYGENTLY*

Honey - *CHANCE EMERSON*

Northern Attitude - *NOAH KAHAN, HOZIER*